Frost Heaves

Murder and Mayhem in a Small New England Town

A. M. Byron

Oakberry Press
Oak Harbor, Washington

"When the two people who thus discover that they are on the same secret road are of different sexes, the friendship which arises between them will very easily--may pass in the first half-hour--into erotic love."

From C. S. Lewis' *The Four Loves*

Thank you to Helen, Wilma, Patricia, Emily, and Mary. You know who you are and how much your interest and support means to me. I would also like to thank the members of my family who put up with my absence from household duties while I wrote and rewrote and rewrote and ...

This is a work of fiction. Names, characters, places, and incidents are either the product of the author's imagination or are used fictitiously. Any resemblance to actual persons, living or dead, or locales is entirely coincidental.

Frost Heaves
Murder and Mayhem in a Small
New England Town

Published by Oakberry Press

Library of Congress Catalog Card Number:
98-92179

ISBN 0-9667645-0-1
First Edition

Printed in the United States of America.

Frost Heaves

Murder and Mayhem in a Small New England Town

PROLOGUE

It all began on a blustery morning in April that would have been more suitable for February weather. The townspeople of New Venice had been harassed by wind and snow for over five months and were getting downright cranky about the situation. Easter was coming in four days, but where was spring? Weather was not to be the main topic of conversation in New Venice by the end of the weekend, however.

Jake Patenaude, the night watchman for the New Venice High School, was just finishing his rounds in the very early a.m. of Maunday Thursday before turning the three wings of the school complex over to the morning janitors on duty. He took his work seriously even though he was not sure whether he had been promoted or demoted from his former daytime janitor job. There had been theft and vandalism in the school from the beginning of the year, and somebody had to do the night watchman duty, he rationalized, but he didn't like it. The fact was, he had a family to support and wasn't in a position to argue with the business manager, who was in charge of the janitors, or the school board, which had voted to hire a watchman for the night hours.

The hallways of the academic wing were dim with the only source of light coming from the emergency lighting over exits and stairways augmented by the flashlight Jake carried in his right hand. He had reached the end of the second floor corridor and turned the corner to descend the stairs to the floor below when he casually glanced over the railing to shine his torch on the bottom of the steps.

Somebody had dumped what looked like clothing items on the stairs, but they hadn't been there on his previous round. So where did they come from? Damn! Had the vandals returned to cause more trouble, he thought, or was it something to do with the other goings-on he had observed for several months. Descending the steps as fast as he could in the dim light, Jake finally got close enough to see what was splayed across the bottom two treads and beyond onto the hall floor.

It was a man dressed in dark clothing lying there, and he wasn't moving or making any sound at all. The man's arms and legs were in impossible positions for a living person, and when Jake inched closer, he could see that his neck must be broken, too. Blood was splashed over the lower portion of the stairwell from a wound on the back of the man's head and had also pooled on the spot below where the man's head lay.

Shining his light directly on the man's face, Jake recognized the distorted features of the school district's superintendent, Dan Frost. He leaned over to feel for a pulse on the super's neck, and felt nothing. Just then the realization of what he was seeing and doing overcame him, and a strong surge of nausea hit him. Swallowing hard, he ran back up the steps to the hallway above where he made the boys' bathroom just in time to regurgitate his last snack of Twinkies and coffee into the wastebasket.

After rinsing his mouth out in the trickle of cold water that ran from the sink faucet, Jake made his way back to the janitors' office in the vocational wing to call 911. When he had made the nature of the emergency plain to the dispatcher, he sat back in the wooden swivel chair and mopped his face with a paper towel he had brought with him from the upstairs bathroom.

The town cruiser was the first to respond to Jake's 911 phone call. The two cops questioned him long enough to figure out what had happened and where before they followed Jake to the scene of Dan Frost's death. No one went close to the body except the one policeman who checked for a pulse. It was obvious that the man was dead, but the motions of looking for life signs had to observed. A call was put in to the state police barracks at once. The three men stood guard over the scene until help arrived.

CHAPTER ONE

A regular school day was scheduled for this disastrous Thursday before Easter. Students, staff, and teachers were expected in an hour from the time Dan Frost's death underwent investigation by the state police personnel who answered the emergency call to the New Venice high school.

Dorothy Watkins, the school principal, and John Lindner, the vocational director, were notified in order to implement plans for an orderly cancellation of school for this day and Friday. The student buses had already left the garage before anyone thought to stop them, and so the first task was to intercept the high schoolers at the front door as they arrived and send them back to the buses for a return trip to their homes. Staff members and teachers were directed to the auditorium for a short program of enlightenment and instruction.

Dorothy and John were good at handing out instructions and what they thought was enlightenment. Together with Dan Frost they were spoken of behind their backs as the "terrible three" because of their underhanded and unfair tactics in administering the school district, in particular the high school. Although

FROST HEAVES

Dan Frost had not been popular with the teachers and staff or anyone else in town for that matter, his death was shocking to everyone present in the auditorium. How could something like this happen to a prestigious person in their community, in their very own high school, in their supposedly quiet New England town were the questions displayed on each face turned to the auditorium stage as Miss Watkins explained, as best she could, what was going to happen next.

The week following Easter was a scheduled spring holiday. This made things easier for everyone after the initial shock was registered and the students returned to their homes for two extra days of vacation time. Secretaries were told to report to their normal duties as there would be incoming telephone calls from parents and the media to take of. Normal shipments of supplies for the school cafeteria and classrooms would be arriving on schedule and had to be received in the janitor's wing before distribution.

Jan Madison left the auditorium proper after the principal's announcements with the other teachers and staff members and headed for the main door to the lobby. The teachers had been told to pick up whatever materials and books they wanted to take home with them and then depart the premises. This was not a problem. The big problem with most of the teachers was figuring out how to tell their spouses and significant others that they were not supposed to leave town until the state police investigator told them it was all right to do so. The vacation plans for many of their families included

5

reservations for Disney World in Florida for the week following Easter.

Jan had no such vacation plans and her boss expected her to be in the office all of this day, tomorrow, and most of the next week. She would have to call him in Montpelier as soon as possible to let him know what had happened. Jan was not a regular teacher, but rather a state program assessor/instructor who did not get the school district's holidays unless they were also state and national observances. Of course she had two weeks vacation time coming to her, but she preferred to parcel it out during the year to her own advantage.

The teachers considered her to be an outsider in their high school with her dropout student population and irregular hours to accommodate them as they worked on the state program designed to get them to graduation in June with the eighteen-year-olds. They probably felt suspicious and guilty about what the dropouts were telling her. The students in New Venice's high school were most often allotted punishment, when behavior problems arose, according to who their parents were and how much money they had. Jan attributed this attitude to the unwritten policies of the "terrible three." She considered her position in the school to be an important one no matter if she got the cold shoulder or not.

As usual, no one asked her to join the discussions going on in groups stationed about the lobby, but Ginny Miller, the adult education secretary, was waiting for her near the door. They tended to support one another because their work with adults coincided, and the other teachers and staff members supposed that they were best friends as well.

"Hey, Jan," she called. "Over here! What a development! Who do you suppose could have done such a cruel thing to our former fearless leader? I know that lots of people were mad at Mr. Frost, but I can't believe anybody was angry enough to kill him."

"I can't believe that anybody had the nerve to do such a thing," replied Jan. "This is a small community. The state police will have no trouble finding out who did it, I'll bet. The two of us could qualify for suspects though, along with all the other people Dan Frost has hurt over the last few years. He made you mad at the vocational meeting on Monday morning, and you know how I feel about my experiences with him this year."

Ginny gasped and exclaimed hastily, "You don't actually think that I would do such a thing, no matter how upset I got over what he said about Eric, do you?"

"Don't worry, Ginny," answered Jan with a laugh. "You'd have to pick a number to get to Dan Frost and take a turn like the people in the Agatha Christie murder mystery."

"How can you say such things?" said Ginny with a shudder. She was not quite up to Jan's sense of humor or her sarcasm. She had been upset all week because her son Eric had been accused of not living up to his responsibilities as a teaching aide in the automotive shop. Several expensive tools were missing and presumed stolen, and Eric was the person who checked such tools in and out of the teacher's office as needed during regular school hours. Ginny had told Jan that Frost and the vocational director John Linder made it sound like Eric himself had taken the items and sold them when the theft was announced to the teachers attending the vocational meeting on Monday. The local police had been called in to check out the garages and pawn shops in the area, but not one item had surfaced as expected. Eric had not been accused directly, but the responsibility was his no matter if there were all kinds of scenarios possible, like the one in the evening classes of adults when the atmosphere was more relaxed than it was during the day. The handling of the problem as it related to Eric Miller was unfair, to say the least. Both Dan Frost and his hand-picked vocational director were becoming junkies for power in the school system and they didn't worry about hurt feelings.

"Let's go over to the cafeteria for coffee," said Jan, feeling sorry that her sense of humor had offended the adult secretary. Ginny did have a legitimate gripe and so did she. It was obvious that this was no ordinary day, however. Neither one of the women knew exactly what category they fell into; staff members who were supposed to stay at school or the ones who were sent home for two extra days of vacation.

"I've got to go back up to my office. We can have coffee upstairs," replied Ginny. "I won't know whether to stay in school or go home until I talk to Lindner. How about your situation?"

"I'll go with you," Jan answered, "because I've got to call Montpelier about what's happened here. I don't have any students scheduled for this morning, but I do this afternoon and tomorrow if it's possible. I'll have to check with George and then make phone calls to the students to cancel if I'm supposed to leave school."

The two women turned away from the front door to the auditorium to walk down several corridors to the vocational wing. Their offices were next door to each other on the second floor. Ginny's was already open, so she went ahead to call the vocational director's secretary. Sis Vachon supposedly would know whether she was to stay in her office all day or go home. Jan fished her set of keys from the bottom of her purse and opened her office to the whoosh of stale air escaping the small, enclosed room. Oh, for a window, she thought one more time as she turned on the overhead fluorescent lights.

There was no outside line available when she tried using the phone the first time. By trying every minute or so, she was able to place her call with the switchboard in the main office and connect with George Wright, her program boss. Filling him in quickly on the reason for her phone call, she remembered that George had known Dan Frost for a long time and was even a very distant cousin. They also belonged to the same old boys' network in the state, although George professed that he did not believe in such nonsense. He was as shocked at the news of Dan's death and the circumstances surrounding

9

it as everyone in the high school was and had to think for a minute about what she should do.

"Has anyone said anything about how the investigators are going to interview the people at school?" he asked Ginny.

"None of that has been discussed with the teachers or the staff other than the night watchman and the administrators at this point, I suppose. No one is to leave town, however," answered Jan.

"Why don't you cancel your appointments for today and tomorrow," stated George. "I'm sure the state police don't want your students coming in while they have enough to do already sorting out people's whereabouts. We'll see about next week on Monday. What time was your first student due in on Monday?"

"Not until one thirty. I was going to work on files in the morning."

"Okay. We'll leave it like that and get in touch on Monday morning. Try to have a nice Easter in spite of all the commotion." George was a pillar of the community in Montpelier.

"Thank you. I will try. I'm singing with the choir at church for two services, and I'm invited to a friend's home for Easter dinner. You have a nice Easter, too."

They both hung up after saying good-by and Jan took out her appointment book to see whom she had to call for cancellation. She made connections with all but one of the students. She could call him from home later on.

When Jan looked up, Ginny was standing at the office door with her coat on. "Let's get out of here and go to Wendy's for coffee," she said. "I take it from overhearing your phone calls that you are to leave school for the rest of the week."

"Right," said Jan with vigor. "I'll meet you in the parking lot outside Wendy's in five minutes." As Ginny turned and vanished down the stairwell, Jan picked up the student folders on her desk and put them in the top drawer of the big gray file cabinet next to her desk. She shrugged into her red jacket and tucked in a white woolen scarf firmly around her neck. With car keys and gloves in hand, she adjusted the door to lock when she closed it and turned out the lights.

Jan had time to think about her relationship with Ginny as she went out the janitors' door into the cold air to unlock her Escort wagon. She could be difficult to deal with in a perverse way when a person was counting on her for support. It wasn't just the fact that she was literal minded and lacking in humor. Ginny was a known gossip and reveled in having new items to put out over the high school grapevine system. Maybe it made her feel good to have the other secretaries and the teachers pay attention to her, or perhaps it compensated for the trouble she had had in the past with her son when everyone was talking about him. Eric had been involved in joy-riding with a stolen car when he was in high school, and it hadn't turned out to be the pleasant adventure as envisioned by Eric when it was all over. Ginny was an only parent, but she made sure the experience straightened him out for the rest of his young life. He was able to graduate from high school and go on to earn a college degree in teaching. The only reason he didn't have a position of his own as a history teacher was the fact that there was a glut in the market and budget problems all around the state at the high school level where he should have been teaching. They had survived his youthful prank, but it now gave the superintendent and the vocational director a good excuse to think of him as a possible scapegoat.

Ginny was waiting for her, seated in her white Suburu in Wendy's parking lot. The two women walked to the front storm foyer of the small restaurant and entered quickly. There was a bone-chilling breeze coming off the immense lake which extended all the way into Canada, and they were both happy to be inside and out of its reach.

Jan's cheeks were as red as her winter jacket and her shoulder length brown hair with the longish bangs was in a tangle. Ginny's short gray-brown hairdo was standing on end all over her head as they hastened to the order counter for their hot drinks. Having lived in the New Venice area for some years, they were accustomed to the wind and the chill of the air coming from the lake, but this never-ending winter had been extraordinarily harsh.

Collecting their coffees, creamers, and sugar, they hastened to a booth near the hot air outlet to warm their bones. The restaurant was nearly empty, which assured them of a privacy they wouldn't have found in the high school. They had come at a good time; after the breakfast crowd and before the lunch bunch.

Jan began the conversation by apologizing for her bad jokes about Dan Frost's murder. "I don't know what comes over me sometimes, Ginny," she said with a sad smile. "I guess it was the irony of all those people in the auditorium pretending that they cared whether Dan was living or dead, and all they really cared about was would it affect their vacation plans. I know you're worried about Eric. Do you think that Lindner has enough balls to carry through with what he implied about Eric and the stolen items?"

"I don't know. Remember how mean he was when he was badgering Jeanne Smith and Linda Schofield out of the school district. They'd cry and start searching through their files to refute something John would accuse them of during a meeting and then come up with the paperwork he wanted to see after hours of looking. Neither one of them had time to teach properly or tutor, which made them look worse than ever," Ginny frowned fiercely.

"Well, Linda finally got a job out of town and so did Jeanne, and now they're doing just fine," said Jan. "It's hard to believe that anyone could be as sadistic as Frost, Lindner, and Watkins when they're on a roll. If you think about it overall, there have been some nice men and women who have left New Venice High School employment within the last couple of years. Remember what's-her-name in the science department and the woman who was head of the cafeteria? I think the "terrible three" are on my case too, and I consider myself to be nice, although independent and sassy at times."

"You're making yourself sound like a bottle of wine that's been aging in the cellar for ten years," replied Ginny with a laugh. "Yeah, I remember them, but I can't think of their names right now either. You don't really believe there's a plot behind all the things that have been happening since Frost became superintendent, do you? I find it hard to imagine how the things that have been going on with you have anything to do with Eric's problem in the automotive shop and those expensive tools that were stolen, for instance. Honestly, you have the greatest imagination of anyone I know. Or maybe you're getting paranoid in your old age."

"Well, I do have the faculty of putting two and two together to make five, if that's a virtue," said Jan. "Also, I was at the in-service meeting with the teachers when Dan announced that he was good at getting rid of people who were not wanted in the school. How that relates to Eric, I don't know. In my case it's easy. I'm not a regular teacher. I'm not a union member, and I hear a lot of stories about how shabbily some of our former students were treated in the past. In addition to those items, my high school diploma program costs money, however nominal, that never seems to make it into the budget. When Dan Frost brought his big hand down on my thigh during the meeting with area superintendents, it wasn't sexual harassment; it was a power play to see what I'd do if he put me in my place in front of all those men. I told my boss what went on and he professed to see nothing. He wasn't about to start trouble. Now I'm wondering if that was the beginning of the campaign to get me out of the way and to get rid of the diploma program."

"What gets me," said Ginny, "is why Dan was in the high school building at that hour of the morning. There has to be something going on that's not on the up-and-up for him to be there at all. I can't seem to make sense of it. I hope that the state police investigator finds out who did it right away, or none of us will feel safe in the school, in the evening hours at least."

"The people in town and in the sending school districts know that the system is screwed up with the "terrible three" in charge of the high school, but how to fix it is another matter. And, it would probably cost the taxpayers money, so the problems are ignored as long the kids keep getting on those big yellow school buses bound for classes every week day." Jan rose to get a refill of her coffee. "Sit still, Ginny," she told her companion. "I'll get yours too."

Just as Jan got to the counter to ask for two coffee refills, Jake, the night watchman, arrived to order take-out for his lunch before he went home to get some sleep. His face was gray and whiskery, and it was obvious that he had just left the school after some repeated questioning sessions with the state policemen in charge of the superintendent's death. He didn't seem to want to talk to Jan, but she asked him about what was happening at school anyway. He told her that there would be an autopsy performed on Dan Frost's body in Montpelier and that any information floating around before then was just rumor. The state police would be making a statement to the public about the results and the progress to date by Saturday at the very latest. He had to come back to work on his regular shift whether he was able to get some rest or not, but he was going to try.

Jan asked for and received her two refills and headed back to the booth where Ginny was waiting. Ginny had gotten more creamers and sugar while Jan was talking to Jake, but hadn't joined them at the counter. She had noticed Jake's reluctance to chat with Jan and thought better of adding to his distress.

"What was all that about?" she queried Jan as soon as she had settled back into the booth again. "He didn't seem to want to talk to you at all."

"I think he's scared witless," answered Jan as she sipped her coffee. "He probably went over what happened this morning a hundred times too many. Did you notice how gray his face looked? Jake is not exactly a young man anymore, and since he's been doing the night watchman job he seems tired all the time."

"Maybe there's something going on that we don't know about," speculated Ginny. "I don't think that I'd want to be in his shoes right now. Finding the body on the stairs like he did would be enough to make me look gray in the face, never mind the fact that he was apparently the only other person in the building."

Jan thought for a minute before she answered. "The police can't possibly think Jake killed Dan," she said. "There's a lot more information to come when the official report from the police is out, I'm sure. He did look frightened about something though."

The two women finished their coffees and prepared to leave the restaurant. It was bundle-up time again, but the wind seemed colder than ever when they opened the outer door and sprinted for their cars. Neither one of them lived far from Wendy's. Ginny's funky little house was on the north side of town, and Jan lived in a modern condo just beyond the center of North Venice in the opposite direction.

Jan thought about her plans for the rest of the day as she drove home. There was the Maundy Thursday service at church that night at seven thirty. She sang alto in the choir and so should be there by seven o'clock at the latest to warm up with the other members. It was strange how the ordinary duties of life must go on, even after the murder of someone you know well.

The wind buffeted her car as she turned to drive along the causeway and cross one of the cement bridges leading into the business district. The huge lake behind Wendy's, Lake Memphre, could be seen between the buildings on her right. New Venice was aptly named with two rivers emptying into the lake between spits of land connected by the cement bridges. There was water everywhere a person looked on the north. To the south and west, the land rose gradually away from the water with streets and homes making up the older residential section of town near the business district. Jan's condo was located on a plateau at the top of the hilly part of town where new homes had been recently built.

The view of the lake on her right opened up
as she neared her gravel turn-off road which
then led to the condo buildings' driveway. The
water was steel colored with a strong current
driving little waves toward the American shore.
The looks of it made Jan shiver even though the
heater in her Escort was going full blast by that
time. The turn-off road was uphill with a curve
about half-way to the condo driveway. A huge
frost heave had emerged just at the spot where
anyone driving up the road had to accelerate in
order to reach the top without grinding away at
the engine's low gear. When it had snowed
recently and before the plow arrived to clear the
road, it was impossible to get to the top of the
hill without a four-wheel drive vehicle.

On more than one occasion, Jan had been
forced to back down the curving hill. Trying a
second time usually did no good, but fortunately
there was a mini-mart located opposite the
gravel road where people could park, overnight if
necessary. During the month of April there had
already been two snowstorms heavy enough to
necessitate parking at the little store. She was
not happy trudging and slipping on the icy hill
while carrying her purse and book bag, plus
groceries if she had stopped at the Grand Union
on the way home from work. The situation also
made her nervous if she had to go out after
dinner not knowing what condition she would
find the road when it was time to return.

The curving road was clear as she made the
turn. With a sigh of relief, she made it to her
parking place outside the condo without trouble
and went to the bank of mailboxes to check her

mail. The wind whipped around her as she extracted a magazine and two long envelopes. "Probably bills," she muttered to herself as she made her way to the big front door of the building she occupied. Once inside, she stamped her feet and put down her purse and book bag to open her own door. This was a routine she considered a major hassle. Pushing the book bag and purse into her little hallway with her foot, she was grateful not to have a couple sacks of groceries as well. The thought about groceries made her remember that she was supposed to pick up cat food. This was the cue for Dickens, her big black cat, to arrive on the scene to check for brown paper bags full of Tasty Treat. Jan picked up her purse and book bag and proceeded into the living room while trying not to trip over Dickens, who was winding between and around her legs.

"Never mind, cat," she said in soothing tones of promise. "I'll find you something good to eat to hold you over until this evening 'cause I have to go out again pretty soon."

Dickens seemed to catch the drift of her conversation because he beat her to the fridge and started to rub the bottom front edge before the words were out of her mouth.

Stepping out of her Easy Strides and throwing her coat over the couch, Jan got busy fixing leftover chicken for the cat's bowl and her own sandwich of whole wheat with mayo and lettuce.

Making a fresh pot of mocha java to go with her sandwich kept her busy for a few more minutes. Dickens got his milk bowl filled before

she poured the first cup of coffee for herself.
With the chores finished for the moment, she
settled into her favorite blue swivel rocker, which
was positioned next to the sliding glass doors
leading out to a small porch facing the lake and
mountain view.

Trying to figure out whether her legs felt
shaky from all the coffee she had been drinking
or if she felt this way because of what had
happened at school, Jan fell into a reverie. Her
eyes lifted to the scene of mountains and lake.
The water was as wintry looking as before, but
somewhere in Canada a spotlight of sun was
shining against the forested hills like the first
promise of spring.

This was her special addiction, besides all the
coffee she drank, sitting in her blue chair gazing
out at the ever-changing scene of lake and
mountain before her. It was also a great waster
of time, but Jan didn't care. It was good for the
old blood pressure to sit and relax. Just then,
Dickens jumped up into her lap and started
purring as he made himself comfortable.
Dickens was good for the old blood pressure,
too.

After sitting and relaxing, she got up and
resettled Dickens in the blue chair. It was
unusual for her to have time off from work, and
she was determined to make it pay for her as she
gathered up dirty clothes and bedding to put in
the washing machine. She also began an early
spring cleaning of her kitchen cabinets as she
waited for each load to finish drying. The
afternoon passed quickly with frequent stops for
coffee and viewings out the big windows.

Patches of blue sky were emerging over Canada, which meant the weather was clearing with more cold air on the way for the overnight hours. Oh well, Jan thought, it's better than another snowstorm.

When it was nearly time to stop and get ready to go to church for the Maunday Thursday service, Jan made a small snack to eat with a final cup of coffee. It was a great temptation to stay home and curl up with a good book, but she was obligated to sing with the choir this evening, for tomorrow's Good Friday service, and of course, two Easter services. What a day this has been, she thought, and it's not over yet. The air was crispy cold as she made the trek out to her car.

St. Luke's Episcopal Church was located one block off the main business street to the right. At one time it had been a residential estate on a narrow lot with a home built at the back of the property. The house had become the parish hall, and the church proper was built at a right angle to it toward the street. It was known around town as the little white church with the red doors.

Someone had arrived early and turned the heat up for the choir practice before service time. Bless him or her, Jan thought as she entered the vestibule. After taking off her coat and scarf, she went to the small music office to collect her robe and music folder. The office was crowded with men and women trying to do the same thing, so Jan stood back to wait her turn. The choir director, Molly Nadeau, turned and saw her standing there.

"What's been happening at the high school?" she demanded to know. Jan remembered that Molly had a daughter in high school who had returned home this morning with news of two extra days off for spring break.

The other members of the choir gathered around her. "I don't know a whole lot more than you folks do. When I got to work, the teachers and staff were told to go immediately to the auditorium for information about something that had happened in the school in the early hours of the morning. As you've probably already heard, Dan Frost's body was found at the bottom of the stairs in the front end of the academic wing. What he was doing there is not known. The state police investigator is going to release a statement on Saturday morning for the Burlington newspaper. Until then, who knows?"

"Only the Shadow knows," commented Molly, who had a quick wit for one-liners. "In the meantime, we'd better get into church and start warming up. It's almost time for the service to begin." Molly was also very practical and life did go on after all.

The service of solemn commemoration of one of the last days of the Lord's life proceeded to the conclusion of the rituals of foot washing and Holy Eucharist. All other thoughts were driven from the congregation's minds until they gathered outside on the church steps and front sidewalk. Their breathing in the cold, crisp air made smoky plumes over each group. No matter how much chaos had been created under the administration of Dan Frost, they could express sadness about his untimely death, and fear that such a murder could have occurred in their small town.

Someone inside the church turned off the outdoor lights, not realizing that people were still gathered there to talk to one another as if there were safety in numbers. The groups hurriedly broke up to leave the comfort of each other's company for individual vehicles parked along the street.

When Jan got back to her Escort, she realized that she hadn't spoken to Ginny nor did she remember seeing her in church. Just as she pulled out from her parking space, Ginny drove by waving good-by. So much for concentration, Jan thought, as she thought of her absorption in the difficult music the choir had lined up for this Easter season.

Another thought penetrated the other-worldly mood she found herself in. Cat food. Dickens needs cat food. The small convenience store at the bottom of her road would be open if she hurried to get there before the door was locked for the night. Damn, she hated being out in the dark and cold, but she had promised Dickens his special cat food.

Jan put the car in the garage for the night when arriving back at the condo. It was much easier to start in the morning when she did, and who knew what the weather might be like by then. Remembering Molly's words, she told herself that only the Shadow knows as she jogged for the front door with key in hand.

CHAPTER TWO

The next morning was cold and gray in spite of the clear overnight weather. Rooftops and lawns on the shady side of the street were covered with frost wherever the snow had melted. It was, however, fitting weather for Good Friday.

Jan did not wake any longer than it took to make a trip to the bathroom the first time. By eight thirty the cat had curled up on her chest to keep warm, but she arose again in spite of him to make a pot of coffee. Dickens was only disgruntled at being disturbed until he heard the refrigerator open when he came trotting into the kitchen just as Jan filled his bowl with Tasty Treat Supreme Fish Dinner. Do you love me for myself or for the cat food I provide, she thought to herself.

She decided to make microwave scrambled eggs to go with a couple slices of toast for her own breakfast. In a way, it was nice having two extra days off this week in spite of the circumstances involved. We should have Thursday and Friday off before Easter anyway, she thought. It used to be that way years ago when I went to school, back in the dark ages.

Jan parked herself in her blue chair near the sliding glass doors and gazed out at the lake. For some strange reason, the water looked almost dark turquoise in color, and it was as smooth as glass. "I never get tired of the way the lake view changes," she said to herself and to Dickens, who had jumped up onto her lap. "I can sit here as long as I want to this morning, and have another cup of coffee, too."

She reviewed her schedule for the day in her head. There certainly wasn't any rush to get to work this morning, but it might be necessary to go to the office if she couldn't reach the one student who needed to cancel his eleven o'clock appointment. There were the kitchen cabinets to finish cleaning if she found herself in the mood. The Good Friday service that she would attend was at seven thirty with the warm-up for the choir a half an hour earlier. That left Jan with plenty of free time, which she wasn't used to having.

She tried her student's telephone number again and was told that the phone was no longer in service. This meant that she did have to be in her office a little before eleven o'clock to intercept him and make a new appointment for next week. There was no big deal about dressing for work, so she put on jeans, a turtleneck, and a sweatshirt after picking up the kitchen and straightening the bedroom.

It was still early for the student appointment, but she decided to leave anyway. Grabbing her purse, her bookbag, and the black plastic trash bag from the kitchen that badly needed discarding, she headed for the door. Dickens was determined to go out with her, under every step she took. Jan did not like to let him out the front door because of the driveway and other owners coming and going in their cars, but Dickens scooted for the shrubbery near the condo foundation where it was safe and he could watch for other cats as he hid behind an evergreen planting.

Jan flung the trash bag into the appropriate receptacle and slammed down the lid before opening her garage door and backing out the Escort. She debated about leaving the door open, but got out of the car again to close it. Who knew how long she would be gone on an unexpected day off when time didn't have as much meaning as it usually did?

Driving down the hill from her condo, Jan noticed a fine slant of rain that wanted to turn to snow hitting the windshield from the direction of the now somber-looking lake. If we could just get past this bad spot, spring will come, she thought as she skidded to the left when she caught the edge of the frost heave on the curve. The bump would not go down until the water underneath the roadway stopped freezing and pushing the gravel upward. Nearly all the roads in the state were staked out with bump signs to warn drivers not to speed over them without thinking about the possibility of being airborne in a direction not intended. Jan found herself thinking seriously about moving to the West Coast to avoid another winter like the one they were still experiencing.

Thinking and doing are two different things, she thought as she drove to the vocational wing of the high school. At least there was no problem with the parking on this day with plenty of space left over from the secretaries' and janitors' spots. They did not have the day off like the rest of the staff and the teachers.

The gloom of a large school building out of action descended on Jan as she entered the side door called the janitors' entrance. She had to use her key to get in, as the wing was not officially open to the public. The janitors' room to her left was dark and empty as she walked to the stairwell in the semi-darkness. She turned on the stairwell lights with another special key so that she did not stumble and fall on her way up to the office on the second floor. The steps were littered with dirt and paper from the last class sessions on Wednesday, but this was not unusual because the vocational wing was the last one to be cleaned after the academic wing and auditorium wing were finished. The janitors had other unpleasant cleaning to do on this day, trying to eradicate the signs of Dan Frost's death. She supposed enough time had passed for the crime scene to be released by the state police investigators.

After Jan had opened her office door, she stepped in and noted once more the backlash of stale air that rushed out to meet her. It was creepy in this part of the building and smelly with the lingering remembrances of hundreds of teenagers and their sneakers. I'm not going to stay very long, she promised herself as she shed her coat and gloves. I feel like I'm totally isolated on a planet in another galaxy.

A. M. BYRON

As the outside door to the janitors' hallway was locked, Jan kept an eye on the clock in order to go down and wait for her student a few minutes before eleven o'clock. There were other ways to get to her office from the academic wing, but students often gave up if the janitors' door was not accessible. She was sure that the academic wing was off limits to students anyway near the front door, with the staircase where Dan Frost's death had taken place just around the corner. There was still plenty of time, but she went down.

The cheerful aroma of freshly brewed coffee greeted Jan when she reached the hallway leading to the janitors' room. Someone was on the ball, she thought to herself, as she peeked around the corner to see who it was. It was Jake Patenaude, still on the premises long after his shift was over.

"Jake!" she gasped in surprise. "What are you doing here at this hour of the morning? I thought you'd be all the way home by now."

"Come on in and have some coffee, Jan," replied the night watchman. "The state police wanted me to go over my statement again this morning after I finished work. I think they want me to make a mistake when I repeat what happened or else they think I'm holding back something. By the way, what are you doing here? I was told that all you teachers had today off."

"Yes, I'll have a cup of coffee with you. I'm waiting for a student to show up. I couldn't get him on the phone to cancel, so here I am.

28

Anyway you know that I'm not one of the regulars."

Jake was a friend of Jan's and had been so from the time Jan had helped his son get his high school diploma several years after he had dropped out of school in his senior year. The high school diploma had enabled Andre to join the Marine Corps, and he had made a success of his second chance to Jake's everlasting gratefulness. Jan knew that the family was dysfunctional, but whose was not these days in one way or another? It always seemed to Jan that the second chance for success afforded by her program was the most humane and economical way to solve the problem of educating dropouts.

"The whole place seemed deserted when I came in a while ago," said Jan. Where is everybody? It was scary up there on the second floor by myself."

"Lindner's around somewhere and so is Sis Vachon," answered Jake. "They had appointments with the state police this morning, too, but I don't know what they can tell them except where they were in the middle of the night, in bed probably. The investigator in charge is Gregory Whitehouse and he is a tough mother, let me tell you." Jake's face was gray with fatigue again this morning, "Who knows what goes on around here lately."

Just then there was a knocking heard at the door, and Jan hurried to let her student in.

"Hi there," she greeted him. "I didn't know if you'd try to be here after Mr. Frost's death or not, but we need to cancel today's appointment and make another one for next week. I tried to get you on the phone, but no luck. Do you have a new telephone number to give me?"

The student was not too unhappy to have his appointment canceled, which made Jan suspicious that he had not finished his homework. She got his new phone number, made another date with him, and bid him good-by until the following week when things would be normal. She hoped.

Jake left to get his sleep in before returning to work that night. Jan ran back up the stairs to collect her things after she had cleared away the cups and sugar wrappers and wiped the counter where the Mr. Coffee reposed. As she was straightening up her desk and putting the student folder back in the file cabinet, John Lindner appeared at her doorway, having approached silently on his rubber-soled loafers. Jan jumped and Lindner glared at her with dislike gleaming in his icy-blue eyes.

"What are you doing in the vocational wing today?" he asked. "All the teachers and most of the staff do not have school, so what are you doing here?"

At once, Jan was on the defensive and angry. She could not stand Lindner's rude approach toward conversation at the best of times. "I had to come in to work because there was a student who couldn't be contacted for cancellation of his appointment today. I didn't think you'd want him wandering around the school looking for me, so I came to catch him at the janitors' door. I'm just leaving."

"That makes a pretty good excuse," Lindner replied. "Just don't come back trying to find out what's going on, and I don't want any gossip coming from this corner of the building either. You adult ed people don't belong here with your dropouts and losers in the first place. I'm sure you'd be much better off away from the high school altogether."

"I'm sure, too," answered Jan with mock sweetness. "I know what all you vocation administrators are afraid of. You're scared silly that the adults in this area will find out how much they are entitled to by state law because you'd have to foot the bill for training classes. Most people believe that needy adults should get another chance to make something of themselves for their own sakes and for their families' sakes because that would be better for the community in the long run. The short term view of life under your nose doesn't change anything for the future."

"Just lock up your office and get going," reiterated Lindner. "I don't need any soapbox speeches from you, thank you very much." He stalked away down the hall, but the effect was ruined by the soft whisper of his rubber-soled shoes.

Jan put on her coat and scarf, muttering to herself as she turned off the light and locked the office door. Actually, she was surprised that she answered up as much as she had. It probably would be a good idea to change the location of the diploma program if there was that much animosity against it. She was lucky to have had an office in the school for nine years at that.

Jan had been married for fourteen years before her husband was killed in an airplane accident in Maine. She was well provided for, and she was thrifty and smart with her investments. If Dan Frost and John Lindner had thought to intimidate her, as they had tried for the past four months, with Dorothy Watkins' blessing of course, they were barking up the wrong tree. Jan thought again about her options as she reached her car and got ready to leave the parking lot. She could have the diploma program moved to the state employment office complex, she could quit her job as soon as graduation was safely passed, or she could leave New Venice completely and move to Seattle in the state of Washington. Her cousin, and best friend while growing up, lived there and had been writing to her for several months about the moderate temperature, the flowers, and all the things to do and see. She decided that the best option could be a combination of the three.

Driving home she thought about the chaos caused by the terrible three's administration. Besides the unfairness and cronyism, if that was a proper word, there had been disasters of another kind. A teachers' strike in the fall had delayed the beginning of classes until October. The item in contention was the medical care policy of the school. The teachers had caved in and agreed to pay a greater proportion of the cost, which elated the school board and Dan Frost no end. The sense of frustration with the superintendent, who dominated the board in ways not altogether proper, lingered on after five months. It was picked up by an evaluation team that had come in January. The consensus was that the rift should be healed as soon as possible as the poor educational atmosphere was affecting the students and their parents.

A second problem involving the school was a rumor floating around the district that an administrator or administrators had been taking kickbacks from the construction company that built a new addition onto the junior high school. In a small, closely knit town like New Venice where many people were related by blood and marriage, it was difficult to keep such a rumor under wraps, especially since the construction company, Smithfield's, was owned by a prominent local family. Of even more importance, was the suspicion that the same situation would arise when an addition at the high school began in early summer.

In March, the cafeteria staff, janitors, bus drivers, and secretaries asked for a raise at contract signing time and threatened to strike if they didn't receive it. They got what they asked for, but the scuttlebutt was that the school board was angling for a private company to come in and run the school buses with their own drivers next year. To make matters worse, the cafeteria was going up for bids to private companies, too. All these changes were seen to be retribution by the board and superintendent because of the pay raise.

The public school board meetings began to be held at ever-changing hours of the early evening in mid March. Jan had heard that her diploma program was under attack at one meeting that was supposedly private and closed to the public.

She was determined to go before the board to present the facts, before things got out of hand without a single consultation with her about the history and mission and purpose of the program. Fortunately, Ginny had found out that the next meeting was to begin at six thirty instead of the usual seven thirty, which had also been changed to seven o'clock one week ago. As a non-scheduled speaker, there was plenty of time for her presentation because the scheduled people didn't know that they were supposed to be there at six thirty. While Jan was speaking, Dan Frost sat at a table opposite her chair talking and laughing in an undertone to his chairperson. Jan made her presentation and answered questions posed by the board members and left clenching her teeth in anger. She had to admit that the flack against her program quieted down afterward though, so it seemed worth the anger and frustration. The basic problem was that the vocational department had not paid its share of the cost of the program, which had been agreed to by contract with George Wright several years before. The cost was nominal in the first place, and the manner of payment could be up to creative bookkeeping for the state educational department accounting system in the second place. There should have been no problem.

Arriving home at last, Jan let herself in the condo front door. Dickens decided to come in with her, and so she was soon involved with kitchen chores for herself and the hungry cat. Good Friday was a proper day to assess her thoughts about her job and the people she worked with, but enough is enough.

FROST HEAVES

While she and Dickens ate, Jan decided to watch TV. It was a treat to choose among the daytime programs she never had time to watch when she was at work, but it got a little boring. She picked up a novel she had been trying to read for several days and turned the sound down until three o'clock when an interesting talk show came on. The program was all about the deadly new viruses emerging from the tropical rain forests of Africa; it was enough to scare the wits out of her, but at least it held her attention. When the program was over, Jan made a private little analogy to the scary happenings emerging into the daily life of New Venice.

She picked up her book again, but couldn't concentrate on it with her thoughts all in a jumble over what was happening at school. It might be a good idea to get serious about moving the program out of the vocational wing. With all the hullabaloo over Dan's death, it would seem a natural situation with no connotations of having been asked to leave by Lindner. Besides, the school was so grubby and even frightening when she had to be there in the evening by herself.

Deciding to make the best use of her afternoon and feeling restless again, Jan got out her ironing board and steam iron to press some of the clothing she had washed the day before. She loved the cotton material in her blouses, skirts, and pants, but how she resented the time it took to smooth the wrinkles. Just when everything was Perma Prest and easy to care for, fashion dictated that it was not the fabric finish of choice any longer. While she was at it, she lined up the things she would be wearing that night and on Easter Day.

Remembering that she should make a phone call to her friend Marianne, she quickly finished her tasks and put away the iron and ironing board. Marianne Mackenzie was a good friend from the old days when Jan's husband had been alive. She lived on the outskirts of a small neighboring village with her husband Sam, who sold farm equipment and supplies from the large barn on their property. When Jan phoned, Sam answered from his office and buzzed for Marianne to pick up the telephone in the house. Marianne was in the kitchen making cookies and continued taking pans in and out of the oven as she talked. They chatted awhile about what had happened at the high school. The news of Dan Frost's murder had been in the state's leading newspaper that morning, Marianne told her. Jan had not known that it would be state news this soon; the article also mentioned that the official police and coroner's statement would be included in Saturday morning's issue.

"Sam found out something interesting last week when he was out near Barton on a selling trip," stated Marianne. "Did you know that Dan Frost, John Lindner, and Dorothy Watkins have been buying large blocks of acreage out there near Town Road 15? Sam was not all that interested in the news at the time, but he did come home and tell me about it. He has since decided to keep his ears open when he's out that way because the whole thing sounded strange to us when we thought it over."

"Well, I'm certain no one in town has the scoop on this piece of news, or it would have been on the grapevine in no time flat," answered Jan. "Where is this land supposed to be, anyway? Is there something special about it? Had the three of them formed some kind of business group?"

"Hold on a minute, Jan, that's three questions there," remonstrated Marianne. "The farmers out that way seem to think the land is very special. It's close enough to the interstate to be good for anything that doesn't own a dirty smokestack. Remember the time we went to a big antique sale out that way, and we said how beautiful the farms and open pasture land were in that spot just north of the village. That's where the main pieces are that they bought, especially one lovely farm, and the rest is more open pasture with some woodland. It's acres and acres, and it didn't come cheap, either."

"That lovely piece of property belongs to the terrible three?" squealed Jan. "What on earth did they plan on using it for? Some farmer's widow owned most of it, I'll bet, and was holding on to get the best price possible."

"That's what Sam thought, too," said Marianne. "Now that Dan Frost is no longer alive, I suppose we'll be hearing lots more about the deal."

"Not to change the subject, but I am changing the subject. What time are you looking for me on Sunday for dinner, and do you want me to bring the relish tray when I come or something else?"

"I'd like to say bring yourself and nothing else, but I'm not going to have time to get the veggies bought and fixed. I'd really like you to do that."

"Your wish is my command," replied Jan. "I'll be along after church, and I'll bring a surprise for dessert." Marianne groaned in mock despair over the dessert idea. They were good friends indeed.

Jan put the phone down, went for a cup of coffee, and plunked herself in the blue chair again. Thoughtfully she mulled over Marianne's news about the land purchases made by Dan Frost, John Lindner, and Dot Watkins. Where did they find enough money to buy such beautiful land in large quantities to be meaningful for three people? The unholy three had good salaries, yes. They also had obligations for that money, just like everybody else in town. In fact, Jan thought to herself, their salaries with raises every year were placing them at the top of the local society where a certain lifestyle had to be maintained. They all belonged to the country club and met for golf with family members and friends on a regular basis. All three owned prestigious homes with acreage and had purchased new cars recently. There didn't seem to be anything lacking in their lives such as the obvious material items of vacations or clothing.

Dan had never married, but quite a few enterprising women thought they had the inside track for his affections at one time or another. How much intimacy was involved was not known to the general public. The supposed affairs were probably conveniences on Dan's part. Two of the women had been chairs of the school board, and both had resigned from the board for no apparent reason and out of the blue, so to speak, thought Jan. His home in New Venice was an architect's dream, and he supported his mother in her own home in Montpelier.

John Lindner was married for the second time. He had two high school-age sons to support from his first marriage, and college days for them were coming up soon. Skiing with all the latest equipment was his special passion after the new cars every two years and the golf, of course.

Dorothy Watkins lived with her elderly parents, who didn't do much for themselves anymore. They were hospitalized from time to time with various symptoms connected to heart problems, but nursing home care was not necessary with the private help they received at home, thanks to Ms. Watkins. Yes, thought Jan, they all had their expenses and obligations just like everyone else in town. So where did the big money come from to buy such large amounts of land near Barton?

Dickens strutted by her chair with his tail held high and proceeded to the sliding door to be let out onto the porch. Jan pushed the door to the right and he streaked to the railing where he disappeared down into the bushes. There were advantages to living on the first floor, she thought, especially when one had an outdoor cat. Luckily, the condo association allowed one cat per occupancy, or she wouldn't have bought the place at all. She liked the convenient location and the newness of it while deploring the condition of the road outside when it got slippery in the winter and early spring. Things could change. The town could fix the road some time in the near future.

Jan took one last look out at the lake and mountain view before she arose from her chair, coffee cup in hand, to sally forth to the kitchen to check out her cookbooks for the recipe for chocolate amaretto cheesecake pie. She promised a surprise for dessert on Sunday, so it had to be something spectacular. The recipe was not complicated as she remembered it, but did she have all the ingredients? It was going to be time for church service in a couple of hours, so it might be a good idea to get dressed, go out for something to eat, and hit the aisles of the Grand Union before choir warm-up time.

Jan looked for her recipe just before leaving the condo. It was a clipping from a magazine, and it took her a few minutes to find it among the others stashed in the front of her Better Homes and Garden cookbook. Then Dickens decided to come back indoors, so she fed him and thought to herself that it must be getting very cold again if the cat wanted to come in this soon.

Sure enough, the air was crisp and well-chilled when Jan left the condo to warm up the Escort in the parking lot just outside her dining room window. She turned on the dome light and surveyed the list of ingredients needed for the amaretto cheesecake pie. Yes, she did have to pick up a couple of items if she wanted to prepare her contributions to the Sunday dinner ahead of time. It also felt like an escape from her thoughts about the Dan Frost murder as she pulled out of her parking space and drove down the hill to the main street.

The supermarket was her first stop, and she was in luck finding a parking spot near the front door of the place. It wasn't very busy inside, another stroke of good luck. She picked out a chocolate flavored pie shell and unsweetened chocolate squares in the baking needs aisle, two packages of Neufchatel cheese and a small sour cream container from the dairy section, and two cans of mandarin oranges from their obvious site and proceeded to the checkout counter. She had half a small bottle of amaretto, carrots, broccoli, cauliflower, and celery at home, so she should be all set for Sunday. Thinking of her phone call to Marianne and Sunday dinner reminded Jan that she hadn't seen the paper yet with the article about Dan Frost's death. She picked up a copy of the state's main newspaper and added it to her purchases at the last moment. I'll read while I eat, she thought as she wrote out the check for her groceries. The Burlington paper was usually accurate and not given to sensationalism.

Back out in the parking lot, Jan opened the car door and squeezed the small bag of groceries past the steering wheel to the passenger seat along with her purse. Jerome's Restaurant, where she was bound next, was several miles away near the entrance to the interstate. Friday's evening special was prime rib dinner. She felt due a treat even if she did have to eat alone. The fact was, she wanted to be by herself right then. Time enough for people and chatter when she got to church for choir warm-up.

The restaurant was fairly busy when she arrived. She joined the line of people waiting to be seated when a waitress came by the foyer with a fistful of large menus in her hand.

"Are you by yourself?" the young woman whispered. It was one of Jan's former students. "The small table in the back is free if you want it."

"Yes, I am, and I'll take it," replied Jan. It was the perfect spot for one person in this restaurant because couples tended to reject it as being small for two people.

"It's yours," said the young woman, as she led the way through the aisles of happy diners in their black plastic booths. Jerome's was a popular place to eat on Friday night. "Are you having the special with baked potato and salad tonight?"

"I sure am," said Jan, as she slid into the small booth and started to shrug off her jacket. "And some coffee, too, when you have time, please."

There were fringe benefits that came with the adult education business every now and then. She opened her newspaper and glanced at the front page to see if the article about New Venice was there.

When she finally found the article, it was in the second section with the state/local news, and it was short and to the point. Just the facts, ma'am, she thought to herself. Dan Frost, superintendent of schools in New Venice had been found dead in the high school building early Thursday morning by the night watchman on his rounds. There was evidence of foul play suggested by the state police, who were in full charge. An autopsy was being performed in Montpelier. and an official report would be issued in the Saturday morning issue of the paper.

Just then the waitress arrived with Jan's coffee and a glass of ice water. Jan asked the young woman what she thought about the article in the paper. She had not seen it, and did not know what to make of the news. Her youngest brother was still in high school and had been sent home by Ms. Watkins on Thursday after Mr. Frost's body had been discovered. "Somebody was mad at Mr. Frost for sure this time," she commented.

Jan read through the whole paper while she waited for her prime rib dinner. It was a luxury to have time to sit quietly and read everything, even the funnies. The waitress popped back with her food, and she realized how hungry she was when the aroma of the meat wafted across her face. I really must be nice to myself more often she thought. I might even have dessert for a change. The restaurant had excellent lemon meringue pie that Jan was always resisting.

As she ate, Jan looked out the window near her shoulder at the action in the parking lot. It was beginning to get quite dark outside. Two men came out of the light pooled about the entrance and walked to a car parked in a shadowy corner of the lot near an evergreen planting. One was tall and lean and the other was several inches shorter with a husky build. They were deeply engrossed in conversation as they walked along toward a vehicle that could just barely be identified as a state police cruiser. Jan realized that she must be gazing at the state police investigator, Gregory Whitehouse, and a fellow officer. After finishing her dinner, she decided against having the lemon meringue pie and left the restaurant for choir warm-up.

Nearly everyone was present when Jan arrived at church. The piece that they were singing for Good Friday was complicated and rather gloomy as befitted the occasion. The altos and tenors needed the practice to be confident when they hit certain chords that were difficult and hard to remember from last Wednesday's practice. The choir stopped and went to robe up as the congregation began to gather in the dark and somber atmosphere of the nave. The service was soon completed with the removal of the altar items and all light in solemn procession, and the congregation left in silence.

Jan had headed for the choir office to hang up her robe and retrieve her jacket when she heard her name called as she turned back toward the entrance to leave the building. Someone was waiting for her just inside the door. When she drew closer, she could see that it was Jake from the high school calling her. He was very agitated in manner, and did not want to be seen by anyone else.

"Jake, what's wrong?" she cried out in alarm. They both stepped through the doorway to the front steps without being noticed. "Aren't you supposed to be at work? Has something else happened at the school?"

"Let's get away from here and walk down the street aways," Jake replied without answering any of Jan's questions. "I've got to talk to someone, and you're elected."

"My car's around the corner where it's darker. Let's head that way as we talk."

"I want to tell you that I seen and heard some goings-on at the high school at night over the past few months. I didn't let on to anyone that I knew anything, and I was always very quiet when I made my rounds. I was afraid that I was going to lose my job if Lindner or Frost knew that I changed the order of my rounds because it made more sense to me. You know how bullheaded they could be about changing anything; I just went ahead and did it. There was no formal time punch to worry about. It's just that I was in a different part of the school than they thought I was when they were having some kind of meetings. In the wee hours of the morning the meetings were, and sometimes they were hollering at each other."

"Who are you talking about?" said Jan.

"I recognized Lindner's voice and Frost's and maybe Mrs. Watkin's. There were other people there; sometimes it sounded like two people and sometimes four or five. I was afraid to look for sure. The hallways were pretty dark, but they turned on some kind of light in the room they used. It was a different room almost every time they had this meeting thing and about once a week. Look, meet me at Wendy's tomorrow

45

morning at eight o'clock and I'll tell you all about it. I got to get back to work."

Before Jan could say a word, Jake had taken off down the street. Whatever Jake wanted to tell her, he was afraid of the consequences. Now Jan felt frightened, too, and she glanced around the darkened street to see if anyone had seen Jake talking to her. There was no one. She quickly opened the car door, slid under the steering wheel, and started up out of her parking space. The motor was cold and so was the interior of the car as she chugged up the streets to her condo, nearly stalling out at the first stop sign. Halfway up her street, she hit the frost heave near the curve and almost lost control of the Escort toward a ditch. "Shit," she whispered to herself. "I've got to calm down. I don't even know what I'm scared about." Jake had definitely impressed her with his fear and wariness.

When Jan arrived safely at her garage door, she put the car in park and opened the door. It was a dandy time to think about it, but wouldn't it be nice to have an automatic opener, she thought. I've never minded before, even when there were blizzard conditions, but tonight I want to get indoors as fast as I can.

Dickens was sitting on the other side of her front door when she let herself into the foyer with her bag of groceries, her music folder, and her purse. Jan could never figure out how he knew who it was at the door in time to position himself so neatly in welcome. She realized that he slept most of the time that he was in the house, only getting up to stretch now and then or check out his food bowl before curling up in one of his several napping spots again. Right now he led her to the fridge, and Jan could see that his dish was empty.

"Would you wait until I get my coat off, at least," Jan scolded him, as she proceeded to do just that and throw it over the nearest available chair. After Dickens' dinner was portioned out, he started to gulp the savory fish down as though he hadn't eaten in a week. "You aren't a cat," she told him. "You're a pig in disguise."

Dickens lifted his head from the food dish and looked at her for one cool minute before resuming his gulping.

"I know," said Jan, "if you could only learn to open the refrigerator door, you'd help yourself and not bother me at all." A low purring sound was her answer.

The interaction with Dickens calmed her down, but the fear and uneasiness returned at a lower pitch after she put her grocery purchases away and made a pot of coffee. She scrounged in the freezer compartment for a treat for herself. Waist Watchers Black Forest cake will hit the spot, Jan thought, and I didn't have my lemon meringue pie after dinner. Rationalizing doesn't work when you want to lose weight, but comfort food is comfort food when you need it. At least I can acknowledge what I'm doing and why I'm doing it.

Jan finished her dessert and decided to call it a day. After taking a quick shower and brushing her teeth, she headed for bed carrying the remote for her small TV and a new book on hot viruses in the rainforests. Her eyes closed and the book slid to one side off her chest after only fifteen minutes of reading. It had been a stressful day.

About four thirty in the morning, Jan was in the midst of a horrific nightmare until she got her eyes opened enough to realize that she had been dreaming. Her face was covered in perspiration and her hands were clenched into fists as if she had been fighting; fighting something or someone. Struggling to remember what had transpired in the dream did no good, so she tried to relax to regain the feelings that apparently drove the action. She could recall being angry, which helped her to remember pushing against someone who was threatening her. As Jan thought about it, she told herself that this was the way she always reacted when she was frightened about something--anything from criticism from an authority figure to downright threats of physical harm. It was her survival mechanism, and the nightmare was probably symbolic of fighting back against John Lindner's rudeness to her in her office.

Dickens stretched at the end of her bed and then decided to check out the food situation in the kitchen. He'll probably want to go out after he eats, thought Jan, and I could use a cup of coffee and some toast. Nothing like getting an early start to the day. Dickens finished up the leftovers in his dish and strolled to the patio door to be let out on the porch where he sat for several minutes surveying the gray pre-dawn scenery.

She turned the lights off and sat in her blue chair while watching to see what Dickens would do next. He finally slipped through the railings of the porch into the shrubbery to hunt any small nocturnal animal that was unlucky enough to encounter him. Jan sipped her coffee and nibbled on the toast she had made as she gave some consideration to her position in New Venice and in her adult diploma program. It was depressing to realize that the program wasn't as logical and popular with other members of the educational community as it was with her and her fellow adult teachers. In New Venice there seemed to be a constant reward system for some of the people and a punishment system for others who didn't quite measure up to an unspoken level of excellence. Those members of the community that wished to improve their lot were firmly held in place at the lowest level. Of course, this had to do with economics and available low-cost labor for one thing and fear in some people's minds that there was just so much room at the top for another.

Jan finished her coffee and toast and went back to bed. There is no use brooding over things at this time of night, she thought. It was easy to slip into depression and self-doubt in the wee hours of the morning, especially when you have no one to talk things over with. She pulled the covers up over her head and dozed off.

CHAPTER THREE

Jan got up again at seven o'clock even though she wanted to stay in bed for at least another hour. Saturday morning was her favorite dawdling time over coffee and toast. Then she remembered that she had already been up once and had coffee and toast after letting Dickens out for a pre-dawn hunting trip. Oh well, I'll have another breakfast, she thought to herself as she poured out a bowl of cereal and topped it with sliced banana. When she got out the milk carton for her coffee and the cereal, she thought of Dickens and filled a small bowl with milk for him. Looking over at the patio door she saw him pawing the glass and went to let him in.

"Speaking of the devil, and here he is," she said to Dickens, who was purring in advance of being fed. "There's milk in your bowl and kitty food coming right up."

After finishing her breakfast standing at the kitchen counter, Jan put the promised cat food into Dickens' bowl and cleaned up the dishes and flatware that she had used. She had time to spare before she was to meet Jake at Wendy's, so she turned on her small TV in the bedroom to watch the news as she got dressed. The weather was going to be a tad warmer today and Easter

Sunday was going to be especially nice until early evening when rain was predicted, announced the Channel 8 weatherperson with a slight smirk. He was wrong a good deal of the time, which made for all kinds of jokes at his expense.

It's still sweater weather, Jan thought as she slipped her patterned Icelandic sweater over a navy blue turtleneck. She had decided on jeans and boots and her heavy red jacket for this morning's attire. One never knew what the weather was going to do after you had left the house. It was better to be prepared for the worst at this time of the year.

Dickens sprang onto her bed as she straightened out the sheets and quilt and fluffed up her pillow collection. All at once, Jan remembered her bad dream and fit of depression at the witching hour of the early morning. The distress, which she had buried, returned when she thought of her feelings of anger and readiness to fight. I've never been able to hurt anyone in a fight since I was ten years old, she told herself. Why do I feel like I'd like to push someone down a flight of stairs and then stomp on him to make sure he didn't ever get up again? Jan covered her mouth as soon as she realized what she had just thought. I was mad enough at Frosty to have pushed him down those stairs at school myself. Was that what her nightmare was all about?

It was time to depart for Wendy's. Jan left the condo after turning off the TV and getting into the winter outerwear she had decided on for her early morning jaunt downtown. When she glanced at the lake, it had a rim of ice along the shore just below the street she would be driving on in a few minutes. So it is still pretty cold, she thought as she opened the garage door, backed the Escort, and got out to pull the door down again. I should have my head examined for being out this early in the morning on a Saturday. Then she thought of the fear on Jake's face the night before when he had made this appointment with her.

Making her way safely down the curving hill road to the main street below, Jan decided to stop at the mini-mart to get the Saturday paper. The police report of the circumstances around Dan Frost's death was promised for today's edition, if the promise was to be believed. She could get caught up on the news while she waited for Jake, as it was a few minutes yet until eight o'clock.

Wendy's had just opened when Jan arrived at the outside door. She went in and draped her heavy jacket over a chair back before going to the order counter. Receiving her large coffee, she picked up two creamers and a stirrer as she made her way back to the table she decided on because it was in the corner away from the few other customers present. Jake would like privacy to tell her whatever it was that had frightened him so.

When she opened the newspaper, she saw that the state police statement and the coroner's report had made the front page, with a headline. It detailed the injuries to Dan Frost that had caused Gregory Whitehouse, chief investigator, to be suspicious of accidental death; in addition, there was the bizarre hour of his demise. There was, the article stated, a severe trauma to the back of the head as well as the expected wounds elsewhere consistent with the fall from the upper railing of the stairwell. Evidence of a scuffle on the vinyl tile landing with marks leading to the railing where Superintendent Frost had apparently gone over to his death was noted. If the blow to the head had not killed him immediately, it had incapacitated him long enough for the fall over the railing to the bottom of the stairs where his neck was broken. Jan winced, remembering her dream of the night before.

There were short side articles on the front page chronicling Dan Frost's family background in Montpelier, his educational history at the state university, and his career highlights in the school district of New Venice. Jan had not known that Frosty had spent his whole employment time in New Venice. No wonder he was on the power trip of directing every event and person in his domain ... like a king, she thought. I'll bet he thought I was one of his "loose cannons" to get rid of. Frost had stated publicly at a teachers' meeting that he had done everything that he could to accommodate the wishes of the staff, including deleting the people they didn't like or want around the school for one reason or another. Jan thought of Jeanne and Linda. There also had been a woman science teacher and the business machines department head not granted contract renewals last year. Both had excellent reputations and seemed to be well liked by the other teachers.

Dan Frost also had reasons of his own to want certain people to disappear from his kingdom.

Jan scanned the rest of the newspaper as she sat waiting for Jake to arrive. On the obituary page, a picture of Frost was included with a short biography of his shortened life and career. The photo was grainy, but his sparse hairline and jutting chin stood out in spite of the photographer's art in trying to make his client look like a handsome pillar of the community.

Turning back to the first page, Jan saw that Gregory Whitehouse apparently had no suspects from his investigations so far, but he stated that there was still evidence to be processed with more conclusions to be reported as soon as the processes were completed. The person in the school building at the time of death was questioned, and he was planning queries to all Superintendent Frost's close associates and other members of the school community. There was no firm motive for the suspicious death as yet. Funeral arrangements were pending the release of the body on Tuesday of next week.

By eight thirty, Jake had not come into Wendy's for his talk with Jan. He must have gotten cold feet, and is not coming after all, thought Jan. She got a refill for her coffee and creamers and sat for twenty more minutes looking out the window watching for a sign of Jake's late arrival. At last she gave up and decided to leave for home to prepare her offerings for Easter Sunday dinner at Marianne's.

The morning coffee-and-giant-chocolate-chip-cookie-to-go crowd was lined up at the order counter as Jan made her way to the side door. There was an atmosphere of hushed excitement prevalent as people waiting to be served talked amongst themselves. Jan paused to hear what the topic of conversation was with feelings of dread that she could not rationally account for. She heard one man say, "down by the railroad bridge," and a woman next in line added, "not identified yet." Jan suddenly turned and ran from the restaurant somehow knowing that those people were talking about Jake. He must have had some kind of an accident, she thought; that's why he didn't meet me this morning. Her mind's eye again saw the fear on Jake's pale face as he fled down the dark street on Friday night.

Customers in the parking lot stared at her as she ran to her car. She started the motor before she was firmly seated, closing the door again as she backed out of her parking place. Things like this do not happen in small towns like New Venice, she said to herself as she drove over one of the many bridges that linked various spits of land near the lake. The police station was situated two blocks up the main business street to her right. There was a metered parking spot directly in front of the place, and as Jan rather recklessly drove into it, she thought how silly it was to pay for a parking space there. What an irony to receive a parking ticket because one forgot to insert a quarter into the meter as one reported a burglary, rape, or beating to the police.

Jan was thankful to note that there was nearly an hour left on the meter, as she climbed out of the car, slammed the door, and crossed the sidewalk to mount the cement steps to the heavy glass storm doors that formed the entrance to the police station. The building itself was a red brick antique, but renovations such as those needed to hold down the heating costs had been taken care of during one of the oil crises. The municipal all-purpose room was at the back of the main downstairs hallway, the police offices were to Jan's left as she entered, and a tax office was to her right. There were various other town business offices up a set of stairs beyond the police offices and public restrooms in the basement.

Not knowing the procedure, Jan felt intimidated as she turned to her left and saw that the police offices were all buttoned up in heavy glass over a narrow wooden counter. A notice to the right of a pass-through section stated directions for contacting a human being somewhere beyond the glass panel. At certain hours of the day, a person should push a button to summon help at the counter. Jan pushed the button and heard the buzzer sound on the other side of the glass partition. A woman in civilian clothes responded after a few minutes longer than Jan could tolerate just as she reached to give the buzzer another try. Jan suddenly did not know what to say to the woman, named Debbie according to her identification tag, and she haltingly asked for information about an accident to a man called Jake Patenaude.

"I can't give out anything on an accident," Debbie told her. "I'm the night dispatcher working late because everybody's busy. I'll take your name, address, and telephone number and pass it along to the officers at the scene for you, and they will be in contact with you if you have some information for them. Are you from New Venice? Will you be available this morning at home or at work? Can you wait for just one moment?"

Jan was determined to see the situation through to its satisfactory conclusion, no matter how foolish she felt. "Yes, I'll wait until you get in touch with the officers. I was supposed to have an appointment with Jake Patenaude early this morning, and he never showed up. He was frightened about something. Then I heard people talking, and it seems there is an unidentified body in the river by the railroad trestle bridge. The first thing I thought of was that it had to be Jake. I don't know why exactly unless it was that he was scared of something, big time."

Debbie disappeared into the back recesses of the offices to use the radio. When she returned, there was a distinct improvement in her interest in the woman standing on the other side of the partition. "The state police investigator will contact you at home in about an hour," she stated. "The state police are in charge now."

Jan thanked Debbie and slowly left the building to enter her car. She glanced at the parking meter and saw that there was still a half an hour left for some lucky person needing a space in front of the police station. It seemed like a week had passed since she first woke up to keep her appointment with Jake. Home was a good place to be.

Jan managed to drive safely up the hill to her condo even though her thoughts were not involved with the process in any way. Automatic pilot was the phrase she acknowledged as she parked in the outdoor space beside her dining room window. She walked to the set of mail boxes to see if there was anything in hers after remembering that she had forgotten to check on Friday. Sorting through the contents as she stood there, she noted a letter from her cousin in Seattle and the electric bill amongst assorted junk mail and the church newsletter. Elizabeth never gives up on her campaign to get me out to the West Coast, Jan thought as she let herself into the condo. The utility company never forgets me either, and this can't be good news after all the cold weather we've had lately. She was always astounded at the winter and late spring figures on the bill when it arrived.

She almost tripped over Dickens, who was waiting at his customary post just inside the front door. His expectant pose changed rapidly as he jumped to one side to avoid Jan's booted feet and darted to the front door to be let out.

"I'm sorry," she told him as she opened the heavy front door to let him scoot through. "I'm just not with it right now. I'll make it up to you when you come back in."

She kicked her boots off in the tiny foyer and put the mail down on the coffee table. I'll look at it later, she thought as she took off her jacket and hung it in the hall closet. It might be a lot later if I don't feel better soon. I'm wondering how long it will be before someone calls me about the person in the river. Just then the telephone rang and Jan ran to answer it before it had time to ring twice.

It was Ginny Miller calling to ask if she would be bringing fruit salad for the Easter brunch after the ten o'clock service. There would have to be food available for the choir members after the eight o'clock service as well because they would not have time to go home, as Jan was well aware of. Ginny's managerial tone made her impatient. She was supposed to be one of her best friends, but independent Jan did not like to be managed. Other people who knew Ginny from years before called her a survivor, a person who would go against her friends to protect her own position, and it had become a habit. After all, she was more or less in charge of the buffet. It had to be done right. This was one symptom left over from earlier years when her husband had involved himself with another woman, a best friend of Ginny's in fact, in an adulterous relationship that resulted in his divorce and subsequent marriage to the woman. Jan had not known any of the persons involved beyond acquaintanceship. She was bored with Ginny's past history because of this fact. Ginny carried her head high, and Jan admired her for that, but the important thing right now was to get her off the phone. She almost hung up on her, but managed to be polite as she explained about expecting a phone call that was very important.

Making a pot of coffee would occupy some time as she waited, so she got busy with the bean grinder, filter paper, and water. Walking into the living room, she glanced at the patio door and spotted Dickens waiting eagerly to be let in again. She opened the door to a rush of brisk outdoor air and a galloping cat headed for his empty food dish.

Almost stepping on him again while her thoughts were with Jake and the incoming phone call, she filled his dish to the top and poured out a small saucer of milk as well. When Dickens had settled down to his meal and the coffee had brewed, Jan grabbed her mug of mocha java and sat in the blue chair with the view to the lake.

Maybe spring is on the way after all, she thought as she gazed out at the water. The edging of ice was gone along the shoreline, and the mountain trees in the distance showed a definite haze of red where buds were forming. It would be many more weeks before the lake view would include white-sailed boats, however. Just then the telephone rang.

Jan did not hurry to the phone this time, but picked up after the third ring. A pleasant, well modulated male voice identified itself as Gregory Whitehouse from the state police after she had quietly said hello into the instrument.

"I was asked to contact you by the town police, who were told by the dispatcher at the office that you had stopped in to give possible information about the man found in the river early this morning," Whitehouse stated. "He has definitely been identified by a relative as Jake Patenaude, the night watchman at the high school. I was informed that you had been expecting him to meet you for an appointment at Wendy's at eight o'clock this morning."

"That's right," answered Jan. "He showed up at St. Luke's church last night right after the seven o'clock Good Friday service. He was supposed to be at the school at that time, so he was careful to keep out sight of the other people there. We went outside to talk near where I had parked my car. It just took him a couple of minutes to say that he was scared and that he wanted to talk to me about something. We made the appointment and he ran off down the street before I could question him."

"I am going to use one of the offices at the town hall near the police station," replied Whitehouse. "Could you come down and give me an official statement at three o'clock? I would appreciate any information that you have about Jake Patenaude's death. The connection between Dan Frost's murder and Jake's death is obviously the high school. Do you have anything to do with the school?"

"I teach a state education program for high school dropouts in the adult ed section of the vocational wing," Jan answered. "I knew Jake from seeing him in the janitors' room in the mornings and also from contact when he brought his son to enroll in my program last year. I will be in your office at three o'clock to be of any help I can."

She hung up the phone after saying good-by and slowly returned to her blue chair. This time she did not swivel to look out at the view but sat there thinking about the events of the morning. Jake made me feel frightened when he was scared about what he saw and heard at the high school, but I should have told him to tell the police right then instead of waiting until morning to talk to me. Why didn't I speak up or even go with him to the police station? Maybe he wasn't sure of the meaning of what he heard and wanted my opinion before he committed himself to more questioning with the state police. After all, I felt intimidated just going to the office and talking to the police dispatcher because I wasn't sure of the intuition I had about the body found in the river.

Thinking about Jake's death over and over was not going to solve the mystery, thought Jan. What is going to help is talking to Gregory Whitehouse at three o'clock. In the meantime, she could get busy making the chocolate amaretto cheesecake pie for tomorrow. The recipe was easy enough, but the concentration of what she was doing relieved her mind of fear and guilt about Jake for a few minutes. When the pie was assembled and in the oven, she poured another cup of coffee and sat down in the blue chair again.

I like being independent, but it sure would be nice to have someone to lean on right now. Jan thought about her husband, who had been killed in an airplane accident ten years before. The plane had been a small private one that he used to get back and forth to upper state New York and Maine on selling trips. It made her apprehensive to have him fly instead of drive because there had been three crashes of small planes that year, but Joe quoted the statistics to her on travel safety when her uneasiness made her speak up from time to time. When he had left on his final trip to Maine, she hadn't said anything to him about her intuition of disaster because the weather was beautiful for flying, and Joe was euphoric over an impending big deal at one of the paper mills.

After the crash and his death, she wished that she had tried to persuade him to drive, or maybe she could have gone along with him if he drove, and it would have been a mini vacation. When he was cooking up one of his big deals, however, he planned on entertaining his customers in a big way, including too much drinking at a local restaurant or club. Jan would not have fit into his plans in that case.

As she sat there thinking, Jan realized that she had thought along the same line when she felt guilty about Jake. If, if, if only she had done this or that, but it was already too late to do anything other than try to sort out the reason behind his death. Or reasons, she thought.

The pie had a few minutes to go in the oven when she got up to test it. The kitchen was filled with a delicious aroma, chocolately and reassuring to Jan in her present mood of self-recrimination. "Comfort food to the rescue again," she said to herself softly.

"The only thing is, I have to wait until tomorrow to eat it."

She decided to get started on the vegetables for the relish tray while she waited for the pie to finish baking. If she covered the tray well, they should stay crisp and tasty until dinner tomorrow. Jan obviously was filling the time up with homey tasks until she could leave for her interview with Gregory Whitehouse at three o'clock.

The chocolate amaretto pie came out of the oven looking like a definite triumph for Easter dinner, with the addition of some whipped cream for decoration just before serving. She finished the vegetables for the relish tray and covered them tightly to put in the refrigerator. The cheesecake pie could cool while made herself a sandwich and cleaned up the kitchen.

Jan sat in the blue chair to eat her sandwich and drink her coffee, and this time she swiveled to take in the view as she ate. The sun was shining brightly on New Venice like it meant business for the first time in a solid week of somber grayness. Dancing ripples of blue reflections from the sky on the lake made it iridescent in appearance. The forests on the mountains were showing definite signs of budding trees by forming clouds of hazy pink in the distance. This view is just as good as comfort food, Jan thought.

When she had finished her lunch, she covered the cake to put it in the fridge. There was one more cup of mocha java left, so she poured it into her mug and added milk before shutting the refrigerator door. Dickens food dish still held some savory fish dinner for snacks while she was gone, so he was all set until Jan got back from downtown.

Arriving at the town hall building, Jan parked in the unmetered rear lot where there was one space empty. This must be my lucky day, she thought as she pulled in ahead of a Chevy Celebrity. When she recalled why she was there in the first place, she didn't feel so fortunate; she felt nervous.

The Chevy had to wait to pull around Jan in the tightly spaced parking lot, and as she walked around it to get to the sidewalk, Jan was careful not to make eye contact with the irate woman driver. There was a one block hike up a slight incline to go before she was able to intersect with the main sidewalk leading to the heavily glassed front entrance. Once inside, Jan paused to let her eyes adjust from the bright sunshine outdoors to the gloom of the hallway. A fine mist of perspiration covered her upper lip and forehead, and she fished in her jacket pocket for a tissue to wipe it away, wondering if it was from the exercise or nervousness about the meeting with Gregory Whitehouse. A little of both, she decided.

Checking her watch, Jan saw that it was exactly three o'clock. A door opened near the police partition and a tall, well-built man in uniform beckoned to her. She recognized Gregory Whitehouse and followed him along a short hall to an office on her right.

"I'm Gregory Whitehouse," said the state police officer, extending his right hand, "and you must be Jan Madison from the diploma program at the high school. I attended the graduation celebration in Montpelier last summer, and I remembered you because you gave one of the speeches."

"Well, I'm astounded," replied Jan as she shook hands with him. "I recognized you from pictures I've seen in the newspaper, but I also saw you last night at the restaurant where you ate dinner. I was there for the prime rib special. I want you to know that I don't follow every man

who calls to me from a doorway in town hall."
She laughed briefly and acknowledged to herself
that he was very easy to talk to.

"I admire what you are doing for the people
who need another chance to join the rest of us
tax-paying citizens. Do you have a large group
for graduation this year?"

"Yes, I will have thirty-three. Did you know
that there isn't enough money left in the
program for a celebration this year? It's a good
thing that the adults may attend the regular
graduation ceremonies with the kids if they want
to. I've been thinking of having a small party for
them at St. Luke's church though; you know,
just for this region of the state. It's not like the
old days when the governor came to the
celebration in Montpelier to give the main
speech, but it will have to do."

"Things are tough in Montpelier this year,
including the state police main offices. It looks
like we were all living in some kind of a dream
world that had to collapse when the fiscal
examiners got busy. Reminds you of the feds,
too, doesn't it? Oh, I'm sorry, please sit down.
I'm borrowing this office for the duration of the
investigation. It isn't very comfortable, but I
guess we'll have to make do."

"Thanks, this will be fine," Jan replied, as she
seated herself in a plain brown wooden chair
near the desk Gregory Whitehouse had borrowed
"for the duration." He didn't seem too
uncomfortable in his wooden swivel office chair
behind the desk, even though it looked like his
office furniture had been found in the town
hall's attic.

"I feel good about what I'm doing to alleviate the high school dropout problem, but it's been difficult and lacking in support from the teachers and administration people who think knowledge can only be transferred to students who sit in certain seats for four years. Unfortunately, schooling and learning are two different things. It's been a difficult year for everyone at the high school what with the strike and the tough negotiations for the staff salaries. Now we have the murder of Dan Frost to worry about and possibly that of Jake Patenaude, too; if I'm not guessing wrong by the expression on your face, that is."

"I'm glad you brought the conversation back to the business at hand," said Gregory. "What made you think that the body in the river was Jake's? Why did he want to tell you something, something about the high school that frightened him?"

"That's actually two questions," answered Jan. "First of all, Jake must have thought that I was a trustworthy person to tell his story to, and maybe he was looking for some advice. When I saw him after the church service on Friday, he was so scared that his face was white and wild and he didn't want to be seen by anyone. He certainly impressed me and I got frightened, too. In fact, I didn't use my head at the time. If he was that frightened, we should have gone to the police station right then and there. About thinking that it was Jake in the river, you'll have to chalk it up to women's intuition."

"I guess that I'll have to go along with the women's intuition thing. We men in the detective business call those insights strong hunches, but tell me whatever you can about what he said about things happening at night in the school building."

"He said that he changed his order of making rounds. Apparently he didn't have to punch in on stations at set times, and the order he decided to use seemed to make more sense to him. Mr. Lindner and the business office people got upset if he asked for any changes, so he didn't tell them. He also told me that he'd changed his mind about not saying anything about what he saw in the academic wing because it was obviously weird with the people not turning on lights and all, and the strange times of the night. If one of the group figured out that he was not where they thought he was during the nights in question, he'd be in trouble, and danger I might add. It got hard for him to answer your questions then about where he was at certain hours because he couldn't remember exactly what he'd already told you. He was supposedly the only other person in the building, after all, and the most likely candidate for being accused of murder."

"I did notice some discrepancies when I went over his statement the second time. What I want to know is, did he recognize anyone in the school on the nights when the group was meeting? Did he say that he overheard what they were talking about?"

Jan was going to be cautious when she answered these questions. She also thought that it was disconcerting to have two questions asked of her at once, but she was beginning to trust Gregory Whitehouse. It was apparent that he valued her good sense when she used her personal impressions to answer questions about Jake's troubles. Speaking against John Lindner and Dorothy Watkins, however, was something that called for an off the record agreement.

"I can't tell you any more than what Jake told me," said Jan, as she started to answer the first of Whitehouse's questions. "He said that as he was walking along the halls in the academic wing on certain nights, he could hear voices having discussions or maybe arguments sometimes in one of the rooms. Principal Watkins', he thought; John Lindner's and Dan Frost's, definitely. There would be an additional person there most of the time, but the last two months or so there was at least one other person present too. That was judging from the voices. He couldn't make out what they were saying, and he didn't see who they were because they didn't turn on the overhead lights; they used some kind of small light, Jake said."

"Did he say why he couldn't hear what they were talking about?" asked Whitehouse. "That's just one question, I want you to notice."

"I did notice, thank you," answered Jan. "For one thing, he implied that he wasn't close enough, even with the doors slightly ajar. The classrooms they used are large, and those people were at the farthest point they could get from the door. Jake would have had to stick his head around a corner to see or hear anything up close. Of course, he didn't want to be seen or heard because he recognized Dan Frost's voice even though he couldn't hear what he was saying. I'm sort of filling in the gaps here."

"I'm thinking that he saw or heard more than he told you the first time he spoke to you about the meetings. That's why he wanted to talk to you this morning at Wendy's. Your intuition was right on."

"I'm sure you're right. I feel terrible about not going to the police with him last night. Does this mean that there is definitely more to Jake's death than accidental drowning?"

Whitehouse looked at her thoughtfully before he replied. "It will be official soon. The coroner found a wound to the back of Jakes' head that matches the one that was dealt to Dan Frost. It could possibly be the same blunt instrument, some kind of object heavy enough to take a person out if applied to the right spot at the base of the skull. The medical examination will tell us whether he died from the blow or drowning."

"There was something else that I heard about, secondhand, you understand. It may have nothing to do with what's happened, but you never know. A friend of mine, Sam Mackenzie, is an independent farm equipment dealer, and he said that people on the farms to the south of New Venice are talking about large land purchases being made, expensive ones, near Barton not too far from the interstate. Guess who they say is involved--Ms. Watkins and John Lindner and Dan Frost."

"That's interesting to say the least about it. It could have a connection with what's been going on in New Venice. I have a friend in real estate down that way who can check it out for me."

70

"Well, you know how people love to talk when there's some kind of a smart deal going on that's supposed to be a big secret from the regular folks. It can get out of hand and exaggerated. I don't know how anyone at the high school would be able to tap into the kind of money we're talking about here. The bigwigs have to keep up appearances and those three do a good job of spending their money as far as I can see."

Gregory rose from behind his borrowed desk and put out his hand. Jan gratefully got up from her uncomfortable wooden chair and they shook hands. The interview was over. She felt a measure of relief from the guilt she had been carrying around since hearing about Jake's death. As if reading her mind, Gregory told her not to feel any more responsible than she could safely handle for her own mental health. What happened to Jake was regrettable, but it was probably inevitable given the circumstances. He sounded as if he knew what he was talking about.

"You've been very helpful; filling in the blank spots of Jake's predicament is important for the investigation as is the other information you've passed on. The two deaths are a puzzle right now, but I promise you that the pieces are going to fall into place eventually. I know that solving the part about Jake's death is more of a priority for you from the way you've been talking, and you must tell me more about that some day soon. May I call you on Monday, Jan?" There was a twinkle in his gray-green eyes.

"That will be fine. You know there's officially no school, but I'm not on the regular teachers' schedule. You have my number at home, or I'll be in my office." Jan left the small office wondering over the glow she felt at being complimented by Gregory Whitehouse.

Out on the main business street, she decided to walk down to a small coffee shop located next to the bank where she did most of her financial transactions. The store windows were filled with colorful Easter items, and Jan stopped to look at a clothing boutique's display of spring fashions on the way to her needed cup of coffee. She spotted a light pink blouse that would go well with her navy blue suit for Easter and decided to think about buying it as she drank her coffee. If the price is right, she told herself.

When she reached the tiny restaurant and entered to look for an empty booth, she saw Ginny Miller sitting by herself in one of the booths near the front window. Jan waved and Ginny beckoned her over to the booth. Ginny was smoking one of her beloved cigarettes, but she offered to put it out if it bothered Jan. Jan said no, that a little bit of secondhand smoke wasn't going to hurt her at this stage of her life. It did no good to say anything she knew, because Ginny had no intentions of quitting, ever.

Seating herself, Jan asked what Ginny was up to before Ginny could question her. I'm not going to tell her what I've been doing for the past hour because she'll have it blabbed all over town before the sun goes down, thought Jan. Ginny was a strong segment of the high school's grapevine, and any information given to her would be common knowledge to everyone in all three wings of the school in no time at all. Only the unwary gave her a juicy item of conversation and then suffered the consequences.

"I had to do some shopping for the brunch at church tomorrow," Ginny said. "After I talked to you on the phone, I realized that we didn't have enough rolls to go around for the people staying between services, like the choir members in addition to the ten o'clock crowd. Are you just tooting around downtown for something to do, or did you forget an essential ingredient for your famous fruit salad?"

"No, I'm all set for the salad," Jan replied. "I'll put it together tonight and bring it with me when I go to the eight o'clock service. You'll find it in the fridge in the parish house. I was feeling sad about Jake Patenaude and came downtown to distract myself from thinking about him. Of course, I care about Dan Frost dying the way he did, but Jake's death is much more personal. You did hear about someone finding him dead in the river early this morning?"

"It's all over town. His brother Yves was the one who identified him for the police. I also heard that the state police have taken over the investigation of his death, too, and we all know what that means," said Ginny.

Jan shook her head in confirmation. "Yes, it means that Jake's death is not accidental. The state police do the investigating when there is strong suspicion of foul play, not the town police out here in the boonies."

The waitress came to the table at that point in the conversation, and Jan ordered coffee and a warm-up for Ginny's cup. The news about

Jake had made it around town just about as swiftly as one might expect, she thought. The coffee arrived and the two women said nothing further but were both deep in their own thoughts about conditions at the high school. At least they had vacation week to get their thoughts and feelings sorted out before having to face the teenage students.

"I had a little run-in with Lindner yesterday," Jan stated with a quizzical glance at Ginny. She wanted to note her reaction as Ginny did not seem to care about other people's problems with the vocational director, only her own.

"Oh, was he his usual rude self or did he have a special ax to grind?" queried Ginny in an offhand manner. "Where did this take place? At school?" One of her main complaints was that Lindner came into her office unannounced and took over her computer without asking or caring if she was in the middle of something.

"In my office," answered Jan. "I went to the school because I hadn't been able to reach one of my students to cancel, and all of a sudden, he was standing behind me looking over my shoulder to see what I was doing. I nearly jumped out of my skin because I hadn't heard him coming down the hallway. You know how spooky the high school is when the kids aren't there for classes. He told me to leave right then because it wasn't appropriate for me to be there."

"Was that all," said Ginny. "I'd say he was being his usual rude self. I don't see how he thought you were not supposed to be in your office if that's where you wanted to be. Nobody said anything about not going into the vocational wing, nobody official that is."

"There was something funny, I mean strange, about what he said as I was leaving, though. He told me that he didn't want to hear any gossip about Dan's affairs coming from our corner of the building, as if you could stop anybody in this whole town from talking about what's happened. It was weird."

"Maybe he thought we were going to besmirch Dan's reputation if we told the state police any of the things we have been speculating about for the last couple of months. How would he know what we were saying about Dan anyway? I'm beginning to think we were right when we thought that the phones were bugged. I for one don't trust the P.A. system either. It can be a listening device, too, down in the main office."

Jan looked at Ginny in surprise. She had never heard her speak against the high school and the administration this strongly. The job she had was her key to survival for the next ten years, so it must be the suspicion about Eric and the missing tools and parts in the automotive shop that was getting to her.

"I didn't realize that about the P.A. system," Jan replied.

"Ed Hogarty in the audio/visual office showed me how it works," stated Ginny emphatically. "The switch can be set for outgoing as well as incoming messages in the individual rooms of the school. The teachers have to be sure that their switches are put on "privacy" if they don't want to be spied on. Most of them move from room to room during the day and forget all about it. When we're talking in my office, we're gathered together almost directly under the system outlet. Think about it."

"I'm feeling a touch of paranoia," gasped Jan. "I did say some nasty things about Dan after he clamped his big hand down on my thigh during that meeting with the area superintendents. My boss was no help after I reported what had happened, so I had some choice words for him, too. It's just one big "old boy" network in this neck of the woods, I'm afraid. What else did we say, for heavens sake?"

"Well, I wish that we had known sooner. I can't remember the exact words we used, but the gist of what we were talking about was pretty plain. Lindner's rudeness and the things he said about Eric got me going, and we were already upset about Jeanne and Linda. It would seem like a full-time job to sit around and listen selectively to every person in every room in the school, though. If they're doing it, they've got some kind of a plan which doesn't include random chance."

"You mean they had certain people they wanted to get the goods on, like a black list? In that case, I'm gone, Ginny. We all know who was the head of this operation, don't we? I'll bet Dan got some good ideas at those conferences he went to all over the United States."

"I remember seeing a segment of *60 Minutes* or some other program like that where all kinds of spying was done on employees by bosses and supervisors under the justification of knowing what was going on in the businesses with company time and resources. The issue was privacy of E-mail communications and computer files. The conclusion was that bosses have the right to check on their employees like that because everything in the workplace belongs to the companies in question. The reporters and consultants for the program thought that it was pretty naive of employees to think they had a right to personal privacy at work."

"Naive and dumb and dumber," responded Jan. "We don't know for sure if someone was listening to us talk in your office or not, Ginny. Did you check to see if the privacy switch was on after you found out? When was this anyway?"

"Actually, it was last year that Ed told me about the P.A. system and then I forgot all about it, thinking it applied to the teachers only. Don't ask me why. The other day when I came back from the meeting in Lindner's office where I told him off because of what he was implying about Eric I thought to look up at the switch and it was open to the main office. I shut it off then."

"Talk about locking the barn door after the horse is stolen," said Jan. "I'll never feel comfortable in that school again. George, my boss, was talking about possibly moving the Adult Diploma Program to the new state employment office on River Street. Most of my students are their recommendations anyway, and it would be handy for me to process the paperwork for them. And I hear that they have air conditioning; think about that for those hot summer days coming--some day."

"I don't want you to leave the high school. I'll be all alone up there except for when Lindner comes along to check up on me. You know how he feels about my being there to answer the phone at all times, nevermind if I have to go to the ladies room or leave the office to go downstairs. You've covered for me enough times."

"Look Ginny, if Lindner made that crack about gossip coming from our corner of the building, you can just bet he knows what we were talking about somehow. I wouldn't put it past him to eavesdrop on us or have someone alert him that we were talking in your office."

"Well, I'd never do anything like that!" Ginny replied emphatically. "Anyhow, I'm heading for home."

Jan stared at her in amazement as she abruptly rose from her seat and left the coffee shop. There's something going on here, she thought to herself. Feeling stunned, she ordered a refill for her coffee. As she ran through the conversation with Ginny again in her mind, she stared out the window with unseeing eyes; the words "the lady doth protest too much" entered her consciousness.

When one is taking on the old boys' network or the local chapter of it, at any rate, one must learn to use their rules, she thought. There's some kind of thread that's holding all the things that have happened together, but I'll be damned if I know what it is. But I do think that Ginny has joined the enemy's camp. She's smart but her mouth gets her in trouble.

Jan finished her coffee. Grabbing her purse and the check, she proceeded to the front register to pay the bill. Her thoughts were still on the conversation with Ginny as she zipped her jacket and tugged on her gloves. Of course, private companies in business should demand employee loyalty. Of course, employees should follow company policy, but a school environment is a public domain paid for by the taxpayers. The resources of the school should be guarded against waste and the business office people have to be on the ball. But beyond all that, the employees have a double duty as taxpayers to be watchdogs over administration policies and attitudes because they are on the inside, so to speak. The trouble with that is, we're all kept so busy that we don't have time to pay enough attention to what's going on right under our noses. Whom do you trust? she thought.

Walking back up Main Street, Jan paused at the window of the boutique once more. I could go in and ask about the price of that pink blouse and check the sizes available, she told herself. I don't have to buy anything. A few minutes later she came out of the shop with the pink blouse ensconced in a flowery boutique plastic bag. The price was right, and they had her size. For some reason, she felt a little better. At least she was in control of something.

After remembering that she had parked her car in the lot behind town hall, she hurried to get underway for home. The short trip was uneventful until she drove up her hilly street and forgot about the frost heave again. The small bump and skid did not excite her, but it was annoying to have to accelerate to make it up the hill, watch out for the curvy section, and avoid the frost heave almost in one simultaneous operation. You would think that the high taxes we all pay to live in this part of town would entitle us to a decent road, she thought.

The parking area around the condo buildings was crowded with extra vehicles, so Jan quickly pulled up to her garage and opened the door to park the Escort for the night. The neighbors must have company for the Easter holiday, she thought as she pulled the heavy door down again. Dickens was at his usual post just inside when she got her front door open.

"And what do you want, old bean?" she asked him. "As if I didn't know. More fish dinner and a trip outdoors will fix you up. Did you think that I was never coming home to feed you?" Dickens eyed her accusingly and then relented enough to rub back and forth on her ankles in feigned ecstasy.

Jan put her outerwear aside and walked to the refrigerator to get out the milk for Dickens and then reached up in the cupboard for a new tin of kitty food. When her chores for the cat were finished, she rubbed him behind the ears a couple of times as he ate and then washed her hands. I certainly don't need any more caffeine, she thought, but I think I'll put on a pot of decaf for later on.

While the coffee brewed, Jan made a quick trip to the bathroom, washed her hands again, and got out the ingredients for the fruit salad. It really was no big deal, no matter that Ginny called it her "famous" fruit salad; everybody just seemed to like the combination of pineapple, mandarin oranges, and mini marshmallows in sour cream dressing. Maybe she'd put coconut on top and call it Hawaiian salad this time.

It took no time at all to finish putting the salad ingredients together and then clean up the kitchen. Dickens was put outdoors for a couple hours of prowling the neighborhood. Jan decided to shower and change into sweats for an evening of relaxation--reading or TV viewing or both at the same time as she frequently did. She hadn't eaten dinner, but she wasn't hungry yet. I'll make a sandwich later on to go with the coffee; one of the joys of living alone was doing what one pleased on one's own time schedule, she thought to herself.

By keeping busy in the kitchen, Jan had kept the bad thoughts about Jake's death at bay, but when she had showered and settled down for the evening, sadness came over her in waves as she tried to concentrate on the new book about hot viruses. She couldn't bear to think of him face down in the icy water, all alone in the darkness under the railroad trestle bridge. Once more she wished that the two of them had gone to the police station on Friday night. I usually react fast enough when I'm surprised or frightened, but this time I did nothing constructive; I just ran away.

Of course, some of the responsibility was Jake's, but he wouldn't have liked going to the police with a story that couldn't be proved by hard facts. It would be his word against Lindner's and Watkins', and they had the power on their side. Even if he had gone to the police and had been believed, what could they do for him? Nothing, most likely, thought Jan. On the other hand, she knew that Gregory Whitehouse was staying in town because she had seen him leaving the restaurant that night. Why hadn't she thought of that?

"Shit", she remonstrated with herself in thought. Or had she said it aloud for the word seemed to echo around the room? "Now I'm talking to myself; isn't it bad enough that I hold conversations with the cat. I'm over the edge."

Trying once more to concentrate on her book about hot viruses in equatorial Africa, Jan read for an hour without really remembering later what was on the printed page. She had made a vow never to set foot on the continent sometime during her reading, however. The troubles close to home kept intruding into her thoughts and they seemed more important and threatening than exotic viruses in faraway places. Maybe a good TV program will distract me, she thought as she pressed the "clicker" power switch and surfed the channels for something interesting. An old movie, *The Robe*, was playing on Channel 8, so she decided to watch that in her bedroom. After forty-five minutes of listening with her eyes half open, she passed into the blessed oblivion of sleep during one of the commercial marathons.

CHAPTER FOUR

Easter morning dawn stole quietly into Jan's room through the ivory slats of the mini-blinded windows on either side of the bed. She awoke with a start and became aware of the TV's buzzing signal for off-the-air time. The first thing she did when she became oriented to being awake was to glance at her alarm clock to see what time it was. The second thing she did was turn the TV to an early morning news show to see what the weather expectations were for the day. Thank God it was early enough for her to get ready to go to church for the seven thirty choir warm-up at a leisurely pace. Another thank God was for the promise of a warmer and sunny day for Easter.

After a quick trip to the bathroom, Jan turned the bedroom TV off and did a few arm stretches over her head to get going on her busy day. On her way to the kitchen, she noticed Dickens waiting for her to let him in on the front porch. She opened the sliding door to let him in and followed obediently to the refrigerator.

"Did I forget you last night?" Jan queried. "I didn't mean to leave you outside all night, but you don't seem any the worse for wear." Dickens coat was shiny and fluffy from the cool morning air. He purred and rubbed the front edge of the fridge in anticipation of his coming super fish breakfast. Jan knew that he was safe during the night if he stayed on the porch. Dickens knew it, too. She fed him and started on the makings of a fresh pot of coffee.

When the coffee had finished brewing, she decided that a piece of whole wheat toast to go with it would be sufficient considering all the goodies coming later at church and at Marianne's. Taking her coffee and toast in hand, she sat in the blue chair and turned it to look at the lake. The light outside was still dim at six forty-five, and the view was further obscured by a fine veiling of fog that trailed along the shoreline near town and on into Canada. Clouds backlit by the rising sun, rested on the tops of the mountains in shifting layers that seemed to flow with the wind. As she watched, a faint rosy pink tinted the faraway shrouds, forecasting the beautiful Easter day to come. She sipped her coffee and nibbled her toast in a aura of peace and awe.

Jan sat quietly for a few minutes after finishing her breakfast, eyes on the spectacular sight unfolding before her like a healing gift from God. She said a prayer for the repose of Jake's soul and then, grudgingly, one for the departed soul of Dan Frost. Whispering softly to herself, she prayed that the troubles that had come to New Venice would soon be resolved with justice for all those involved. She also thought to add a request for safety for herself and anyone else who might be in danger.

Dickens came to her chair and bounced up onto her lap. She rubbed his head behind the ears until he turned over to have his belly rubbed, too, nearly slipping off her knees in the process. Dickens was a large cat with some of the tendencies of the kitten he had been still residing under the bulk. Jan sat for five more minutes before getting up, placing the cat in her vacated seat. The blue chair was one of Dickens' favorite nap spots on a rotating schedule of favorites, so he quickly curled up to go to sleep for an hour or two.

After sipping on one more cup of coffee, she washed, brushed her teeth, and dressed for the Easter service at eight o'clock. A minimum of make-up, a pass or two at her hair with the brush, and a mist of perfume finished her beauty ritual for the morning. Slipping on a pair of flat-heeled shoes, Jan went to the kitchen to organize the items she needed to take to church or to Marianne's later on in the afternoon. Deciding that it would be easier to use her picnic basket to carry the large fruit salad, she got it down from the top shelf of the pantry to inspect for dust. A couple of swipes with a handful of paper towels did the trick before the salad was placed inside along with a promised package of butter sticks for the ten o'clock brunch.

She got her navy blue coat from the hall closet, put it on, and decided against wearing boots just for the short walk to the garage. Gathering up the picnic basket, her purse, and her gloves, Jan let herself out both of the front doors after a quick glance at Dickens to see if he was truly settled in for the morning.

The potholes in the gravel driveway were still full of muddy water, but she made it to the garage without stepping into one and pulled up the door. Climbing into the Escort, she maneuvered the basket to the front passenger seat and placed her purse on top. The car started easily after being in the garage all night. She was grateful for small favors as she backed out, pulled the door down again, and left the muddy driveway.

The streets of the town were quiet and Jan's peaceful mood continued all the way to St. Luke's church. It was going to be a glorious day as befitted the Easter holiday. Lugging in the picnic basket after finding a parking spot right in front of church, she reveled in her good fortune and happy mood. Maybe it would be possible to set aside the troubles in town for one day.

After stashing the salad and the butter sticks in the parish hall refrigerator, Jan left for the choir office to robe up. The choir director and her husband, one of the tenors, were there, as most of the alto singers. I wonder if that means anything special, she thought. Like we are the most worried about our parts. I know I will feel better after we warm up and go over some of the difficult parts again. When the organist arrived a few minutes later, they decided to get started, even though all the choir members were not present.

Molly Nadeau, the choir director, led the members in a short prayer, which included an urgent wish that the missing singers would arrive before they finished the warm-up scales.

There was a short round of muffled laughter after the "amen" and the choir started in with the vowel sounds, stretching their mouths to enunciate fully. A joyous atmosphere prevailed, as the other choir members straggled in one by one to the pretended derisive comments of the singers who had been on time. This is going to be a happy day, Jan thought.

After the warm-up was finished, she went to the parish kitchen for a drink of water before the service began. Ginny was there fussing with the tables for the buffet, but Jan avoided any hint of confrontation by wishing her a happy Easter and leaving at once for the church. There was a sad and perplexed expression on Ginny's face when she turned to Jan, just barely in time to say the same, as Jan's backside disappeared through the door.

Arriving at the choir stall in the back of the church, Jan looked over the bulletin for the eight o'clock service and marked the hymns to be sung with the congregation with small pieces of paper. She also noted the prayer book pages, because the eight o'clockers used an older version of the service called Rite One. They had choir music only on special occasions and were very appreciative of the double duty effort of the singers on Sundays such as Easter Day.

Father Gareth Winslow, the crucifer, the torch bearers, and the lay ministers readied themselves at the back of the main aisle along with the red-robed choir members for the march to the front of the church after the opening prayer. The first hymn was sung by everyone as the choir members came back to their seats by way of the two side aisles.

When Jan had seated herself after the beginning ritual, she looked at the backs of the heads of those assembled to see who was present for the eight o'clock service. To her surprise, she noted a tall, well-formed male shape which could only be that of Gregory Whitehouse, special investigator for the state police. "Well, I never," she whispered to herself. Mina, the alto singer next to her, turned to ask her what she had said, but Jan replied that she would tell her later.

She watched Gregory from the choir stall, without his being able to know that she was looking, to see if he was familiar with the standings and kneelings and sittings of the service. He hadn't said that he was Episcopalian when she was explaining about Jake's last visit on Friday night. As the choir rose at special times during the ritual to sing their special offerings for Easter Day, Jan had to concentrate on the alto parts to do her best, but she did see Gregory turn to watch the choir members at one point. She could discern a smile that was directed her way with a brief nod of his head as she was turning the page of her music while the organ played a short interval. Would he take communion, she wondered. Of course, as a baptized member of another faith he was welcome, but still it would be nice if he were an Episcopalian. It would also be nice if I kept my mind on the service, said a stern Jan to herself.

Whitehouse stayed through the whole service and took communion with the rest of the congregation. After the last triumphant hymn was sung, the congregation surged to the door to greet the pastor. Jan waited until Gregory was near the choir stalls to say hello in order to introduce him to Father Gareth.

"Happy Easter, Jan," Gregory called out as he drew near. "Your choir music was perfect, and I enjoyed the whole service. I was feeling depressed after all the autopsy talk and interviews, but this Easter service has made me feel hopeful that things can be resolved, after all."

"Thank you for the comment on the music," replied Jan with a smile. "We certainly practiced enough to get it right. I didn't know that you were interested in a church service, or I would have invited you to come this morning. I always feel better after service each week, too. Sometimes I think that I'm not going to make it through Saturday to Sunday, and I'm crankier than all get out by late afternoon. Would you like some coffee? We have a modest spread of goodies over in the parish house."

"Thank you, I think I will indulge. It's hard to celebrate Easter when a person is away from home and a stranger to all the happy people around him. I do know you, though, here at St. Luke's and that makes it Easter for me this time."

Jan introduced Gregory to Father Gareth as they were leaving the church and explained who he was. The two men shook hands, and Gregory complimented the pastor on his Easter service. Jan gave Father Gareth a hug and turned to show Gregory the way to the parish hall.

"I might as well keep my choir robe on," Jan said when they had reached the buffet table. "We are going to go over the music again in a half an hour or so. This is an all morning affair for me today."

"Tell me if I'm intruding," replied Gregory. "Do you have family members joining you?"

"No, I'm on my own here in New Venice," answered Jan, as she poured a cup of coffee and filled a plate with fresh fruit and a hot cross bun. "My husband died ten years ago, and we had no children. Actually, he was killed in an airplane accident in Maine. Maybe you remember the articles in the newspaper about his flying all over New England on sales trips and his death when his plane went down in the Allagash."

"Yes, I think I do remember. My wife and I lived outside of Montpelier at the time. We had about seven years together in that house until she died of cancer. I'm on my own, too, since then. Gail died a week before Easter after giving the cancer a good fight for over three years. That's why it was so important that I attend service this Sunday."

Gregory filled his plate and poured his coffee. They looked around for a place to sit at one of the long tables near the front window. The room was filling up with choir members and early birds who had come to help with the larger buffet after the ten o'clock service. Jan introduced him to several people who sat at their table. She asked him if his friends called him Gregory or Greg for short as she introduced him, and he smiled when he answered that he was

Greg most of the time. The "Gregory" was for work when he wanted to impress his colleagues and his boss, he told everyone at the table while they ate. Jan liked the way his eyes crinkled at the corners when he smiled. It made him seem less like the state policeman who had come to town to interrogate people about two untimely deaths. She had almost forgotten that fact herself after hearing about his personal life.

"Do you still live in Montpelier?" Jan asked.

"No," replied Greg. "I couldn't stand living in the house that we had bought and furnished together. I kept expecting to see her come around a corner, you know, from the kitchen or the den where she spent most of her time during the day after she got sick. I just couldn't take it anymore, so I sold the house after she died and moved to an apartment in Randolph. Gail was in and out of the hospital until she went into a hospice at the end. There wasn't anyone in either one of our families suitable to care for her at home, and I had to keep working as much as I was able to. The boss was great, letting me have time off to be with her in the hospice care home when she was very ill, but I always felt so guilty when I had to leave. She lingered for a long year after there was no chance for a cure."

"I know what you are talking about," said Jan. "I sold our house a little over a year after Joe's death. My condo has been home ever since. I've learned to be independent, and I know that I can take care of myself in any normal kind of emergency, if there is such a thing. The problems at the high school don't come under the heading of normal, though."

91

"Be careful, Jan. I don't think that it's over yet."

"I will, Greg. I have a really bad feeling about going back into the building, but I have my students to think of. I'll probably see a few of them this coming week if I can get them to come in for appointments. It's so spooky in the vocational building when the regular classes aren't in session that they don't like to be there, even if it's to their own advantage. Then there is my problem with Mr. Lindner, the vocational director. He dislikes me and the whole idea of a second chance for dropouts. There's something else going on, something not right, but I don't have any idea what it's all about."

"Make sure the office people know that you're there when you come in and check with them every once in a while. I'm going to have to leave now. Thank you for your hospitality today. It's made me feel much better. I'll call you tomorrow."

"Please call me. I'll be at my home number or the school switchboard can put you through to my office if I'm allowed to be there," Jan answered as Greg rose to leave.

She walked him to the door and said good-by. Turning to her right, she saw Ginny peeking at her from the kitchen area.

"How are things going for the big buffet?" Jan called to her.

"Just fine, but we could use some more help in a few minutes," Ginny replied. "Who was your visitor? He's very handsome in a rugged sort of way. I've seen him somewhere before, haven't I?"

"Maybe you saw his picture in the paper during one of his investigations. His name is Gregory Whitehouse and he's with the state police. I think he will be in town as much as possible until the two murders are solved. Everybody in town hopes that he will be able to solve the murders soon; just about everybody, that is."

"You mean everybody except the person who did them, don't you. It sounds like there is a connection, but who am I in the world of murder investigation? Have you seen the Burlington paper? Poor Dan Frost's funeral will be held on Wednesday in Montpelier. There was nothing about Jake's yet."

"What's this about "poor" Dan Frost? Now that he's dead, all is forgotten and forgiven, huh." Jan was beginning to sputter with indignation before she remembered what day it was and where she was. "I've got to go over to the church for a short rehearsal, but I should be able to help for a few minutes when we set the food out after the service. Then I have to scoot because I'm going out to Marianne's for dinner this afternoon."

"Lucky you; I've got fifteen people coming for dinner later on, about five o'clock or so. Eric and his girlfriend should be at the ten o'clock service, so maybe they can help the cleanup crew."

"Well, I wish that I could stay and help too, but I can't this time. I'll see you later."

Jan left for the church and the rehearsal feeling slightly guilty. I shouldn't worry about not helping more this time, she thought to herself. Every time we have a potluck dinner or celebration of some kind, I do my best to see that everything is cleaned up afterward. Ginny could sure make a person feel shitty sometimes.

The choir members were nearly all assembled again when Jan regained her seat in the loft, as they too had stayed for breakfast after the eight o'clock service. There were two additions to the music that had been sung at eight o'clock to practice, but they went well, as did the rehearsal of the pieces already performed once. Only one of the other altos asked Jan who her visitor was at the earlier service. The woman's eyes widened with interest when Jan explained the circumstances of Gregory Whitehouse's attendance at church and the breakfast.

Most of the choir stayed put after the rehearsal because the congregation started arriving early for the next service. The main doorway was clogged with parishioners greeting each other. Easter Sunday was very popular with those people who attended church only occasionally, and extra folding chairs were being put out in the side aisles and at the back of the nave for the expected overflow. There would be no marching around the church aisles for this service. Jan was grateful to sit in her seat in the choir loft and read her program leaflet, for she was feeling very tired all of a sudden.

The service of an hour and a half passed in a blur. The choir rose and sang at the appropriate places, but Jan had trouble concentrating on what she was doing. Her Easter Sunday emotions had been spent at the eight o'clock service, and apparently it was for many of the other choir members, especially the women who had children that had gotten up at the crack of dawn see what the Easter bunny had brought.

Daydreaming through the second time around for the sermon, Jan thought about what a strange place the world was today. Here we all are, celebrating Christ's rising from the dead and the Easter bunny boodle all rolled up in one day of pageantry, ritual, and secular jollity. No wonder the children are confused. The same goes for Christmas, she thought. And in New Venice, Vermont, we must also suppress for one day our morbid thoughts and fears of a double murder last week. And there will be consequences that follow after the perpetrator is caught. If he or she is caught. Sometimes I think that we have to be mentally ill to be able to put up with all the things that are happening around us.

The service finally ended with the last hymn, and Jan rose quickly to go to the choir office to take off her robe and put her music folder away. Hurrying to the parish house afterward, she tried to shake off her depressing thoughts as she exchanged Easter greetings with several people also headed that way. I'm going to be great company at Marianne's this afternoon if I don't get over this mood I'm in, she told herself.

Working at the simple task of laying out the various bowls and platters of food, Jan was able to hold her moodiness in abeyance for the next half an hour. The women helping chattered amongst themselves as they passed each other on trips to the kitchen and back to the buffet tables in the dining room. Everything was ready just in time for the arrival of the parishioners, who knew from experience not to arrive too soon from the church proper. The food looked scrumptious, but Jan did not stay any longer than it took to check with the kitchen crew that everything was under control. She retrieved her picnic basket, called out her good-bys, and left the parish hall for the return trip to the condo.

Dickens was waiting for her as usual as she got her door open. He would be the first order of business, Jan decided as she filled his food dish with fresh fish dinner. Dickens was suitably appreciative of this attention to his needs and purred as he gulped at his food. That's a good trick he's got there, gulping and purring at the same time, Jan thought while pulling items to go to Marianne's out of the fridge. The platter of raw veggies and the chocolate pie fit into the picnic basket just fine with a little padding of folded newspapers.

It was not necessary to be dressed up for dinner at Marianne's, so the next order of business was changing from her navy suit and new pink blouse into a pair of black slacks, a white turtleneck, and a red cardigan sweater. The weather was holding at warm and sunny, but it was not the time to give up turtlenecks and sweaters yet. Jan straightened up the bedroom, used the bathroom, and walked back to the kitchen to see how Dickens was doing. He was ready to go outdoors, so she let him out onto the porch where he found a patch of sun to sit in while he surveyed his territory for other cats and neighborhood dogs.

FROST HEAVES

Jan gathered up the picnic basket of food and her purse to place them on the coffee table in the living room while she got her red jacket out of the closet. When she turned to pick up the basket, she noticed the mail she had thrown down on the coffee table the day before. The letter from her cousin in Seattle was on the top, so Jan guiltily opened it. It was an Easter card with a note inserted describing the nice weather Seattle was having for April. Elizabeth really did want her to move out to the West Coast, Jan thought, as she put the card and note down to gather up her basket and purse again.

The trip out to the small village where Marianne and Sam lived was harrowing as frost heaves were still evident and even prominent in some instances along the way. Oncoming traffic made it impossible to dodge them all. Most people who used this state road had the bump locations memorized, but Jan's preoccupation with her thoughts of the two deaths and her possible involvement with what was going on at the high school did not contribute to her driving skill. Visions of Seattle's spring-flowering plants in her mind contrasted with the bleak views of tangled weeds in the fields along the roadway. There were even dirty spots of snow tucked into the hilly shadows. This is a very difficult place to live, Jan thought to herself as she drove the last mile into the village. People who live here year around pride themselves on being able to cope with the horrible weather in the winter, but I'm not sure I want to do it anymore.

The road to Marianne's house was on the other side of the village to the right. The hard surface of the road abruptly deteriorated into country gravel plus muddy potholes. Jan's Escort slid to the right several times, but she had slowed to moderate speed to compensate for the difficult spots. She arrived at their lane and accelerated to make it to the top of the steep driveway. Speaking of coping, she thought to herself as she parked her car to the side of the other vehicles lined up in front of the garage.

Sam was in the garage working on his inventory of farm machinery parts. He greeted Jan warmly and helped her with the picnic basket of food as she climbed out of her car. The doorway to the kitchen was at the back of the garage and up a short flight of stairs. Marianne had heard her car arrive and opened the door for her immediately. They greeted each other with happy Easter words and hugs before proceeding into the warm kitchen beyond a short hallway.

Jan unpacked the veggie platter and the chocolate amaretto pie. Dinner was almost ready, so the veggies were set out for appetizers with a simple dip that Marianne had in the refrigerator.

Within ten minutes, Sam came in from the garage and went to wash up for dinner. There would be just the three of them this Sunday. The Mackenzie's only child, a grownup son, was visiting college friends for the holiday. Jan set the veggie platter and dip on the coffee table in the adjoining family room, and the three of them sat chatting idly while the roast fresh ham on the kitchen counter rested for the recommended time before slicing.

"How was your Easter service at Sacred Heart?" Jan inquired. Marianne and Sam attended the Roman Catholic church in the village.

"We went to the early one this year," responded Sam. "The eleven o'clock service is so crowded that it has become distracting. It was great when Rick was young, but now I think we prefer going when it is quieter."

"You're right about the crowd at the later time," Marianne agreed. "Did you have a nice buffet after your ten o'clock service?"

"It certainly looked great with a lot of fabulous food brought in for the tables," Jan said with a smile. "I stayed long enough to help get the dishes put out, and then I left. I really got all pooped out what with all the practices and worry about the music going right. I never seem to remember from one year to the next how tiring it is to get up for the early service, get everything together to take to church, practice one last time, and then perform well. Of course, we all tell ourselves that we are not performing, but there is the strain of wanting things to be beautiful for both services."

"I know what you mean," answered Marianne. "I was the lay reader for the first service. I'm always afraid I'm going to stumble over the words or somehow disgrace myself, but it turns out okay every time."

"How do the people of New Venice seem to be coping with all the tragedy?" Sam asked. "We heard about Jake Patenaude's death last night."

"I'm glad you asked me that," Jan answered soberly. "We were all wrapped up in our Easter doings at church, which seems callous. People can't focus on tragedy all the time when there're other obligations to take care of, the daily types of things and the special ones like preparing for Easter. As for myself, I feel involved because of my friendship with Jake Patenaude. He was frightened and wanted to tell me something on Friday night after the church service. He scared me, and it's as if I went brain dead. Instead of insisting that we go to the police station immediately with the information he said he had about what's been going on at school, I let him get away from me. I find that feelings of depression come over me every few hours even when I'm not actively thinking about what has happened."

"We didn't realize that you were so involved with Jake Patenaude's death, Jan. He must have seen or heard something at work the night Dan Frost was killed, I'll bet. Something else, Sam found specific information yesterday about those land purchases out near Barton," Marianne chimed in. "And we wanted to let you know right away. When we were talking about it on the phone, the subject sounded a little bit like country gossip, but Sam says it's true and it's a big deal."

"Yes," Sam said with a frown. "I spoke to a Mrs. Morely who owned most of the land, and she confirmed that she had sold it to three people, two men and a woman who worked at the high school. She got a good price, too, according to what she told me. There were other considerations involved with the sale, however. From what I've been able to figure, it must have been something to do with an agriculture school, according to her understanding. I don't know anything more about that part of the of the deal, though." Sam's eyebrows shot up and his brow furrowed all the way to his wispy brown receding hairline. Deals of this magnitude were not common to the New Venice area.

"What I can't figure out is where they got that kind of money," Jan declared.

"Me either," agreed Sam and Marianne in unison.

"I had an interview with Greg Whitehouse, the state police investigator, Saturday afternoon. It wasn't the official one as an employee of the diploma program at the high school. It was about my worries when Jake didn't appear for an appointment we had set up for Saturday morning. He didn't show and it started to get late, so when I heard customers talking about someone being found dead in the river, I was sure it was Jake. He had wanted to tell me something important that morning. My crazy intuition had kicked in, and I had to tell someone, so I went to the police station. Greg got in touch with me after I got home. I went down to his office at three o'clock to tell him what I knew. He also seemed very interested in the land purchase deal, rumor or no rumor, and said he had a person to check it out with in Barton. I felt a whole lot better after I told him about Jake and all. He also told me to be careful if I went up to the vocational wing to work with my students this coming week. Even though I'm not particularly happy about the situation, I'm not going to let it scare me off.

Graduation time is getting close, and I do think that if anyone can get to the bottom of the mess, he can. I was impressed."

"What's he like?" Marianne asked rather breathlessly. "Is he married or anything?"

Marianne was always trying to fix Jan up with men she thought were eligible. She and Sam were very happy together, and she wanted Jan to have the same good relationship with a suitable companion. Jan, however, prided herself on her independence and avoided most of Marianne's proposed introductions and arrangements. They both understood the other friend's perspective and laughed about it sometimes when they were in a reminiscing mood.

"Let's get dinner on the table. I'll fill you in as we go along," said Jan. She looked at Marianne's small, sweet face surrounded by soft brown curls and sighed. Marianne was a true friend, one who cared about Jan's welfare as much as she did for her own.

"First of all, I should tell you that he came to the eight o'clock church service and seemed right at home with the ritual. I would guess that he is an Episcopalian who goes to church regularly. We had coffee and something to eat together in the parish hall after the service while I was waiting to warm up for the ten o'clock."

Marianne had started to slice up the ham. She stopped to give Jan a good look as she and Sam passed to and fro carrying mashed potatoes, green bean casserole, and hot rolls to the table from the kitchen. Jan knew that she was blushing when Sam started to laugh.

"You'd better tell all," he said with a grin. "She'll never be satisfied until she gets all the details."

"All right, you devils, I liked him a lot," she admitted. "He's tall and well built with brown hair and gray-green eyes that sort of twinkle when something amuses him. His wife died of cancer five years ago, and he's still trying to get over it. I told him about Joe's death, and he remembered the articles in the newspaper about his plane crash in Maine. We sort of hit it off with our memories of the past and the guilt feelings."

"I don't know why you feel guilty after all this time. It isn't that Joe was a saint or anything. He knew that you worried about his flying over the Allagash, especially after the other accidents with small planes that year, and he proceeded to do just as he pleased." Marianne was indignant.

"I realize that I shouldn't feel guilty, but my heart still nags at me for not insisting that Joe drive on that last sales trip. It was kind of like I had an intuition of what was going to happen. I never talked about it to anyone, but maybe I should have."

"Why did this Gregory Whitehouse say that he felt guilty?" asked Sam.

"He feels that he didn't spend enough time with his wife because of having to work," answered Jan. "There was no one in the family to help take care of her at the end. She went into a hospice house in Montpelier, and Greg's boss was good about letting him off work to be with her as much as possible, but it wasn't easy for him to get up and say good-by when he had to leave."

"Did she linger long in pain, do you think?" queried Marianne. "That probably is part of the guilt--you know wanting a loved one to live and get well when you know that the best thing is for her to pass on because of the pain."

"I'm sure you're right, Marianne," replied Jan. "It's just hard to let go of someone you love. When Joe died in the crash, there was a possibility that he might have survived and was out there where it was difficult to find him right away. I had a couple of days of hope, and then it was over when the site was discovered with no survivor. I think that it was easier on me than on someone in Greg's situation."

"I think you're both right. But it's hard to figure someone else's feelings out if you've not walked in his shoes." Sam was ready to eat. "Enough of the sad talk. Let's dig into this great-looking dinner. Bless this food and us that eats it."

"Sam, you fool," remonstrated Marianne. They were all smiling when they sat down at the table, however.

Dinner, consumed with gusto, lived up to its delicious looks and aroma. They helped themselves to small second portions, vowing to save room for the dessert of chocolate amaretto cheesecake pie topped with real whipped cream later on after the dishes were cleaned up.

"I'll put on a pot of coffee, and while it's brewing we can go for a short walk to wear off all the dinner we ate," Marianne declared emphatically. "You know how it is at our age, the pounds go on in a flash but take weeks of starving to get rid of."

Jan agreed to the walk idea, but Sam opted for TV watching in his favorite recliner chair. They all knew that he would be taking a nap within ten minutes of whatever program he picked to watch. Sam did not put on weight like the women did and felt free to tease them as they went out the door.

"That Sam is too much sometimes," complained Marianne. "If he wasn't such a good guy, I'd tease him right back about that double chin he's working on. When he's out on the road with the farm stuff, it's quite a heavy duty job he's got, you know, loading and unloading from his truck and helping the farmers set up the equipment he brings them. It keeps the rest of his body in shape, anyway."

"It wouldn't be fair to pick on him for the small stuff," answered Jan. "We'll make it our little secret. Men are lucky anyway when they want to take off weight 'cause it seems to roll right off if they give up beer and desserts for a while. We don't want him to give up dessert today, do we?"

"Certainly not. How about giving me the real scoop on Mr. Whitehouse while we're walking. I noticed right off that you were calling him Greg."

"I finally asked him about the Gregory when I was introducing him around at church because it got to sounding so formal."

"Do you think he's someone you could have a relationship with?"

"To tell you the absolute truth, yes. He seems like such a straightforward guy with lots of common sense, and he's sensitive to other people's problems to boot. He's going to call me tomorrow."

"If he turns out to be the kind of person you've been waiting for, I'm glad. I know how much you've had to bear lately with the high school administration acting like they're plotting against you and the diploma program. Maybe you would be better off if your office could be moved to the state employment office."

The two women walked briskly down the gravel road as far as the farmhouse situated about a mile from the Mackenzie place. They turned around for the trip back to the sound of a big black dog's barking because they had crossed some invisible territorial line. A teenage boy came out of the barn waving at Marianne and yelling to the dog to stop.

"It seems like we've done this before," commented Jan as they ignored the barking and continued with their conversation. "Won't that dog ever get to know us?"

"Probably not," answered Marianne. "He barks at me when I walk alone, too. To get back on the track of what we were talking about, doesn't it seem to you that things at school were going along like everything was normal while all the time there were undercurrents that were just waiting to burst out to the surface?"

Jan stopped in her tracks for a minute, staring at one of the ubiquitous "Bump" signs planted by the side of the gravel road. "It's sort of like the sign there, reminding us that water has seeped under the roadbed to produce either a pothole or a frost heave. Dan Frost's death has upset the status quo and brought all the hidden trouble to the surface."

"That's an analogy you'll want to save for the future, I'm sure," replied Marianne with a grimace.

The two friends reached the Mackenzie place and trudged up the steep driveway in silence. When they were inside, they directed their steps to the kitchen after slipping off their muddy shoes. Peeking into the family room, Marianne saw that Sam had indeed drifted off to sleep in his chair in front of the TV set.

"Sam's asleep, but he can catch up on dessert when he wakes up. I'm glad he's snoozing. He can use the extra rest."

Jan cut the pie into small pieces for the two of them and topped it off with whipped cream. Neither one of them felt a twinge while enjoying her dessert. After all, they had walked off a few calories from dinner and therefore were entitled to a bit of chocolate and whipped cream.

"Let's have a cup of coffee and clean up our dishes before I have to leave," said Jan. "I've got a busy day tomorrow with four students coming in for assessment of last week's homework, and I know you are traveling with Sam tomorrow on his deliveries. Are you getting a really early start?"

"Yes we are," answered Marianne. "The farmers are up early, of course, and it takes time at each stop to unload and chat a bit. We can't just drive away without being friendly to the customers, you know."

Half an hour later, Jan was on her way home with some goodies from dinner packed in her picnic basket for a meal later on. It had been a nice Easter day in spite of all the upsets and sadness in New Venice.

Dickens ran out into the driveway from a clump of bushes as she neared her garage. While this worried her, she was pretty sure that he did not have a premature death wish and so would be wary as he approached the Escort. By the time she had parked the car and shut the door, he was scampering for the front door to be let in.

It's as bad as having a kid to worry about, she thought as she unpacked the basket and put her booty away in the refrigerator. Dickens was putting on his "I'm starving" dance about her feet, so she fed him first before putting on her sweats to call it a day. In another half hour, she had made herself comfortable in bed with her book and glasses near-by in case the TV viewing didn't hold her interest. Fifteen minutes later. she had dozed off to the purring of the muted program sound.

CHAPTER FIVE

Monday mornings were not her favorites. Jan awoke at six thirty and groaned with a feeling of fatigue for the whole coming week pressing down upon her forehead. Dickens was not having any trouble facing the morning, however. He stretched luxuriously to full length and gave a little squeak of contentment and then rose to nudge Jan on the chin. Thusly reminded of her duty to cat and employment, she slid out of bed, carefully retrieving her glasses before they hit the floor. Noting that her reading light was still on and that the TV set was humming in the background, she realized that she had had a good night's rest in spite of how she felt at the moment. With the TV sound adjusted to a moderately loud level so that she could hear the newscast as far as the kitchen, she made a trip to the bathroom and then to the fridge for milk and cat food. Dickens followed her steps all the way to make sure he got his breakfast first.

Deciding to take an aspirin before the impending headache got a lasting grip on her face, Jan reached into the cabinet to her right for the pill bottle she had put there where it would be handy to a glass and the water faucet. Am I organized or what, she thought to herself as she swallowed the small tablet. Probably or what. She chuckled as she leaned against the counter trying to think what would go well with aspirin for breakfast. She put on a pot of coffee, grateful to be up early again so that she did not have to make any momentous decisions right away.

Five minutes later with coffee cup in hand, Jan sat in the blue chair and turned to look out the sliding glass door as she did nearly every day. There wasn't much to see this early as the dim morning light obscured more than it highlighted, but the promise of a small patch of blue to the northeast was showing amongst the smoky-looking gray clouds. It might be a nice day after it gets going, she thought, and the weatherperson was indeed promising sunshine and warmer temperatures from the bedroom television set.

Traffic with headlights still on began showing up on the road below, glowing through the haziness. I'll have to get going pretty soon, too, she thought as she watched pick-ups, passenger vehicles, and large trucks bound for the local Grand Union go by. For now though, it was pleasant to watch other people on their way to work and sip coffee in the comfort of her blue chair.

After fifteen minutes had passed she went back to the kitchen for a glass of orange juice and two pieces of wheat toast. Munching and sipping her way back to the blue chair, she began to plan the day in her mind. She had two students coming for appointments before noontime. If she got to her office by eight o'clock, she'd be ready for the first one, who was scheduled to arrive at eight thirty. Each of the appointments took about an hour of one-on-one contact, so the second student was due in at quarter to ten. Holiday weeks, however, were not good for keeping to a normal pattern because the students were not as interested in keeping their appointments. Some of the men and women did not like the atmosphere of the school at any time, but managed to get to her office in spite of their feelings. Others did not like the school when it was empty of the regular students even though it was quieter and better for concentration. Jan tried to balance her time so that she always had work to do correcting papers or managing her files even though the students did a no-show on her. Most of them were courteous enough to call and let her know they weren't coming, but a few just stood her up, no matter how many times she scolded them. Today was going to be one of those trying days she had from time to time.

Jan got up from her chair just as Dickens strolled by asking to be let out for the morning.

"Good-by, pest," she told him as he squeezed past her legs. "Remember now, I'm going to work today, and I won't be back until four o'clock. I'm sure you understand every word I say to you. Not."

With a whisk of his tail, Dickens was gone through the porch railings into the bushes below. Jan checked her closet for something to wear and decided to be informal in jeans, cotton turtleneck, and a navy blue cardigan in keeping with the casual type of week she had going.

After showering, she poured one last cup of coffee to sip as she dressed. Her mind was running a mile a minute with thoughts of her other appointment at noontime with Greg, if indeed he did call her office. Would they just have coffee or would they have lunch, too? Should they go Dutch for the meal or make a vow to take turns picking up the tab? Would there be other lunches or dinners out together? Boy, am I ever out of practice with this stuff, she thought as she finished the coffee and went back to the bathroom to brush her teeth.

On her way out the door at last, her eyes fell on the card and note from her cousin that she had left on the coffee table. If I have a few minutes to kill, I'll write back and let Liz know that I appreciate her offer and that I'm still thinking about joining her in Seattle after my students graduate in June, she thought. I can visit and check the place out when I take my vacation time. If I like Seattle, I'm out of here.

Arriving at the parking lot near the vocational wing, Jan remembered that she had promised Greg that she would let the office people know she was in the building seeing students. Her first stop was the vocation office to say good morning to Sis, the director's secretary, and to inspect the cubbyhole mailbox for envelopes from the main program office in Montpelier. She collected two large manila missives from the box and noted the adult diploma return address as she continued down the first floor corridor to the academic wing. Apparently it was no surprise that she was in to see students this morning.

Hoping to get a glance at Dorothy Watkins' conniving face in the main office, she was disappointed. Two secretaries were busily typing at their desks, but the principal was not in yet for the first morning of the spring vacation. As a salaried administrative employee of the school district, she was obliged to put in a few hours each day at her own discretion. Jan didn't know how she'd react to a conversation with Dorothy, knowing what she had found out about her from Sam and Jake. Jan knew that her own face reddened easily and that her expression showed clearly what she was thinking most of the time. She had never been able to hide a secret thought from her mother or anyone else all her growing-up years, and nothing had changed even though she was now in her forties. Realizing this fact had kept her on the straight and narrow pathway when she was young while her friends were getting into mischief at school and at home. "Saint Jan" they called her derisively and that made her mad. The tears came later in the privacy of her own room.

"I just wanted to let you folks know that I'm in my office most of the day if any of my students call or come in the main office to inquire about me," Jan called out to the first secretary to look at her with inquiry in her expression. "Is anyone else in upstairs in the vocational wing?"

The younger of the two women answered that she didn't know. Replies of this nature were often given to the students when they came in to the main office asking for information, and Jan had confirmed this during her nine-year stay in the high school. It made for some merry mix-ups, as Jan called the confusion caused by the secretaries' not getting up to find the proper answers.

"Well, anyway, if a call comes through the switchboard for me, I'm here," Jan called out as she turned to leave the office. I'll take the scenic route back to the vocational wing, she told herself, not realizing what she was thinking. The darkened hallways to the back of the building were quiet, but she could not help glancing with curiosity at the stairwell where Dan Frost's body had lain last Thursday. In the past, she had said the very same thing to herself about the scenic route when she decided to walk down the main corridor of the academic wing and turn toward the vocational wing at the last cross hallway. She guessed that she wouldn't be saying that again.

When she got to the stairwell in her building, the light was out. Taking her key, she turned it on and noted with disgust that the filth from last week was still present on the steps. Somebody's going to break his neck on these stairs some day, she thought, and wished she could scour out the words from her mind again. "How long will this blundering on my part go on?" she questioned herself. "I hope that I don't say anything like what I just thought out loud in front of a student or anyone else, for that matter."

"'Saint Jan', indeed," she muttered, as she opened the door to her office. The air inside the room was stuffy like it always was when the office was closed for an extended period of time.

There was an additional scent present that made her wrinkle her nose in apprehension, however. As she tried to think exactly what it was that was different, male sweat and cigar smoke came to mind.

Jan put her bookbag, purse, and mail down on the gray metal desk that sat perpendicular to the far wall and surveyed the small room. There were a long all-purpose table also placed in a perpendicular position just a few feet from her desk, two small tables along the right wall, and a large bookcase on the near wall next to the doorway. A three-drawer file cabinet, placed at the free end of her desk to form a partial panel of privacy, and assorted chairs completed the furnishings of the room. There was no window to open for ventilation, so the door stayed ajar all the time when she was in the room with students.

Having had people make jokes many times about her intuitions, Jan was wary of jumping to conclusions or articulating what she felt on certain occasions, like what she was feeling right then. Someone had been in the room over the weekend. Her textbooks and reference books were slightly askew on the tables and in the bookcase. There was that smell that made the hairs on the back of her neck stand on end. She quickly checked the desk drawers and the file cabinet contents. Nothing was missing that she could think of. The recorder/player was in its usual place in the lower desk drawer, and it was the only item that would attract a juvenile thief.

There was the logical conclusion that a janitor had been in the room, cleaning the floor, but on second thought that wasn't very logical after all.   Jan took care of the dusting and sweeping in her small office herself.   The tile floor got washed and waxed twice a year and that was it. The janitors knew that she was not a member of the regular school staff and so left her to fend for herself. That's not to say that the rest of the vocational wing was immaculate because it wasn't even close to being neat most of the time.   Grubby would be the word that came to mind, as if the students who occupied the building weren't worthy of clean halls and carpeted classrooms like the students in the academic wing.

What should I do about this, Jan thought in apprehension.   There's no proof that anyone's been here and taken anything that belongs to me or the program. I don't want to be here by myself, though. She decided to go down to the vocational office to ask Sis if there had been anyone around cleaning offices or doing repair work of some kind. The electrician moved things around when he had to change the wiring for new lights or outlets for electronic equipment.

Sis was opening and sorting mail when she got to the downstairs office. She looked up and smiled at Jan as she had not when Jan was in the office before.

"I hear that you have a new gentleman friend," she stated. "What do you think of our fearless state policeman investigator, anyway?"

Jan was nonplussed. "How did you get the idea in your head that he is anything special to me?" she asked.   "I've met him twice, once because of the murder investigation that's going on and once at church, for heaven's sake."

Sis didn't bat an eye at Jan's retort. She was an old hand at the end of the grapevine which extended into the voc office. "Well, Ginny was just here a minute ago, and she filled me in on all the news as usual, right or wrong. She's got a meeting with Lindner and Dot over in the other wing. Don't know what it's all about. Come to think of it, they must be getting ready to dump on somebody. That's the way it works around here. Secret meetings. Nobody's supposed to know. You think I care? No way. I just want to get my kid out of here with a diploma and then I'm leaving."

"Yeah, I know how it worked all the other times, as with the two women from our end of the wing who shall be nameless. Maybe they're just having a regular Monday morning meeting. What I really came down to ask you is this, has there been anybody cleaning offices upstairs or making repairs over the weekend?"

"Are you kidding?" Sis replied. "Did you get a good look at the halls and stairwells? Lindner was here because he left work for me on my desk for today, but that's it. They haven't replaced poor Jake yet, so there wasn't even a night watchman on duty."

"It looked to me like someone had been in my office and moved things around just enough to make it noticeable to me. Nothing was taken, though, or vandalized like kids do when they go on a rampage. Besides, kids wouldn't find anything in my office interesting anyway."

"You're probably right about that, Jan," replied Sis with a grin. "I've seen all those textbooks and program workbooks you have in your office. If I was a kid, I'd steer clear of all those possible learning opportunities. They might expand my mind and it would explode or something. Did you check your answer booklets to see if they were all there?"

"I went through everything in my file cabinet, and not a piece of program material is missing," answered Jan. "I don't lock it up because I thought the office door lock was enough. The only thing I noticed beyond that is the smell in the room when I opened the door this morning. It was a combination of sweat and cigar smoke ... hard to explain. You had to be there, I guess."

"Well, if anyone was there, he didn't clear it with me on Friday. Nobody smokes on school property when they might get caught, but some of the guys don't care on the weekends. I'll keep my ears open and let you know if the school electrician was in though. Lindner sometimes doesn't tell me about repairs or changes until a bill comes in and I don't know what to do with it. It will make you feel better if you can explain things, like you said. We've got enough trouble going for us."

"Right! I've got to get back upstairs. A student is coming in about now, I think. You know how it is during a holiday week. If I have any good news about men friends, I'll let you know myself, and you can tell Ginny that if you want to. See you."

When Jan returned to her office, there was no student waiting for her. It was still in the realm of possibility, however, so she sat at her desk putting together a packet of materials for the next week's homework to give to him after today's assessment was finished. Within five minutes the student, Jim Green, arrived out of breath and full of apologies for being late. They both sat at the long table, one on each side, and Jan began the questioning for assessment of his last week's homework. She wrote his replies on her form until they came to the part where she passed over a sheet of questions that had him working on his own. It contained a mixture of business math, simple geometry, and English essay types of problems. Jan got up and handed him a piece of scrap paper to do his figuring on and then left the room to let him work in privacy. This was standard procedure for the adult diploma program, trusting the student to realize that cheating would only hurt his or her chances for a regular high school diploma--a basic necessity for employment.

The door to Ginny's office was open, and she had been busy making a pot of coffee. Jan decided that she would have to act as if she knew nothing about the launching of her apparent friendship-with-Greg Whitehouse news onto the school grapevine. Ginny often caused trouble with her news items, but she seemed to get a kick out of the furor stirred up when the denials and counter charges started flying. Some of the teachers and staff members vowed never to tell her anything she didn't need to know to do her job.

"Good morning, Ginny," Jan called out, as she reached for a coffee mug. "I've got a few minutes to kill while Jim Green finishes up his answer sheet for Booklet Four. I'm really impressed with his dedication and his intelligence. He'll be able to graduate this year for sure."

"I'll bet his wife and little girl will be glad to hear that. He should have graduated six years ago, and would have if he'd paid more attention to school work than he did to partying and drinking," replied Ginny. "Hi, yourself. Are you in the office for the whole day or what?"

"All day," said Jan, as she poured coffee into her mug and added a spoonful of creamer. "I have two appointments for this morning and two this afternoon, but I'm sure that I'll have at least one no-show. How did the brunch go at church after I left?"

"Everything went along very smoothly, but we had a ton of food left over. All the helpers had goodies to take home with them after we got the place cleaned up. How're Marianne and Sam doing? I haven't seen them in ages."

"They're fine. It was just the three of us for dinner. Marianne and I went for a long walk afterward to work off the old calories before we indulged in dessert. The whole day was great."

"I was so tired after everyone left my house late in the afternoon that I took a nap at the wrong time and then I couldn't sleep all night," said Ginny. "How did you and that Gregory Whitehouse get acquainted anyway? Did you meet him someplace before he showed up at church?"

"I thought I told you that I had an interview with him about Jake's wanting to see me Saturday morning," answered Jan. "He was very nice and agreed with me about letting him know what was going on with Jake before he was killed." She smiled to herself at Ginny's transparent attempt to lever information out of her. "Maybe I didn't say anything to you about Jake or my interview with the police investigator. I was very upset and afraid for Jake and for myself before I spoke to him. It didn't seem right to talk about Jake's problem to anyone else. When Greg appeared at church, I was very surprised because I didn't know he was Episcopalian. I would have invited him if I had known."

Ginny gave Jan a hurt look. "No, you didn't tell me any of what was going on." There was another took in her eyes that Jan did not like. It could have been resentment and anger combined.

"It's up to the authorities to sort things out now. Have you had your interview with the state police yet?" Jan asked. "I believe they are going to be very thorough about finding out what has been going on around here for the past year or so. It's obvious that something's gone wrong to cause two deaths within a period of two days."

"Nobody's contacted me so far. The main office secretaries and Sis have talked to Inspector Whitehouse. If they wanted to see me, I think that they would have told Lindner first, but I just got out of a meeting with him and Dorothy and nothing was said."

Jan refrained from asking what the meeting was all about. "I've got to go check on Jim," she said and left the room with her coffee cup in hand.

Jim had nearly finished his mini-test, so Jan sat quietly at her desk until he glanced up to say that the work was completed. She went over the homework assignment for the next week with him, and they agreed on an appointment time. Jan showed him a few corrections that he needed to make in his previous week's work and praised him for his persistence in pursuing the requirements for graduation. Jim's face beamed with pride as he rose from his chair and thanked her for her help. There goes a man who has seen the light, she told herself. It makes my job worthwhile, no matter what the superintendent said in his closed meeting or what Toady Lindner thinks.

She left the room to get a refill of coffee and noted Ginny's absence. Returning to her desk, she quickly did the corrections needed on Jim's homework and mini-test. All of their transactions of the day were noted on a separate sheet of paper stapled to the inside cover of to his folder, and it was returned to its place in the file cabinet drawer.

Taking a peek around the doorway of her office, Jan saw that her next student was just emerging from the stairwell and heading for the office. I'm batting a hundred percent today, she congratulated herself. So far, that is. This appointment would be short because the young woman was doing pre-testing on reading comprehension using the cassette player for instructions and questions. She was only allowed to do this test today, and most of Jan's students breezed right through it.

After a few minutes of general conversation, Jan set the woman up at one of the little tables. She explained the working of the player and warned her that the test was a listening one as well as a reading comprehension test. The student could take her time and reread anything she wanted to, and the cassette player was completely under her control as far as rewind and fast forward were concerned, Jan said. She told her that she would leave her alone to work along at her own pace and would return from time to time to check on how the test was going. After giving the instructions, she left the room.

Ginny was seated in front of her computer when Jan reached the adult ed office door. She seemed to be in trouble over a project she was doing, so Jan did her best not to disturb her as she reached for the coffee pot and fixed herself one more cup. There was a "Higher Education Journal" article that she wanted to read while waiting to check on her student's progress, so she settled down in one of the red plastic lounge chairs with her coffee. When the phone rang several minutes later, they both jumped up to answer it at the same time. Ginny won the honor of answering and passed the phone over to Jan, saying that it was for her. This happened often enough when the switchboard operator of the moment did not realize that Jan had her own telephone in her office. It was Greg, asking if she was free at noontime for coffee and/or lunch at the coffee shop downtown. Jan told him that she would be and promised to meet him at twelve o'clock on the dot.

After she replaced the receiver, she could see that Ginny was clearly upset over something that Jan could not figure out at once. It could have been the computer project, her meeting with Lindner and Watkins, of anything else unknown to Jan, but it was clear that she was going to vent her anger and frustration.

"I wish that you would take your phone calls in your own office," Ginny spat out with enough venom in her voice to set Jan's face aflame with resentment. They both knew that it was someone in the main office that had made the mistake, and Jan reminded her of that fact.

"By the way, Ginny," she retorted, "have you checked to see whether the privacy switch is on for our infamous listening device, or doesn't it matter to you, after all."

"You think you're so smart with your new boyfriend and your wonderful program and all," Ginny replied. "You'd better be ready to pack it up and move on and pretty soon."

"What brought this on?" answered Jan. "Was it your meeting with Lindner and Watkins this morning? Did you make a deal with them to cover Eric and his job, or was it your own position you were interested in saving? You don't have to work yourself up to a case of hate for me to make yourself feel better about turning traitor. I thought you wanted me to stay because it would be lonely for you up here with only Lindner for company. And, who is going to answer your phone for you while you're running the halls spreading gossip wherever you go?"

"I don't know what you're talking about," Ginny retorted.

"You don't know that your nickname is 'the town crier' and nobody wants to tell you anything that doesn't pertain to your job for fear that you'll spread the news all over school? I've tried to be a friend, but things have gone too far now. By the way, who was it that told Sis that a new man friend was in my life? It couldn't have been you, could it?"

"I don't know where Sis got that information. I certainly didn't tell her anything," Ginny lied vehemently. Her face was pinched and gray-looking with spite. "Just take your old coffee breath out of here and don't come back."

"It's only to my advantage to do so," replied Jan. "This filthy building and its rude inhabitants has gotten on my nerves, big time. It doesn't matter if I'm here with students or at the library or the employment office--to me or my boss, and you know it."

"Lindner has already called and written to your boss complaining about you."

"And you filled him in with all the information you could think of, too, I'll bet." Jan turned and left the office, ostensibly never to return.

Back at her desk, Jan reached for the telephone to call her boss in Montpelier, but changed her mind deciding to call from her home phone. The young woman student told her that she had finished the booklet she was working on but wanted to check her answers one more time before she turned it in. Jan was grateful to sit quietly at her desk and recover from her angry words with Ginny. As she thought about it, she knew in her heart that there was something going on with Ginny that she did not understand.

When the student had finished checking her answers, she gave the booklet to Jan and they made an appointment for the next week at the same time.

There was half an hour left before she was to meet Greg for lunch. That was plenty of time to drive to the condo and make the telephone call to her boss in Montpelier. He would be likely to be there on a Monday morning taking care of paperwork and planning his itinerary around the state overseeing the various program sites. Jan grabbed her purse and jacket, turned out the overhead light, and locked the door on her way out of the office. She took the stairs on the run while at the same time being careful not to stumble. As she made the turn out of the stairwell and to the right, John Lindner was standing near the corner blocking the way. When he saw who it was plowing into him from the stairwell, he smiled a very unpleasant smirk as if to say to her, I know why you're in such a big hurry. Jan apologized and kept on going to the outside door. Her car was parked nearby, so it took her only a few minutes to climb in and back out of the parking space.

Trying to get her breathing under control, Jan consciously took in air and exhaled again in a regular rhythm as she drove. Traffic along the causeway and bridge to the main street was at minimum. There were no stoplights anywhere between the bottom of Main Street and her condominium, which made the trip short and smooth. She left the car in front of the building where parking was forbidden and dashed inside to use the phone. As the telephone began to ring in the Montpelier office, she remembered to look out toward the front porch where Dickens patiently waited to be let in.

George Wright answered the telephone himself. It was lunchtime and apparently everybody else was gone for that reason or otherwise away from his or her desk. Jan quickly explained who was calling and why to him.

George was a kindly older man who was looking forward to retirement at the end of the school year, but he was also a player in the state politics game even if the stakes were small potatoes at his level. However, he had not been successful at getting more money for salaries out of the federal pot for two years in a row. Several of the adult diploma program's teachers were disgruntled by this turn of events because they worked very hard in offices where they had little support other than his monthly visits. George would arrive on schedule bringing supplies and good news about coming staff meetings and seasonal get-togethers as usual, but there was little he could do for them when there were disputes in the individual high schools involved with the program. At this point in his life, he didn't want to make waves with his superiors anyway if it would only mean hard feelings and no concrete action for the better.

All the school districts around the state considered themselves autonomous and were not apt to consider the overall state picture after they had captured their share of the state aid money. The bad news was that information or misinformation was passed around by school principals and superintendents at their high administrative meetings where cooperation would better serve the citizens of the state who paid their salaries through taxation. Jan thought about the situation once in a while when the power brokers for the state money pitted themselves against their opponents in the individual districts and the infighting got dirty. No changes for the benefit of the students came out of the clashes, no matter how many times they were proposed, because someone at a high level of administration would lose money, territory, or power in the process. Someone on Jan's level would always be too busy working with those students every day to grasp all the ramifications of what was going on.

"What can I do for you, Jan," said George in his jovial voice. "How's everything in New Venice if you discount murder and a state police investigation in your workplace? I was going to call you to see how things were going. It's just one disaster after another up there in your corner of the state."

"Some people in the vocational building think I'm the disaster," answered Jan. "Have you finished opening your mail?"

"There wasn't much to open this morning," said her boss. "Why do you ask? It can't be that there is anything wrong with your work for the program or I'd have heard about it."

"Well, I think that you will be getting a phone call and a letter pretty soon complaining about my presence in the high school. The adult ed secretary informed me a few minutes ago that you had already had a phone call from John Lindner requesting that I be removed to other premises. The excuse is gossip and spreading lies about the efficiency of Mr. Lindner, which upsets the vocational wing personnel much more that murder does, if you can believe it. The business of not paying for the adult diploma program to the state coffers or the undermining of my work during school board meetings has nothing to do with the whole affair, I suppose," Jan answered sarcastically.

"Did John speak to you directly about this at any time?"

"He never speaks to me directly about anything," replied Jan, "unless you count last Friday morning when I went in to meet a student who couldn't be reached for cancellation. He yelled at me that I shouldn't be there after Dan Frost's murder because it was inappropriate, and then he said that I didn't belong in his building at all. I've also learned that the main office has a way of listening in on conversations that take place in the adult ed office, but I'm sure I'm not the only one who has made remarks they didn't like. It's just that the diploma program doesn't seem to have a real home or support there since Lindner's been in charge."

"I'm sorry you have to go through this trouble right now when there is the police investigation going on in addition to everything else. Have you been interviewed by the state police for any reason?"

"Yes, there is a question of why the night watchman at school would want to speak to me privately on Saturday morning. I kept the appointment we made because he was a friend, but the guy never showed up. His was the second murder. I had this intuition that's whose body it was they found in the river before it was identified, and I went to the town police to report in. Poor Jake was terrified about something to do with Dan Frost's murder in the school building. He told me that he had seen Dan and other people in the academic wing at odd hours of the night, but he never heard what it was all about. Now I think that he knew much more and wanted some advice about what to do."

"My God, Jan, I never dreamed that you were this involved. Is there anything that I can do for you?"

"Remember that talk we had about moving the program to the employment office on River Street? I think that it's time you looked into it seriously. There must be room in that great big building they have now."

"I'll do that right away. Don't worry about Lindner's calling me or writing letters. I'll handle it."

Jan thanked him and said good-by. It would be wonderful to get away from all the trouble at the high school. After finding her office disturbed, there was no way that she could remain there even if Lindner loved her. George was fairly good at the political maneuvering, and he was a genuine fan of the adult program as well as being the supervisor. He could get her office into the state employment building if anyone could.

Jan sighed with relief at mission accomplished and left the condo for her lunch with Greg.

When Jan had found a decent parking place downtown and walked to the coffee shop, she was right on time. As she stood at the entrance waiting for a booth seating, Greg came in behind her.

"We're two punctual people, I see," observed Greg. "Do you think we can get a booth near the window?"

"That's where I'd like to sit, too," said Jan. "It looks like we're in luck if we don't mind waiting for the waitress to clean off that table over there." She signaled the hostess that they would like the booth just being vacated by two elderly women who were taking their time gathering up purses and various shopping bags.

Jan slid in on one side of the booth and Greg took the other seat. Fortunately, the waitress was prompt in clearing the table and wiping it clean. The menus were tucked under one arm as the she finished arranging the salt, pepper, and sugar containers precisely in their designated spots on the far side of the table.

Nothing on the menu was expensive, and Jan knew it by heart except for the specials of the day paperclipped to the front page. She decided to order the green salad and half a sandwich special made with sliced turkey and all the fixings and coffee. Greg opted for the meat loaf with mashed potatoes luncheon. After they finished ordering, they sat in silence for a few minutes, looking out the window at the traffic going by and at the shoppers who were passing on the sidewalk just outside.

"See anyone you know?" teased Greg with a smile. "Small towns are great for gossip. We might be an item for the daily news by now. Let's see, we've been here about ten minutes. That's long enough, I'm sure."

"You're right," Jan answered back in the same tone. "The next thing we know they'll be announcing our engagement on the society page. The only problem with that is they'll have to wait until Thursday because that's the one day of the week there is a society page." The waitress brought their coffee and cream and promised to be right back with the rest of their lunch. They were silent again.

"Did you find out more about the land deal?" asked Jan in a quiet voice that wouldn't carry to the other customers.

"Not yet," replied Greg, also speaking in a lowered voice. "The real estate person I told you about is working on it. He'll call me or leave a message in my office as soon as he learns anything significant."

"My friend Sam more or less verified it on his last delivery route. I was at the Mackenzie's house for Easter dinner yesterday; I think I told you about that, if I remember correctly. Everyone out Barton way is agog with the news of the price paid for the land. He didn't say who the original tale-teller was."

"I took a ride out there yesterday afternoon. I'm pretty sure that I had the right area because I stopped to ask directions at a farm. The land deal was extensive and it is as beautiful as you said. There's something cooking."

"I had an interesting morning," Jan said ruefully. "The adult ed secretary told me that I was as good as gone from the high school because the director had called in a complaint about my behavior and he had also written a letter to that effect to my boss in Montpelier."

Just then their food arrived. They were silent again as they adjusted silverware and napkins. The waitress sang out an "enjoy" and then was off to serve her other customers. The restaurant was becoming very busy and the noise level was definitely high but cheerful. People were glad to be inside out of the rain that had begun slanting in from the west and hoping that the rain would stop before they had to go out again. It was supposed to be a nice day, but northern Vermonters could not always count on the weather report being right.

Greg said that he was sorry to hear that she was being punished unfairly for something that was a group activity in the vocational wing. "There's probably more to your banishment from your office at the school than you know," he stated. "You should hear all the complaints and innuendoes I've been privy to in my investigation of Dan Frost's murder. Most of the unhappiness of the staff and teachers centers around Mr. Frost and the other two administrators--Mr. Lindner and Miss Watkins. Did anything unusual happen besides your run-in with that secretary?"

Taking a bite of salad at that moment occupied Jan until she had chewed and swallowed. "Sorry," she said. "You caught me for a minute. In fact, something did happen that was strange. You know me and my intuition. When I opened my office door this morning at eight o'clock, there was this smell that rushed out at me that was ugly sweat and cigar smoke, I guess. I figured that a janitor or the school electrician had been there over the weekend fixing something or changing the wiring for some reason or other. It happens every now and then, but I never caught that scent before, and when I asked in the voc office, the secretary told me that no one had been authorized to do any work at all. I looked around my office to see if anything was missing, but nothing was. All my books and things were disarranged slightly though. It gave me a creepy feeling."

Greg stopped eating with a forkful of meatloaf halfway to his mouth. "I asked you to be careful," he said in a stern voice. "Did you report in to the main office like I said you should?"

"Of course I did," replied Jan. "I can see that someone is nervous about me because of what Jake may have told me. Jake didn't get around to saying anything important, but how does that nervous somebody know that?"

"Let me think about what you just said for a few minutes," Greg said, as he continued eating in silence. "Have you figured out what you are going to do for an office yet?" he asked after five minutes.

Jan put her empty salad bowl to one side and contemplated starting on her sandwich. It would be hard to talk once she got took that first bite. "I called my boss about what had happened from my home phone. He told me to hang on long enough for him to arrange a move for my office to the Vermont State Employment Building. You know, down on River Street. Actually, he hadn't received any letter or phone call like Ginny said, but I guess it's in the works. Ginny gets carried away with the information she receives and then she can't keep her mouth shut. I used to think that she was a good friend."

"Do you have to go back to school after lunch for student appointments?" asked Greg.

"Yes, I have to be there about half past one," replied Jan. "Then I have to stay until four o'clock after another person comes at three. I'm not on vacation like the regular students and teachers. The holiday weeks are not very busy, though, because my students insist that I must be in Disney World with the other teachers and their families."

"Most of the regular teachers are angry with me and the system because I asked that no one leaves town this week. No one's in Disney World from New Venice this week."

"That's pretty harsh of you," said Jan. "It couldn't happen to a better bunch of rats-- people, I mean."

"That's pretty nasty of you," returned Greg with a smile. "You shouldn't talk about those folks that way."

"It's not hard to find fault with them. They aren't very friendly toward me on a regular basis. They must know that I hear the horror stories from my dropout students about how unfairly most of them have been treated. There's a code of punishment for the difficult students and another one for the sons and daughters of the so-called elite of New Venice. Of course, that holds true for the way the administrators and the school board operate, too. All the kids know about the favoritism that goes on."

"This is a fine mess we've got here, Ollie. I hope that you get your office moved this week at the very latest. Call me if you need help moving file cabinets or anything."

"Let me catch my breath here. I'm starting to get frightened again."

They finished their meal in silence. When it was time to leave, Jan tried out her going Dutch for the lunch idea, but got shot down at the cashier's desk. Greg paid and left the tip for their waitress. Jan was beginning to feel very comfortable in the company of the tall, lean state police investigator as she thanked him for lunch and walked as far as her parking spot with him.

"Remember what I said about being careful when you are in the school building," Greg reminded her as they parted. "I'll call you in the evening to check on what's been happening in the moving-of-office department, if it's all right."

"Okay. Thank you. By the way, do you have the information about when Jake's body will be released by the medical examiner?"

"I'm sure that it will be tomorrow some time. There should be a funeral notice in the paper then. I'll call you tonight; don't forget." They said their good-bys and parted.

Jan drove slowly back to the high school with automatic pilot in control again. The rain had stopped, and the streets were free of traffic. She found her favorite parking space in front of the janitors' entrance vacant and accepted her luck gratefully. It might be cold and raining again when she left work at four o'clock.

The hallway was brighter than it had been in the morning, but someone had turned off the stairwell light again. She fished in her purse for the light key to turn it back on. The stairs were still dirty and sticky from the previous week's onslaught from the vocational students. When she got to the top landing, she decided to visit the women's rest room located down the upper hall to the right before opening her office door. It, too, was a filthy disaster area, smelling of cigarette smoke and urine with used paper towels strewn on the floor near, but not in, the trash container. Make-up and hairs littered the sinks, and someone had left an obscene message written in lipstick on the mirror. Jan used the facilities quickly and washed her hands in the trickle of cold water that came from the one operating faucet.

I should report this mess to Dorothy, she thought. We don't know when some bigwig might be visiting the adult department to discuss a community project, and then wouldn't we all be embarrassed. Stopping in mid stride in the hall, she remembered that this was not her responsibility and it never had been, actually. She opened her door and began preparing for her first afternoon student appointment.

The time passed quickly until two forty-five, when a small break time occurred, Jan rose from her chair behind the desk and stretched. The first afternoon student had been successful in completing his homework, and his appointment hour flew by. Jan had time to assess his program sheets and return the folder to the file cabinet. Feeling competent and efficient, she decided to make a trip down to the main office to see if she could waylay Dorothy to complain about conditions in the vocational wing. Better to register what was happening than have the authorities ask you later why you hadn't, she thought to herself as she walked through the hallways. The shit could hit the fan, so to speak, if someone important made an inspection visit to the building. There was also a fairly active citizens' advisory committee which held meetings in the voc wing every two weeks, and no one would be happy if those people saw the condition of the building.

It was not that she cared about embarrassment for the administrative people. It was just so obvious that someone should make a complaint. Ginny could take care of this type of thing, but Jan knew from experience that she wouldn't for fear of making waves and possibly losing her job if there were too many complaints from the adult ed department.

Dorothy Watkins was standing near the counter of the main office talking to the secretaries when Jan came through the door. She was leaving for the day with her gym bag in hand and did not look pleased at being delayed, even if briefly. Jan wondered whether she had undergone another round of questioning with the state police. It was hard to keep her thoughts and emotions from her face as she spoke to Dorothy about the filth in the voc wing, knowing what she did about the clandestine meetings in the academic wing and the land deal.

"You really should speak to Mr. Lindner about this matter," Dorothy stated. "He's in charge over there and you know it." Dorothy inspected Jan's face carefully as she prepared to step around her and head for the door.

"I can't talk to Lindner. He doesn't listen, nor does he care about the appearance of the stairs and rest room; I know this from other occasions during holiday weeks," retorted Jan. "You must have an inkling of who might be visiting the adult department even though the regular students aren't in session. In fact, it's a darn good time for a VIP to come in because it is quiet. I'm just letting you know what's going on for early warning in case there's trouble. I've registered my information. You are the person ultimately responsible." Jan could be as blunt and to the point as Dorothy in tone of voice and authoritarian manner.

"So be it, Jan Madison," answered Miss Watkins. "You've done your duty. I'll speak to the head janitor about this and I'll also let Mr.

Lindner know what you've told me." She made a move toward the door again, but Jan blocked her way.

"I know that I'm only a guest here in the high school, but I'm also a taxpayer in this community. When I see something wrong, I feel obliged to talk about it. There hasn't been much of a welcome for my program or the dropout students felt lately since John Lindner was hired and I resent it. I've heard enough horror stories about how they were treated from ninety percent of my students, and although I know there are two sides to every tale, I believe them when they tell me they were shown the door without any kind of intervention on their behalf. I have been told that I don't belong in his vocational wing by John Lindner. Well, I'm working on that thought with my boss George Wright, and we expect to move the adult diploma program office to the Vermont State Employment Building by the end of the week, if possible. That's another early warning for you." Jan whirled around and ran from the office.

"Not a very professional attitude," sniffed Watkins. The secretaries raised their eyebrows and stared down at their computer keyboards.

Every time someone feels and speaks strongly about an issue around here, it's called unprofessional, thought Jan as she raced through the hallways to the voc wing. I gave her the facts, but I couldn't leave out the emotion. Paaardon me! When she arrived at the stairwell to her second floor office, Ginny was coming down the last flight to the fire door at the bottom.

Their eyes met, but they didn't speak. There was a wealth of information exchanged between them with that one glance. Jan was on the outside looking in and Ginny was firmly ensconced with the in-group.

The remainder of the afternoon passed without incident for Jan. Finishing with her last student, she put all materials away in the file cabinet and then sat at her desk thinking about her program's future. There were no students scheduled for Tuesday morning. Jan would have plenty of time to organize the items in the office for a move if she heard from her boss that a deal with the state employment manager had been struck. However, feeling a compulsion to do something that showed progress was being made, she went downstairs to the janitors' entrance to see if any empty boxes were piled nearby awaiting pick-up by the town disposal truck. There were several computer paper boxes lying there that were perfect for packing up the program files and books, and she also found two small cartons that would be fine for items from her desk. When she returned to her office and started placing things in the cartons, it made her realize that she had made the transition in her mind to move on with the diploma program. Figuratively and literally, she was out of that office. Putting her jacket on, pushing the two small boxes out into the hall, she locked up and left the room.

CHAPTER SIX

Jan sat quietly behind the steering wheel to catch her breath, realizing what she had done. She was not going back into the vocational wing again until it was official that the program was to be moved somewhere. In retrospect, it was a done deal when Dan Frost had clamped his hand down on her thigh, under the table of course, at the meeting with the area superintendents and her boss. The act and his subsequent rudeness had set the predictable consequences falling in place after that initial touch like dominoes lined up on their small ends. She wasn't quick enough to catch on until this very moment. Feeling sick to her stomach, Jan drove home and parked in the garage.

Dickens made a dash for the front door as Jan removed her purse and her appointment book from the cartons on the back seat of the car, leaving the boxes where they were for the time being. Remembering to check the mailbox, she veered to the right, disappointing Dickens greatly. There were two junk mail envelopes and a plain white one with crude pencil addressing to be extracted. Jan hated the Monday mail, which had little significance beyond advertising and solicitation, and wondered why she had bothered to look. Entering her own hallway at last with Dickens, she narrowly avoided treading on his hind legs as he wove his way around her feet while trying to direct her immediately to the refrigerator.

"Okay already," she told him as she piled her jacket, purse, and appointment book onto the blue chair near the sliding glass doors. With his food dish filled with fresh super supper, Dickens would be out from underfoot while Jan prepared her own dinner.

Picking up and putting away the items she had thrown on the blue chair was second on the agenda. Checking the fridge for something for her own dinner was next, and she settled for salad and microwaved sweet and sour chicken by Lean Cuisine. It wasn't quite enough to fill her up, but she hadn't fully recovered from her queasiness anyway. I'll need one pot of decaf, she thought, and proceeded to get out the fixings for the last cups of coffee for the evening. The daylight was fading as she settled into her favorite chair, cup of decaf in hand. The mail had been deposited on the floor.

Something was jiggling away in her brain as a reminder that there was unfinished business left over from her busy day. It escaped her, however, when she tried to get specific about what it was until her peripheral eyesight accidentally picked out a corner of the weird envelope with its penciled address lying on the floor near her chair. "Oh, yeah, that's what I forgot to do," she said to herself as she pulled it up from the floor to be examined more closely. When she opened the flap she found a piece of lined paper inside, torn haphazardly from a tablet made for children. The message printed in large capital letters warned her to "MIND YOUR OWN BUSINESS OR ELSE."

The words were so melodramatic they made Jan laugh at first. Then she remembered what had been happening lately in New Venice and a chill went up her spine. Trying to be logical did no good because she couldn't think what she had done to upset the unknown author of the note so much that he or she had to contact her in this manner.

Then the telephone rang, as if on cue from the stage direction in a mystery play. Jan jumped with a nervous twitch and then rose from her chair to answer it. There was a deep silence on the other end of the line after she said hello. She said hello once more, but there was no response other than the sound of muffled voices and clinking noises in the background. Finally a whispery message came over the wire. "THIS IS YOUR LAST WARNING!"

Jan felt her usual reaction to such goings-on kick in. In an angry voice she got in one reply before the line went dead. "Who are you; and what are you talking about?" she yelled into the receiver. Of course there was no answer to her retort.

With the phone dangling from her hand, Jan started to shake as the aftermath of her anger turned to fear. She replaced the phone in its cradle and sank to the floor when her knees failed to hold her up any longer. Just then the telephone rang again. Before she could make herself pick up the receiver, Jan had to work up her anger to override the fear she was experiencing.

"You yellow-bellied bastard!" she cried loudly. "Don't you dare try to intimidate me over the phone ever again!"

Greg's voice answered her calmly, "I'll never do it again, I promise. What's happening?"

"Oh, Greg," she cried. "I'm sorry I screamed at you like that. Someone just called before you did and warned me to mind my own business or else. I thought the person was calling again."

"Could you tell who it was?"

"No. That was part of the scariness. The voice was disembodied like someone sending a message from outer space. The other part of the scariness is I don't know what he or she was talking about."

"Hold on. I'm coming right over with my aide, and then you can give us all the details."

"I've got something to show you, too, that I got in the mail," Jan told him. "How long before you get here?" She gave him the directions to her condo from his location at the town hall office.

"It shouldn't take any more than five minutes," he replied quietly.

Jan sat back down on the floor with the telephone receiver in her hand. The mysterious caller was not going to have another chance to intimidate her if she didn't hang up the phone. She watched the second hand go around the numbers on her kitchen wall clock for three minutes and then went to the bathroom sink to splash cold water on her red hot cheeks. At least they felt red hot, but her face in the vanity mirror looked pale and pinched. That's an interesting reaction, she thought to herself, trying to be objective and logical and failing miserably. At least I'm not crying. Then she burst into tears just as her doorbell chimed. Running to the front door, she made sure that it was Greg on the other side before she opened it. The man she had seen accompanying Greg at the restaurant was standing behind him.

They all walked into the living room after Jan made certain that the locks were in place. "I'm glad you got here so fast," she said. "I've been having some strange reactions to that phone call I got, and look at this thing I got in the mail today."

"Slow down a minute," replied Greg. "First of all, this is Bill Rainey, my aide. He can take some notes when we settle down to business." He took the lined paper Jan had received by the tip of the corner. "Do you have the envelope it came in?"

Jan wiped her eyes and tried to appear calm and collected. "Yes, it's on the floor over by that blue chair," she answered. "Ye gods, I never gave fingerprints a thought. By the time I got the darn thing opened and read, it was probably too late anyway."

"Well, you never know how sophisticated people are nowadays," Bill Rainey said as he bent over to retrieve the envelope. "Have you got any plastic bags I could use to put these two items in? We didn't come prepared to collect evidence, I'm afraid. We were in kind of a hurry."

The plastic bags were produced and then Jan told the two state policemen everything that had happened since her return to the condo that afternoon. Dickens came to where she was sitting in her blue chair and jumped up into her lap to curl into a furry ball of warm comfort.

Greg looked over at Bill and nodded. They had clearly decided something with the glance that made Jan feel secure and competent again. It meant that there really was nasty business going on in New Venice that had centered on Jan Madison. She was not an hysterical female who was imagining things to focus attention on herself. It meant that the state police were taking her story seriously, and that they would do their best to protect her from whomever it was out there in the darkness that wanted to do her harm. She scratched Dickens behind the ears while he purred loudly into her tummy.

"The person who is responsible for all the chaos in this area right now is playing for high stakes, and he or she doesn't dare let down one iota for fear of losing the game completely," stated Greg emphatically. "There may be more than one person involved; we don't know yet. Can there be a piece of evidence that Jake wanted to show you or give you before he made up his mind what to do? Maybe he left a message for you, hidden in one of your books in the program office. It would explain your intuition about someone searching through your things. They weren't desperate enough to make a mess while they looked, so it seems that they are not quite sure about your relationship to Jake. They were clearly afraid of what he had seen or heard while he did his rounds in the academic wing, however."

"That's the trouble with this whole day's scenario," answered Jan. "If I have a piece of evidence, I don't know what it is or where it could be hidden. Because of the note and the phone call, I now can say that I'm not imagining that my office was searched though. It makes the person or persons look kind of stupid, doesn't it?"

"Desperate and not too bright, but dangerous nevertheless," Bill added, as he folded his small black notebook with a decisive snap. "I agree that the perp has a lot to lose. He won't dare rest until he has every possible situation covered to his advantage. His or hers," he added. His blunt features under the short blond crew cut looked tired and worried.

Greg got up in preparation of leaving. "We'll have someone watch your condo building tonight, just in case our mystery person decides to carry his search to one more level--your home. Lock up well when we leave, check all the windows, and put a stick or something in the patio door track. If you leave the outside lights on and several lamps lit inside, it will make it difficult for anyone to sneak by us."

"I've got just the thing for the patio door," said Jan as she arose from her blue chair with a disgruntled cat in her arms, "A baseball bat."

Before the two state policemen left, Jan fished around in the front hall closet for the baseball bat, which had been relegated to the most distant corner along with an old black umbrella. Both had belonged to her husband Joe, who carried them around for years in the trunk of his Lincoln Continental. "You never know what a person will need when he's on the road," he'd said when Jan questioned him about giving the bat away to a child or buying another umbrella that was more presentable. When Jan cleaned out his car after his death in order to sell it, she couldn't bring herself to throw away the two items so connected to her husband's personality and her memories of him.

With the departure of her protectors, Jan set about locking up and checking window latches. The bat went into the track of the sliding door, and the designated lights were turned on. She felt safe enough to read her hot virus book for an hour while sitting in the blue chair, after the porch door drapes were pulled. When her eyes started to droop, she poured the last cup of coffee into her mug and headed for bed and perhaps one TV prime time program before conking out for the night. It surprised her to find that she was more concerned about a strain of the deadly virus Ebola escaping from a lab near Washington, D. C., than she was about her own situation, which seemed melodramatic and unreal. After fifteen minutes of TV, her eyes closed for the last time as she dropped into a deep sleep. Dickens was curled over her feet for most of the night. Neither he nor Jan was bothered by all the lights she had left on.

CHAPTER SEVEN

When she started dreaming in an early hour of the morning, it was a crazy combination of carelessness in a laboratory with people entering offices and homes that did not belong to them to search for papers and vials of stolen viruses. Finally waking up in a tangle of sheets and quilts, Jan was covered with perspiration. She had been running from someone who wanted to hurt her at the end of the dream. She tried to remember what her dream had been telling her to do to save herself, but failed to bring back anything more than the feeling of terror experienced as she ran. Dickens had disappeared, probably disturbed by Jan's thrashing feet and/or a compulsion to check out his food dish in the kitchen.

It was nearly time for her alarm clock to go off. She made a trip to the bathroom after shutting it off and then continued on into the kitchen to make the morning brew of high test coffee which would really bring her back to life. What the day would bring was up for grabs, she thought as she took out more kitty food for Dickens, who was hunched over his bowl licking up the last of his supper leftovers.

"Waste not, want not," she told him as she scraped the last morsel out of the small tin of special treat for him. He didn't get the expensive stuff very often.

As was her habit when she awoke early enough to dawdle through breakfast, Jan made two pieces of toast and carried them, carefully balanced on the top of her coffee mug, to the blue chair near the sliding glass doors. She had time to consider orange juice and cereal later after the coffee got her brain in gear.

It was apparent from her dream that yesterday's events had bothered her more than she was willing to admit to herself or to the state policemen who had come to her rescue last night. But after calming down from her reaction to the mysterious and threatening phone call, it seemed ridiculous to keep carrying on about it. Locking the windows and door and getting out the ball bat had helped to make her feel secure again. Of course, knowing that arrangements had been made to watch for intruders near the condo went a long way to alleviate her fear too. When a person hits a high of fear, what does she do for an encore but go into denial, she decided. That reminded her of the weird behavior of heroines in gothic novels who thrived on denial right up to the climax of the last scene. Her dream had shown her that intellectualizing about fearful events only drove the emotions to the subconscious where they replayed until some kind of resolution came about.

So much for the dream of a few hours ago, she thought as she sipped coffee and looked out at the awakening scene of everyday activity

151

downhill from the condo. A bread truck pulled into the mini-mart's parking lot, and the car delivering the Burlington newspaper was close behind it. The stream of vehicles heading into town still had their lights on although the darkness was abating rapidly. Jan went to the kitchen to see about a real breakfast. She was probably going to need it.

Greg called while she was getting ready to prepare some eggs. She had just decided to make a cheese omelet and was at the refrigerator peering into its interior for the small package of sharp cheddar she knew was in there somewhere.

Greg told her that the men watching her condo had had a quiet night with nary an intruder in sight. Jan replied that she had felt safe with them looking out for her welfare and thanked him for the protection.

"It's possible that I can pick up the rest of my things to move to the employment building this afternoon," she informed him. "I'm waiting for a call from my boss this morning before I do anything."

"That's the way to handle it," replied Greg. "Are you positive that he can arrange the move that quickly?"

"Yes I am," Jan stated firmly. "Because it's been discussed before, and the program is related directly to many of the people visiting the employment offices. Nobody wants to say that they out and out sponsor the diplomas for dropouts, those who need the basic credentials to get work the most, but let's face it, the referrals come from there every day of the week and they have to process the paperwork. There's nothing like working for an orphan outfit like mine with low pay and few benefits even though it has proven itself to be successful as hell."

"It's about time that the state people acknowledge what the program is doing for communities and families, especially in a high unemployment town like New Venice."

"I know, but it seems hopeless somehow. You know what happens when there are state budget problems. The powers that be want to sacrifice the library hours, the public park maintenance, and programs like mine to make things balance. I wish they'd start at the top and reduce a few administrators' salaries and benefits. Speaking of public funds, how did you manage to get help for me last night?"

Greg's smile came over the phone like a beacon. "Bill and I managed to share the watch last night, but I have time to figure out what to do for the next couple of days now. Don't worry about that part; just concentrate on setting up your new office space and making whatever arrangements you need to with your boss and the employment office manager."

"Sorry about the soapbox harangue," apologized Jan. "I know that you agree with me about the program work. Thank you for everything you and Bill have done."

"Don't mention it," answered Greg. "I'll be in touch with you about four thirty if you need anything heavy moved."

"I'll plan on being here for your telephone call," promised Jan.

She finished the whisking of eggs and grating of cheddar for her omelet. It turned out well in spite of the interruption of the phone call or maybe because of it. How did I ever get into such a mess, she thought as she sat in the blue chair eating the omelet. I'm used to being independent, but I haven't been doing such a good job of it lately.

Actually, it was because she was independent that she got on the wrong side of Dan Frost and John Lindner. They were afraid that she was informing her students of their rights in the school district. The state government had created an entitlement for adult students that was not covered by state funding, and the cost of advanced training courses for former dropouts would upset the district budget for sure. There was no actual power on her side when she insisted that the school district had failed the very students that had the most need. The long term benefits of a well-educated and informed population participating in town government and paying taxes were self evident to her. What her program stood for in the community should provide enough clout to get recognition for the students as they began major changes for the better in their lives, she thought. It was the first step and an inexpensive one. Apparently the powerful administrators wanted those same people and their families to maintain the status quo at the low level that had been their place since before World War 11. There was no more room at the top or even the high middle; Dan Frost and the men and women connected to him had been running the whole show.

Now that Dan was dead, who would emerge as the leader of the all-powerful elitist clique? There was big money involved, no doubt. Even in a small town like New Venice, there were opportunities for the unscrupulous to tap into large funds meant for government and state sponsored projects within the school district. Jan felt discouraged when she had suspicions of wrongdoing that no one wanted to investigate for fear of upsetting the power brokers. But what had she done to attract notice to the extent of a warning note and phone call like that of last night? If, as rumored, the top administrators had been acting together to gather in kick-backs from two large construction jobs for the school by the same local company, couldn't they also be bribing union officials and town bureaucrats to cover up their illicit activities? The land purchases by Frost, Lindner, and Watkins involved huge sums of money and where the three had found the financing to go forward as far as they had was a mystery to Jan, Marianne and Sam, and a group of savvy farmers in the area where the purchases had taken place.

Greg Whitehouse, as state police investigator, was obviously suspicious of someone or a group of someones because of Dan Frost's murder. Then Jake Patenaude's death the very next night must have confirmed the fact that something big was happening. He had the preliminary information about the land purchases and Jan's connection to Jake from her interview, which was made significant by the search of her office and the threatening note and phone call of last night.

The memory of the abusive behavior of Dan Frost in the name of power came back to her, and she wondered if the other women who had abruptly left the employment of the school district had had similar experiences to hers. John Lindner had impressed her as a toady favorite of Dan Frost's, a person who could do no wrong in the superintendent's eyes because he had been hired as an enforcer. When it came to harassing employees on Frost's blacklist, he made an excellent assistant. Jan wasn't the only one who thought Lindner had been hired for that very purpose.

Dorothy Watkins was another puppet of Frost's when he wanted to make a move on a blacklisted teacher. She also set up all kinds of meetings and seminars for the purpose of engaging the teachers and the public in debate about changes needed to go forward into the twenty-first century, but nothing concrete ever came of it. The leaders of committees were always hand-picked by Dorothy and Dan as cronies or colleagues who were easily controlled. Until Jan had noted that fact, she had been impressed with the meetings and proposed changes for the future, but apparently it was all busy work to keep everyone from noticing what was really going on.

Jan's train of thought came to an abrupt end with a second summons to the telephone. She hoped that it would be George Wright calling, and it was her boss on the phone from his Montpelier office.

"I've got great news," George told her with glee sounding in his voice over the wires from the state capitol. "Grace Evans has agreed to provide space for the diploma program in the employment building. They have plenty of room it seems, and it makes good sense to her to have you and your students working out of that office complex. Congratulations on your leaving the vocational wing of the high school as soon as possible."

"Well, break out the champagne," Jan cried out in relief. "I'm practically out the door at this minute. Someone has volunteered to help me move the file cabinet and the heavier boxes, but the small stuff is already packed and ready to go. When can I move in? I don't want to disrupt their work during business hours."

"I'll be up to help you this afternoon. Grace is staying in the office later than usual today to catch up on her computer work, so you can start moving in at four thirty when all the employment appointments are finished. I have to sign some kind of contract with her, and you will have to check out all the office provisions you'll have at your disposal, like the use of the copier and so forth. It should work out perfectly for everyone."

"I feel so relieved." Jan let out a long breath to punctuate what she had said. "There are a couple of things I didn't tell you before because I wasn't sure about their significance myself. On Monday when I opened my office door at school and looked around the room, I was surprised to feel that someone had been in there searching through my books and my desk and the program file cabinet sometime over the weekend. I asked around to see if the person could have been a janitor or the school electrician doing some repair work. I found out that nothing had been authorized by the voc office."

"You should have told me," responded her boss. "Was anything stolen or trashed?"

"No," answered Jan. "It was very subtly done, like a search in a spy movie. It has something to do with my connection to Jake Patenaude, the night watchman who was killed sometime Friday night or early Saturday morning. I told you about that when I called you yesterday. There are two other things that happened later on in the day that confirmed that I'm supposed to know about or have evidence from Jake that will incriminate the person or persons who are responsible for the murders apparently. I haven't a clue what it is, but someone sent me a warning letter, and then I got a last warning to mind my own business over the phone. I was completely terrified and called the state police investigator. He and his aide watched my condo all night, just in case the threatener decided to pay me a personal visit."

"I had no idea that the situation had reached this level already," stated George. "Would you rather throw in the towel and go on vacation instead of trying to continue working under these conditions? For the record, I'm recommending it." Jan knew that George was an old hand at covering his ass on all occasions, and this occasion was a biggie.

She pretended to contemplate his offer of vacation time for a few minutes. "My students are nearly all ready for graduation, but you know what happens when the big day gets close.

There are eight of them who can make it if I inspire them to work just a little harder in addition to the ones who have it made but need to get their essays in for correction, and then there's all the paperwork that goes with this business. I'd prefer to stay in operation until every student is completely finished."

"You're a brave soul, but maybe not so smart to stick around where the threatener can touch you whenever he feels like it. You have no control over what might happen other than being extra careful." George was definitely not happy.

Where were you when Dan Frost put his big hand on my thigh and when he was carrying on during my presentation to the school board? Not able to speak up then in my defense, thought Jan. He sounds guilty of something.

"The state police have other angles to work on besides my connection to Jake at this point," stated Jan. "But I will feel better when I move out of the voc wing away from Lindner and his friends. They will be happy to get me out of the way, too. Whoever is threatening me would be crazy to carry things any further. I'm supposed to be thoroughly intimidated now."

"We can talk about this when I get up to New Venice. I'll meet you at the high school some time after four thirty, probably closer to five o'clock if I get stuck driving behind a logging truck. You know how that goes."

"That will work out just fine for me," agreed Jan. "I have a phone call coming in to me at home at four thirty to see if I need help moving the heavy stuff like the file cabinet, but that shouldn't hold me up. Can we meet in the parking lot near the janitors' door? I don't want to go in the building by myself after the secretaries have left."

"Okay, that's settled then. You still have all your keys just in case the place is locked up don't you?"

"Yes I do. Thanks for your help, and I'll see you about five o'clock."

After hanging up the phone, Jan got another cup of coffee, but she could not resume her reverie of earlier in the morning. She sat in her blue chair and contemplated the scene outside the sliding doors. The sun had come out in full splendor after chasing away the mists over the lake. The foreground view of her scene was getting very busy with heavy traffic on the road below as people from the outlying villages came to town for work or shopping. Everything looks normal as apple pie, she thought. But it's not. All the things that have happened at the high school affect everybody in town one way or another, but there they all are, pretending that it is just another Tuesday.

As was her customary behavior pattern, Jan felt the strong urge to do something that represented progress of a sort. She could not go to her office at school, but she could get dressed, go into town to get a paper, and do some grocery shopping. Deciding on a reasonable course of action made her feel energized and part of regular daily life again.

The sensation of being in limbo, waiting for something to happen passed as she dressed casually for the short trip into town.

Dickens showed up just in time to go out the front door with her. He quickly disappeared on errands of his own as she backed the Escort out of the garage and closed the door.

Noting the frost heave near the curve of her hilly street, Jan steered carefully around it to the road below. She decided to drive directly to the Grand Union supermarket because it was possible to buy both the state and local newspapers there when she shopped for groceries. Wendy's restaurant was located a block away on the other side of the little mall, a convenient place to pause for coffee afterward as she caught up with the news.

The thefts of school property that had occurred in the vocational wing were under investigation by the local police department, and suspicion of financial mismanagement was a problem for the state auditors. The two problems were being taken care of in an official manner that was no business of Jan's, and yet she did want to know if there had been any progress made.

After making her selection of items needed for the next few days and not forgetting to pick up Dickens' favorite canned treats, Jan proceeded to the check-out counter where the newspapers and magazines were displayed. The two she wanted were there even though it was early for the local paper to be out. With her plastic bag of purchases in hand, she walked to her car and stashed it in the back seat after taking the two papers out to read at the restaurant.

It was such a glorious day to be out in the comparatively warm sunshine, Jan closed and locked the door of the car in order to stroll the short distance to Wendy's. She passed a jewelry store window and paused to inspect some earrings displayed in the window. Another store window beckoned her to go in and see what was new in craft supplies and various dry goods materials. It was good to have time to do these small explorations, but Jan was accustomed to being busy at work on a Tuesday and it made her slightly uneasy. At least she had no important appointments with students for a couple of days, and life would resume its normal pace later on that week in her new office. She made a mental note to herself to leave a memo on the door when she left the vocational building instructing the students where to go for their next appointments if she could not reach everyone by phone. It would also be necessary to inform Dorothy Watkins and John Lindner in an official manner that she was leaving even if she did not want to see their smug expressions of satisfaction. Maybe she would write notes to them and avoid the situation, she thought.

Reaching Wendy's entrance at last, Jan went in and ordered a large coffee, picked up creamers, and walked to a booth near the window. She spread the local paper out on the table after settling in and removing her jacket.

The smaller headline to the right was about the solving of the thefts from the automotive shop at the high school. Jan scanned down the article for the name of the alleged thief, finding it in the last line of the first paragraph. It was one of her former students who was being accused. She felt sick with dread as she slowly sipped her very hot coffee and read the article carefully. The young man, Richard Perkins, had been living in New Venice for only a year and a half, it stated, having moved from the Boston area where he apparently had contacts for selling the stolen items. There were further investigations being conducted as to the possibility that one or more persons other than Perkins were involved. Jan had liked Richard and admired how he applied himself to the program material. His graduation had been a major highlight in his young life because he had not been successful in academic work up to that time. He knew that he was one of her best students last year, and was very proud of himself.

She was appalled at the story. Even with the words "alleged" and "apparently" inserted, there was no leeway for doubt that Richard was the culprit. After his arrest and arraignment, he had made bail and was awaiting trial, the news article went on. Jan could have cried for him right there in Wendy's. She wondered how he had found the money for bail when he didn't even own a car. His living arrangements were haphazard at best when he had been studying for his diploma last year, mostly crashing with friends as far as she could tell. If he had money lately, she hadn't seen any evidence of it out on the street where she sometimes met him walking to his job ride site. Maybe his family is helping him, she thought. One brother lived in New Venice, but the rest of his folks lived in Massachusetts somewhere.

Taking another sip of the hot coffee, Jan read through the pages of the paper until she came to the obituary notices. The private funeral date for Dan Frost in Montpelier was mentioned along with the notice of a New Venice memorial service to be held the following Monday at the Methodist church at ten o'clock. Jake Patenaude's service was to be held on Saturday from the Roman Catholic church in Barton. She had forgotten that Jake and his family lived so far out of town that their home really was in the Barton area for church and schools. Jan's diploma program covered the high school there as well as another small high school to the north of New Venice.

When she looked up from the newspaper, she saw Marianne coming through the main door. Marianne waved and joined her in the booth after collecting her coffee and fixings.

"I thought you had to work today," Marianne exclaimed breathlessly. "I was in the Grand Union and I saw your car when I came out with my groceries. I figured that you had walked over to Wendy's and I did the same thing. It's gorgeous out, isn't it?"

"It sure does beat the weather we had last week," replied Jan. "I'm supposed to be working, but today is the day for the big move from the high school to the employment office. I was going to call you as soon as I got home. There's a lot of stuff going on that I have to tell you about, but I was feeling a little strange this morning and wanted to sort things out for myself before I called."

"So Lindner finally got his way, huh?" said Marianne sympathetically. "You should care what he thinks about anything. Did you read this morning's Burlington paper yet?"

"I bought the paper, but I've been reading about a former student of mine, an adult student, getting arrested and the obituary notices in the local rag," answered Jan. "Have you read this one? Here I'll take the Burlington paper and you can have the local one."

Marianne showed her the article about John Lindner on the front page of the state/local news section before she started to read the story about Jan's student.

Jan couldn't help but rejoice as she read the Burlington reporter's article about John Lindner's questioning by state auditors regarding missing funds from a federal program that he was in charge of. The monies had been awarded to the New Venice high school to remodel a computer lab for the use of vocational and handicapped students who somehow had been left out of the general excitement of the twenty-first century changes proposed for the school. Lindner had falsified his reports to the government officials checking on how the money had been spent so far.

"I didn't think Lindner was stupid," stated Jan, as she continued reading. "I know he borrows ideas from people without asking and is rude and lazy, but I think he'd have to be very desperate to do something like steal federal money right in front of the school business manager. By the way, I didn't see any sign of a new computer lab anywhere in the voc wing the last time I was there. The classrooms haven't even been upgraded to carpet yet, as promised at a school district public meeting of several years ago, and the place is always filthy."

"You told me about that, Jan, several times," Marianne exclaimed. "I remember your saying something was wrong about the management of the voc building. Are you really moving your office today, so soon?"

"Yes, I am." Jan paused a moment, taking her eyes from the newspaper. "It's pretty sad that the kids aren't treated equally in New Venice. There's a real clique that rules the area like it was a kingdom or something, and they intend to keep the status quo from days of yore no matter what it takes. The only way John Lindner could get away with mismanaging federal funds is with the help and blessing of several other people. Everyone in the state thinks that this is a little old isolated area of no importance that no one checks up on. The computer world is changing that attitude. I'll bet that the business manager, Reg Lessette, is the next person we'll be reading about in the Burlington newspaper."

"Several interesting things have been happening to me on account of Jake Patenaude's wanting to tell me something," she went on. "Somebody is afraid that I have incriminating evidence against him or her. I had a warning letter and a threatening phone call yesterday, and I had to call the state police about what was happening because I was frightened out of my wits for a while there."

"Are you sure you don't know what it is that they are afraid of, whoever they are?" asked Marianne in horror.

"Absolutely sure," answered Jan. "I've thought and thought about what it might be, and the only thing I can come up with is maybe there's a note somewhere that Jake wrote to me before he was killed. If some thugs really searched my office as I'm positive they did, they'd have thought of that possibility, too. But they obviously didn't find anything because their harassment continued with the warnings."

"Do you want to come out to our house for the duration?" queried Marianne. "You know we have room for you and Dickens."

"No. Thank you very much for your concern," replied Jan. "The state police were watching the condo for me last night, and now the local police will be helping out as well. There's been too much going on in this town for anyone to ignore, and as you can see by the newspaper article, more officials are taking part in the investigations. I think that my threateners feel that I've cut and run as long as I'm not in the voc wing. Anyway, I wouldn't want you and Sam to be involved in a dangerous situation because of me."

"Well, Sam would say the same thing about having you stay with us, and he's prepared for break-ins because of his business. Think about it," Marianne pressed on.

"Thanks, but no. I'll stick it out as long as I can," answered Jan. "I'm convinced that the people behind the threatening think they have me thoroughly intimidated. I'm being careful, though. George Wright is coming at five o'clock to help me move out of the voc building, and Greg Whitehouse promised to help get the heavy stuff over to the employment office complex. I won't go into the school again by myself."

"Good thinking, Jan. Be extra careful," said Marianne. "By the way, how is your friend Ginny doing? Didn't you say that her son Eric was practically accused of stealing some expensive tools from the automotive shop?"

"Something's happened there, too. Eric's apparently off the hook because that Perkins kid that I had for a student has been formally accused of the thefts. Ginny was acting awfully strange about the whole situation, however, like she and I were on opposite sides of a war, and her side was winning. I didn't get it."

"That's weird, but I trust your intuition, Jan. My coffee's gone, and I've got to get going, too. Call if you need us. 'Bye."

"I'm going to stay for a while and finish reading the papers. I appreciate your offer of help, and I'll be careful," restated Jan as Marianne rose and left the restaurant.

The newspapers and a coffee refill occupied Jan for another half an hour. Talking things over with Marianne had stimulated her thinking about all the New Venice happenings and especially thoughts of what Jake had possibly left behind him before his death. She remembered how frightened he had been and how white his face had looked on Friday. If he had been desperate enough, he would have left her a note, logic told her. Where would he leave a note in her office so that she would be sure to find it if anything went wrong? It would have to be a place that had something to do with his son, she thought. The searcher didn't know about Jake's son and so missed a clue as to a specific place to look for a note.

Then Jan remembered that she had a box of small items from her desk in the back seat of the Escort. Among the items was a file box of 3x5 index cards she had used to keep track of all her graduates from the very first group. She had taken pictures of most of them and mounted them on the cards with interesting updates as the years rolled by. The evidence of how well they were doing in the real world was her proof that the diploma program was definitely worthwhile. Jake knew about the file box. It would be a logical place for him to leave a note, near his son's card.

Jan quickly gathered up her papers and purse to leave Wendy's. Her mind was swirling with the thought that she was about to find a clue as to why she had been undergoing all the harassment. On her way out, she bumped into two construction workers who were standing in line at the order counter. They looked at her with the disgust reserved for weird older-type females.

The walk back to her car in the Grand Union parking lot took only a few minutes. She climbed into the back seat next to the box of belongings from her office and started rummaging through the items she had placed there. At first she thought that the small metal file was still in her office, but one more pass at moving the notebooks, folders, and office accessories aside revealed it to be on the very bottom in the corner. After quickly pulling the box up and forward, Jan held her breath as she opened the lid. The alphabetized cards slipped through her fingers as she searched for the name "Patenaude." There it was at last, but nothing extra was written on the front. She turned it over to look at the back for some kind of message. There was nothing. Her disappointment was as palpable as a blow to the mid section.

Then, when she sat rubbing her fingers over the card as if wishing for a genie to appear and solve her problem, she noticed that it didn't feel right. Taking another card out for comparison, she saw that Andre's was thicker. Her heart gave a thump as she looked again. Sorting through the items in the carton, Jan found a letter opener and used it to pry the other card from the back of the one she had placed in the file box. That old fox, she thought to herself, he's glued two cards together and put his note to me inside. All the materials he needed were right there in my desk. He probably was aware that the atmosphere didn't feel right after he came on duty, but was hoping it was just a bad case of nerves on his part. The poor guy.

The note that Jake had left her was on a necessarily small piece of paper. Jake had used both sides and covered them with very small printing. Jan was grateful for the printing because she knew what Jake's handwriting was like.

The first sentences went over what Jake had told her on Friday night after the church service. From there, Jake went on about being definitely able to identify the voices--Frost's, Lindner's, Watkins', Reg Lessette's, and a local construction company owner's named Smithfield. Later on, there had been a stranger at their meetings with a soft voice that Jake could not identify as a local person. He thought that it had an uppity New York City accent. He never used his flashlight and was very quiet when he spied on the group, but once he thought that he had been seen. It had been reassuring to him after a day or two that he hadn't been seen when nothing was said. This was probably wrong, and Jake wanted to talk to Jan before he made the big step of going to the police. He hadn't come forward because he was afraid to lose his job. There was something else that made him change his mind. He had picked up some scraps of paper one night after a meeting when everyone had left, and he had listened to the conversation on several occasions. Jan would know where to look for these pieces of evidence, he wrote.

Jan sighed. She did know where to look, but nothing could be done about it until her two protectors accompanied her to the program office. She felt the guilt creeping into her mind again as she thought of that Friday night when she might have saved Jake's life.

She had to find Greg, and do it right away. After tucking the small slip of paper into her wallet, Jan climbed out of the back seat of her car and sat in the driver's seat ready to go to the police station with her note from Jake. As she pulled out of the parking lot, she glanced at the corner near the jewelry store and saw the two construction workers watching her with interest. She froze for a moment. almost stalling the Escort. Were they looking at her for a reason?

Am I a paranoid person or an observant one, she thought as she drove along the causeway and over the cement bridge to the business district. The police station where Greg's office was located seemed hours away as if she were driving in slow motion. There were no parking places in sight as she finally neared the red brick building housing the town offices and the local police department. I'll have to try the ones around in back, she thought unhappily. She didn't want to have far to walk because her heart had started pounding as if she had just participated in the Boston Marathon.

Nevertheless, she speed-walked around the side of the building to the front entrance, pulled the heavy glass doors open, and raced up the steps to Greg's temporary office. To her dismay, there was no one there. She decided to check with the local police for information on his whereabouts. Knocking on the glass panel of their office brought an older cop on duty to the panel where he asked how he could be of help.

"Do you know where the state police investigators are?" she asked while trying to get her breathing back to normal.

"No ma'am, not right at the present moment," he answered. "Can I help you with something?"

"My name is Jan Madison, and I need to get in touch with Greg Whitehouse as soon as possible. I have some information for him. I promised to get in touch with him if I did come across this information."

"Are you the same Jan Madison who owns the condo we'll be keeping an eye on?"

"Yes, I guess so." Jan was getting frustrated and her face and voice showed it.

"Do you want to wait for him to come in?" asked the policeman. "I could try to catch him on the radio."

Jan thought for a couple of minutes. If Greg was out of town, it would take him some time to get back to his office from wherever he was. She mulled the problem over and then told the officer on duty to try and track him down and give him a message.

"Tell him I'll be at home, staying there until I hear from him one way or another," she said. "It seems the most sensible thing to do. Please tell him that the information is important."

She turned away from the glass panel and went down the stairs and out the front door again. The beautiful spring day had turned gray and the wind off the lake had picked up. Jan leaned into it until she reached her car. Living through the rest of the day while she waited to hear from Greg seemed impossible.

At two thirty the telephone finally rang. Jan hurried to answer it on the second peal, and sighed with relief. It was Greg.

"Where are you calling from?" she asked him. She definitely wanted to know how long it would take him to get back to his office.

"I'm in Barton. The New Venice police just caught up with me. I've been interviewing people over here about the land deal circumstances," he answered. "What's up? The message I got said that you had some important information for me. Are you all right?"

"I'm okay," she returned. "I found a note from Jake in a pretty good hiding place he thought of. He also gave me a clue as to where to look for more information, but I need to go to my office to check on that."

"Don't you dare go by yourself. Wait for me to get back to town." Greg's voice left no room for debate. "Will you be all right for another hour or so?"

"I think so," said Jan. "I'm sitting here in the condo trying to keep myself occupied so that I don't think about looking for the evidence Jake left me, now that I know where to find it. The only thing that works is reading that book about the hot zone viruses. It's so horrifying it would take a person's mind off any other subject for a while, anyway."

"Keep reading," replied Greg. "I'm giving a quiz later on this evening when we go out to dinner."

Jan laughed. "I'll be waiting right here. Hurry."

After hanging up the phone, Jan poured herself another cup of the decaf she had brewed when she returned to the condo. Sitting in her blue chair, she swiveled toward the sliding glass doors to check the lake for change-of-weather signs. The beautiful spring day was definitely gone now. Gray-green lake water was topped with white froth, beaten to the shoreline in waves by the whip of the north wind. The temperature would probably fall into the freezing range again tonight, thought Jan. The lake was a pretty good indicator.

Turning back from the lake view, Jan picked up her hot virus book again. Within a few minutes she became absorbed in her reading, taking sips of coffee without really looking at the mug in her hand. At quarter after three, she heard a clicking sound at the porch door, and put down her book to let Dickens in. He rubbed against her ankles for a second and then made for the kitchen. Jan rose and went to answer the cat's summons for more fish dinner and fresh milk.

The time then began to drag. Three thirty came and receded slowly into the past.

She tried to read once more and found it impossible this time. Dickens went to the porch door and butted his head against it several times before stretching up as far as he could in pretense of opening the door by himself. Jan was amused and gave him a good between-the-ears rubbing before letting him out. He quickly disappeared into the evergreens.

At ten minutes to four, the doorbell rang and when she ran to answer it, there was Greg.

"At last," Jan exclaimed as she ushered him into the living room. "I was beginning to worry that something had happened, like an accident or two flat tires or something."

Greg laughed ruefully. "It's hard to break away from the people being interviewed after you have squeezed the information you need out of them. They want to feel justified in telling you about other people's business whether it's for a good cause or not. I try not to leave them feeling guilty about it. When we need witnesses in court, it's best to have left them with their self-respect at interview time. It's one of my own theories. However, it's made you have a hard time waiting for me, and I apologize. I know you are excited about one of your theories right now."

"First of all, look what I found in the metal file box that I put in my car," Jan told him. "It certainly was a theory that helped me find this little slip of paper that Jake left for me in my office." She passed over the note to Greg, who read it quickly.

"He's confessing that he did snoop around after he noticed those meetings going on in the wee hours of the morning," said Greg. "How did you know where to look for the note?"

"I was sitting in Wendy's drinking coffee after talking to my friend Marianne when logic took over and *voilà*! Remember when I said that I had made up my mind to get out of the voc center and packed up the small things from my desk and file cabinet to put in my car? When I asked myself where I'd hide a note that I didn't want found by the wrong people, like Jake wanted to do, I thought that I'd hide it in something that pertained to my son. Actually, the file box where I found the note holds a collection of cards with pictures and information on former graduates. Jake's son graduated last year and then joined the Marine Corps. His life has completely turned around for the better. Jake was proud of his success and grateful for his second chance to make good. That doesn't mean anyone else paid attention to what happened in the past, and that's why the clue was missed by the searchers."

"But," said Greg, "the searcher could have found the note just by dumb luck, couldn't he or she?"

"I'm glad to hear that you are bearing in mind that the search was an equal opportunity project," exclaimed Jan. She then explained how the note had been pasted in between two of the file cards where it had remained undetected.

"Jake did well, didn't he?" said Greg. "I suppose it was actually easy after he figured out what to do and when all the things he needed to use were right in your desk drawer."

"That's true, but we need to find the evidence that he stashed somewhere else in my office. The logical place to look next is my file cabinet drawer where I keep my old student folders. I clean them up every summer after graduation and put them away for safekeeping until George picks them up for permanent storage in Montpelier. Lately there has been a lack of space for all the folders from every teacher in the program, so I still have Andre's folder and his portfolio of completed work. Those are the two places to check out."

"It's early for us to meet your boss, but we could go over to the voc building now if you want to," stated Greg. "You still have all your keys, don't you?"

"Yes, I do," answered Jan in a breathless voice. The excitement of a treasure hunt was building up in her mind. When she looked at Greg, she could see he was feeling the same way. They made perfect companions for the next step in Jake's paper trail.

Greg had been driving his own car and wearing civilian clothing for his interviewing chores. He figured that it would be helpful not to appear intimidating when he talked to the real estate people and the farmers over in the Barton area. There was no rule that he had to wear his uniform when it would antagonize the people he wanted to have open up for him.

Jan admired the way his dark gray trousers and navy blue sweater fit his lean body as they prepared to leave the condo. She pulled on her red woolen jacket over the white scarf and tugged on her gloves. It was going to be cold out. Greg had a warm jacket in his car, he told her as they locked up and left.

It took only a few minutes to drive down the hill into the business district, over the cement bridge, along the causeway, and up the winding street to the high school buildings on the other side of town. Jan had her janitors' door key ready as they arrived at the voc building parking lot.

With a mixed sense of high adventure and dread, she let them into the murky hallway next to the janitors' office where only a low watt desk lamp was dimly glowing. Taking Greg's hand, for support as well as guidance, Jan turned the corner and proceeded to the stairwell leading to her office. Of course, the stair lights were not on, so Jan used her light switch key once again. The place was still a mess, and they both held their breaths for a moment against the foul odor coming from the enclosed stairwell.

"Is this place always so dark and dirty?" queried Greg as they emerged from the fire doors into the second floor corridor.

"During vacation days and through the summer; yes," answered Jan. "It's the last section of the three wings to be cleaned as a rule. I finally protested the way the wing was kept up, especially the stairs and the rest rooms, but I got nowhere with Lindner or Ms. Watkins. I may not be a regular teacher, but I do pay taxes for this school and its maintenance."

She turned toward her office door to unlock it as Greg commented, "Good for you."

The familiar whoosh of stale air rushed at them as she opened the door and turned on the overhead lights.

"Do you see how I was able to tell that someone was in my office on the day it had been searched? The smell of cigar smoke and and body odor was unmistakably different from the usual stale air."

"I get what you mean," said Greg. "After all the years you worked out of this office, you'd know. And you followed up on your suspicions, which was the right thing to do. After all, you have confidential material about your students in that file cabinet." He indicated the gray bulk of a cabinet at the end of her desk.

Jan smiled at him. "It's so nice to talk to someone sensible. When I was disturbed about the strange smell and disarray of things in the office, nobody cared enough to discuss it with me beyond the report I gave to the voc secretary."

Greg returned her smile and patted her forearm. "There's a good reason for that, believe me. Where should we begin the search for Jake's notes?"

"I put my old student folders in the bottom drawer of the file cabinet. It's a real messy system I've got going in there, because it was supposed to be temporary. The finished portfolios are in the big boxes under the table. Jake was visiting me the morning I was putting things away after graduation, as memory serves me. He was feeling so good about Andre that he stopped in to say thanks again. We could start with the folder, I guess."

Jan pulled out the heavy drawer. The contents did look haphazardly filed, but she soon found Andre's manila folder in approximately the correct spot. It was well worn and rather grubby looking, befitting a student folder that had gone back and forth from home to program office for nine months.

"There are several places in amongst the papers that would make good hiding spots," said Jan as she spread the folder and its contents out on the long table.

"Let's start at the beginning and work toward the back," replied Greg. "Remember Jake was no fool when it came to hiding things. If we examine every scrap of paper and then lay it aside, we'll not miss anything that looks unusual."

They carefully scrutinized the sheets and scraps of paper in the folder and found nothing. Jan was disappointed at their lack of success until she thought to pry out the staples holding a page of student transactions and appointment listings to the back of the front cover of the folder. "This looks like it," she exclaimed excitedly.

Two thin sheets of paper were concealed there. Jan pulled the first one out and passed it immediately to Greg. The sheet was covered with columns of figures in a fairly orderly manner, which indicated that a person who was familiar with financial matters had used it to demonstrate totals to others in the group. The back side of the paper was set up as a preliminary profit and loss statement. It needed analyzing, Greg told her, but his gray-green eyes were sparkling over the possibilities.

The second piece of paper had Jake's printing on it, back and front. Paragraphs were headed by dates, which indicated that they were summaries of the meetings Jake had accidentally or deliberately overheard as the secret group continued to meet in the academic wing of the high school. Jan wondered to herself what Jake originally had intended to do with all this information. The word blackmail entered her mind.

They both glanced up at the same time, and a wealth of information passed between them as the look lengthened to a gaze of understanding and victory.

Greg quickly stowed the papers back in the folder and placed it in the file drawer. "Just in case someone comes along that we don't want to deal with right now, let's pretend that we're here to move you out of the office and that's all," he stated. "It's about time for your boss to arrive, so why don't you go get him, and I'll guard the evidence while you're gone."

"Good thinking, as the kids say," replied Jan as she headed for the door. "Remember Lindner creeps up behind you in his rubber-soled loafers, so be on the lookout for him."

"I'll watch out for him, don't worry about that," he promised with a grin.

Jan ran to the stairwell and down the steps two at a time while clinging to the wrought iron banister. When she got to the outside door and looked out the window, she could see George's car parked to the right. He saw her wave and came to the janitors' door to be let inside.

"You're not here alone, are you?" he exclaimed, as they walked through the corridor to the stairwell.

"No, I'm not," stated Jan firmly. "I wouldn't do that. A friend is here to help move the heavy stuff, as promised, and you'll never guess in a million years who it is, so I'll tell you. It's Greg Whitehouse, the state police person who is in charge of the investigation of the two murders involving the high school. And he's in civilian clothes. We've become quite good friends. Do you know him from the offices in Montpelier?"

"Not personally," said George. "He has an excellent reputation, however, and I've heard his name mentioned in connection with other investigations."

"Well, helping me move to the employment offices is above and beyond the call of duty, I'm sure, but the business of Jake's murder and my warning note and phone call seem to tie together. Everybody's watching out for me right now, and I appreciate it." They arrived at the program office and Jan introduced the two men.

"Where should we start?" asked Greg.

George told them that there was a modern desk unit and a file cabinet set up for her use in the employment office. The unit included shelving for program materials and reference books, and there was an old metal government desk that could be used by the students.

"As long as I don't need to move the file cabinet after all, I guess that we can load up the contents in those boxes over on the other side of the table," Jan said. "There are plenty of them for the books and extra stuff. I packed up the small things from my desk and put them in my car, Other than that, I'll just take down the pictures and posters and I'm ready to go."

The packing proceeded smoothly. Greg made sure that he kept an eye on the box that held the precious evidence from the bottom drawer of the file cabinet as they loaded up the two cars in the parking lot. No one interfered to ask what was going on. Jan was not surprised, but felt that Lindner must be lurking about somewhere in the building. Her moving was too much of a coup for him to miss. She kept her thoughts on the modern building she was going to, the window she'd always wanted, and the air conditioning available when the weather got hot. It was not going to take long to forget the dirty halls and rest rooms and the spy-master political atmosphere.

The employment office was a mile away from the top street of the business district hill and to the right on River Road. Grace Evans let them

in with the first load of folders and books after
they hit the buzzer near the office door. Jan's
office space was set up at the rear of the large
partitioned room, next to the windows on the
left. It looked very efficient with a space for her
typewriter, plenty of shelves, and a modern
posture chair for her use. I'll be able to have
plants, she thought, noting the large
windowsills.

Grace and George went to the manager's
office to go over the details of the contract for
space that had to be agreed to and signed for the
state accounting office. That gave Greg time to
put Andre's student folder in an evidence bag
and mark it. Jan and Greg moved back and
forth from the cars, unloading her boxes of
papers and books. Things were nearly all put
away when George brought the contract out for
Jan to sign. She signed it and went to Grace's
office to say thanks. It was all too good to be
true.

They bade Grace good-bye after arranging
with her that Jan would start seeing students on
Thursday morning. That would give her time to
get settled in, meet the employment counselors,
and learn the routine of the office.

George decided to get on the road for home as
his wife was expecting him for dinner whenever
the business in New Venice was completed. Jan
and Greg waved their good-byes and headed for
their dinner date at Jerome's Restaurant on the
northeast edge of town near the interstate
entrance. "It isn't prime rib night," Jan told
Greg laughingly, "but they always have a great
menu of steak and seafood." All the packing and

moving had given them both hearty appetites, and they could hardly wait to talk about the papers they had discovered in Andre's student folder.

The restaurant was not excessively crowded when they arrived, judging by the cars in the parking lot. Greg found a space near the entrance and guided her to the door with a soft hand pressure in the middle of her upper back. Jan had lived independently for so long that his touch was almost shocking. It was wonderful to have the door opened for her in such a caring way. A small part of the wall of independence she had built up around her soul began to crumble slightly.

Greg asked the hostess for a booth near the window but toward the back of the nonsmoking section where they could have some privacy to talk about the events of the afternoon.

"It's nice to take you out to dinner on such a day of successful collaboration. This is a celebration, actually," began Greg, as the waitress brought their menus. "We should order champagne, but I'm on call while the investigation is still in progress. How about two cups of coffee and we'll clink crockery instead?"

"That's fine with me," answered Jan. "Coffee's my drink of preference, as you know. For a minute there, I thought I noted a hint of conclusion to that word investigation. Are you that far along in solving the murders and the mystery around them?"

"I wish I could fill you in on all the details because we've worked together so well, but I can't right now. You've had enough attention from the people responsible for the evil going on in New Venice." Greg studied her serious face with affection. "We'll keep an eye on the condo for intruders, but you have to be careful wherever you are."

Jan noted the affection in his voice and a little more of her independence wall started to crumble. "Well," she said, "I've seen the papers that Jake hid, and we can't change that. Won't the people that have been looking for them so diligently guess that we've been searching for them too, and that we've been doing the searching together, not to mention that we actually found Jake's evidence?"

"It's their own stupidity that clued us in to the fact that Jake did have evidence that was worth hiding," stated Greg. "When they started harassing you, thinking to scare you off giving evidence to the police, it doubly confirmed that there was something to look for. Of course, if they had found it first and destroyed it, the story would be different, but they didn't have the inside information about Jake and Andre Patenaude that you had."

The waitress returned with their coffee and took their dinner orders. They solemnly clinked cups and laughed companionably.

Jan thoughtfully gazed into Greg's eyes. "I couldn't make heads nor tails of that paper with all the financial figures. Do you have any idea what it was?"

"I have an idea about what the figures are for because they will dovetail with the other financial evidence we've been gathering since the first of the year. Things have really gotten out of control in this school district, and the State Education Department wanted to know what was going on. I was picked for the job, and now it's blown up into two murder cases before the financial evidence could be verified. There's been a group of people from out of state working on a scheme to wash illegal money in this area with the help of some legislators in Montpelier. The local administrators were conned into going along with their plans." Greg paused as their dinners arrived; steak medium for him and baked seafood for her. "The state legislature has been influenced by the bad guys just as if our little rural state was a playground for out-of-state crooks."

"I had no idea that the school district's problems were so involved or widespread. All I knew was that the atmosphere at school was rotten, and that people in town were doing their best to ignore it. You know me and the intuition thing. When the state evaluation team picked up on it by talking to the teachers and students, it made me think more seriously about it. Also, our administrators were undermining decisions that were made about student behavior on a favoritism basis. The kids knew all about it and were angry, which encouraged theft and vandalism in retaliation."

Jan felt a headache coming on in spite of the good meal in front of her. There had been too much activity and upheaval.

Greg put it into words for her. "It's been a very busy but productive day."

They continued eating in silence for a while. Jan was defying the headache by finishing her

187

fish dinner. When the waitress came around with a fresh pot of coffee, she asked if they would be having dessert. Jan went on with the defiance and recommended the lemon meringue pie for herself and Greg.

"Sounds good to me." Greg was evidently a hearty eater who didn't have to worry about his waistline. "I passed up a good lunch in Barton at the diner because I was running late with my interviews. Ordinarily, I don't have dessert because the state police have a weight program going on, and the sweet stuff does me in. It's easier for me to prevent the pounds than try to take them off later."

"It's my favorite," Jan replied, "of all the pies I've eaten anywhere. I do have to pass it up more often than not, though." She was secretly pleased that she was wrong and that Greg had to go without dessert as a regular habit just as she did and smiled inwardly as he ordered two pieces of the pie.

They finished their desserts and last cups of coffee. Greg had to return to his temporary office to write up his reports for the day, and Jan felt her on-coming headache getting closer by the minute even if she had enjoyed the dinner and conversation. They parted at the front door of her condo like old friends with a hug and short kiss, to Jan's surprise, but she had to admit that she liked it.

There was no Dickens waiting for her inside the door as she opened it and stepped inside the small hallway. Remembering that she had let him out before going to the school, she looked out on the porch to see if he was waiting for her.

He wasn't there either, but that didn't mean much. When he got through gallivanting around the neighborhood and was hungry, he'd be back.

She got into a hot shower after taking two aspirin to combat the dreaded headache, and found that her preventions had worked as she drifted off to sleep with a small smile on her face.

CHAPTER EIGHT

Greg drove directly to his office after leaving Jan at her condo front door. The local police were busy with a group of people arranged in front of the glass panel talking loudly with ferocious gestures, so he slipped around them to his office without being noticed. Turning on the small desk light with one hand and then tugging his jacket off with the other, he glanced around the small room now made even smaller by the shadows crowding in around his desk from all corners. He was surprised to notice that in spite of his busy day and the noise from the melee outside the door, he was whistling "What a Wonderful World" in a sibilant undertone. What's more, he had been doing so all the way to his office.

Settling into the rickety wooden swivel chair, he pulled out the evidence bag containing Jake's two papers that he and Jan had found in Andre's student folder. He had marked the particulars of time and place found along with his initials and hers at the top. It was going to take him a minute to sort the day's happenings into the categories of the information already known.

The state's attorney general had most of the information he had gathered about the missing federal funds in his office already, but the other evidence gleaned from Greg's investigation of the past few days was still circumstantial and not enough to move on. The murder of Dan Frost seemed to be one of passion and fury while Jake's death was obviously a cold-blooded cover-up for what he might have known about the financial manipulations being discussed at the clandestine meetings at the high school. What was needed was a scenario that tied all the information together in a logical sequence.

Greg buried his face in his hands while he tried to think. There could be two murderers on the loose in the New Venice area even though the weapon used to bash the men's skulls matched in configuration with the fatal wounds. That seemed screwy to him somehow, and not likely. He had no authority to search people's cars or residences for lead pipes or any other type of weapon at this point. The vocational building was full of good hiding places, but his aide had not come up with anything likely when he had enlisted the local police in a search. In order to solve the double murders he'd have to interview or reinterview all the participants in the unauthorized meetings at the high school as named in Jake's note. He'd have to get a handle on the thinking and planning that went on during those meetings. Lindner was already in hot water over the missing federal funds, which made him a prime candidate for spilling the beans on the rest of the wrongdoing. Greg made a note on the legal pad in front of him to call the state's attorney first thing in the morning to see who would have the honors. The next best candidate would be the contractor named in Jake's note, a Mr. Bob Smithfield. Information about his alleged payoffs for contracts was only just beyond the rumor stage. Neither he nor Lindner knew that Jake's information was in the hands of the state police, although they were plenty worried about it. Ms. Watkins, the high school principal could wait for another round of interviewing for the present time.

In review of his notes from the trip to Barton, Greg realized that a pattern was forming, slowly but surely. It appeared to him that the three administrators had started out with a legitimate business plan which would be lucrative, long-term, and community oriented. Mrs. Morely, the owner of the land they coveted, would not come down on her asking price at first. Greg couldn't blame her for that because the multi-acred farmland was beautiful with rolling meadows hayed to country club perfection, a sparkling stream and springs system for water, a maple sugar orchard, and immaculate home buildings. Mr. Morely had retired ten years previous to the time of the administrators' interest. The barns were rented out to neighbors for young stock as were the fields for haying. The barns were his particular pride, always kept in perfect condition even though he had retired.

Mrs. Morely had insisted on having a lovely home in spite of her husband's interest in barns and livestock. The square white farmhouse with its huge front porch was surrounded by extensive lawns, shaded by old sugar maples and embellished with trellised flower gardens on one side, with a kitchen garden in the back. She had also insisted on a separation of barn and house atmosphere by enforcing use of a back porch and utility room for changing of barn clothes and boots. The Morelys had loved their farm and had had the money to keep it in excellent condition. Only one thing was missing. They had no living children to pass it along. Nevertheless, Mrs. Morely had kept the farm after her husband's death, managing it as they always had. She was admired and loved by her neighbors as well as the friends of all ages she had accumulated in Barton.

One of Mrs. Morely's main interests beyond that of the farm was the education of young people in the Barton area. Many a college-bound freshman had been helped on the way by a financial contribution from her through the local bank. Greg had found out about Mrs. Morely's philanthropy from his real estate friend who was on the bank's board. There were other things learned from him that helped to explain the three high school administrators' behavior.

When she reached the age of seventy-three, Mrs. Morley had taken a fall in the back utility porch and broken her hip. It was in the late summer of last year just before school started. Luckily, she was found by one of her young neighbors within an hour because he had come to help her pick vegetables in the kitchen garden that she still maintained. Josh had rushed to the phone to call his mother, who came running across the field to call 911 for an ambulance. Mrs. Morley had been called "a tough old bird" behind her back for quite a few years because she always survived the various crises presented to her after her husband's death. This time, she had to go to the Evergreen Nursing Home presumably to recuperate, where she found out that her hip had broken before she fell, not because of the fall.

The doctors' bills, nursing home fees, and hired help salaries to keep up the farm finally convinced her to start thinking about selling it. About this time, the three administrators from New Venice started visiting her on a regular basis. Greg knew that they talked about wanting to buy the land from her again because he had interviewed one of the nurse's aides who had come and gone in Mrs. Morley's room on her regular routine. They told her over and over that they were planning to establish an area agricultural/educational school on a working farm, such as hers could easily be again, to demonstrate that diversification and hard work could bring back the successful family farm. This sounded like music to Mrs. Morley's ears. When they told her that they had to get a break on the farmland to get started, she demurred and said she would have to talk to her lawyer. Then they brought out the computerized plans for dormitory, kitchen, dining, and classroom buildings that would have to be built behind the farmhouse. When they showed her the figures for needed water, sewage, and electrical updates, she succumbed to their plans. What a wonderful opportunity it must have seemed to her, thought Greg as he reviewed his notes. They were even going to name the school, The

Morley Agricultural College. After that, no one could talk her out of the idea.

Jan would have loved the plan, too. In his mind's eye he could see her eyes sparkling with enthusiasm. Too bad it all turned out to be a fairy tale. There was not a shred of truth in the plans for a school as time went on, as far as anyone could verify with hard facts. The group had done a good con job on Mrs. Morely.

His thoughts came back to Jan; how beautiful she looked in her red wool jacket with the white scarf just peeking out at the collarline, how her bangs slid down to meet her reading glasses when she was concentrating, how dedicated she was to helping young adults get a good start in life.

A little discipline is needed here, he told himself, if I'm going to finish my report and send it off in the mail tonight. Working diligently for the next hour, he decided that Tuesday's activities had been well covered with summaries and receipts, as necessary. It was time to lock up and head for the motel room he was sharing with his aide, Bill Rainey. Contrary to the bad news of the happenings in New Venice and Barton, he found himself whistling again as he prepared for bed, to the complete amazement of his roommate.

Gregory Whitehouse was known to be the most responsible and meticulous investigator in the upper-middle ranks of the state police force. However, his wife's long illness and death had taken its toll of his former personality traits of good humor and readiness for any kind of horseplay. Friends and colleagues of long standing wished that he would not be so constantly serious and dedicated to his work. The work consisted of contact with the seamier side of mankind's behavior on a regular basis, which of necessity called for periods of happiness and fun for balance. Greg just couldn't seem to get the hang of it again, even when he tried hard to please his friends. They finally gave up inviting him out or fixing him up with wonderful women that they knew would be perfect for him. His sadness and guilt were beginning to fade away for long stretches of time, but when he was tired or particularly discouraged with a police case, they came rushing back to haunt him once again. Whistling was something he'd not done for years; it was an outward manifestation of an inward contentment.

CHAPTER NINE

Jan woke at eight thirty, which was a pretty good indication that it was exhaustion that kept her from waking at her usual earlier hour. Of course, Dickens was not there to nag her for breakfast, and she had completely forgotten about setting her alarm clock the night before.

Thinking about Dickens got her going. After a trip to the bathroom, she went to the front sliding door to see if he was waiting on the porch to be let in. He was not there, but Jan wasn't worried. It was not unusual for him to be gone for several days; Dickens was neutered, but he still went through the rituals necessary to maintain male dominance in the neighborhood. Jan hoped that he wouldn't come home bloody and battered as he had done in the past.

Checking the morning view of the lake, Jan was happy to see that there might be another spring day coming to New Venice for this Wednesday. Overnight temperatures had been down near freezing, but the very visible blue skies and sunshine would warm the air as soon as the early morning mist dispersed. The surface of the lake was nearly hidden from view, but small patches near the shore looked smooth as glass. She felt a ripple of contentment in her upper mid-section where she supposed her soul to be. The sensation had been missing from her life for several years.

Preparing her first pot of coffee for the morning occupied the next few minutes. It was becoming habit; taking her time, enjoying the lake view, and watching the news on TV while sipping coffee and munching toast. When had she last felt so relaxed and happy just to vegetate at home? It wasn't like being on vacation because she always went somewhere new with a friend, and in the end the days off had been stressful as well as exciting. It must be the spring weather and the new office location combining to make her feel this way. It couldn't be the fact that she and Greg had hit off as well as they had. Or could it?

Just then the telephone rang, and Jan hastily got up to answer it with thoughts of Greg on her mind. It was Ginny calling to tell her that she, Ginny, had been invited to ride in Lindner's van to Montpelier for Dan Frost's funeral at eleven o'clock. Jan had it on the tip of her tongue to say "why are you telling me" or "who cares" when Ginny burst out crying.

"I have to leave for school to meet Lindner and his friends in a few minutes, but I want you to know that I do care about all the things Frost, Lindner, and Ms. Watkins did to make you miserable at school. Your troubles there were just like the problems the other women went through except it took longer to get rid of you because of the state program you work in. That business of Dan fondling your thigh at the supervisors' meeting is also typical of what the other women experienced. I checked."

"For heaven's sake, Ginny, what brought all this on?" exclaimed Jan in anger. "Did you get to feeling guilty or what?"

"There was guilt and maybe jealousy, too," replied Ginny. "Most of all, I thought I could protect Eric from prosecution for those automotive shop thefts. Lindner leaned on me to join in the getting rid of you, and I agreed to it. He implied that he could fix up the problems in the shop if I helped him. The adult student was supposed to take all the blame, but Eric confessed to me that he's involved too. We've been to see a lawyer and Father Gareth at church. He thought that I ought to apologize to you as a first step for my own piece of mind."

"Well, I did wonder what was going on," returned Jan. "I mean we were all in on the derogatory conversations about Lindner and Dan. You know that Lindner is in hot water himself over missing federal funds for a computer lab that has never materialized in the vocational wing, don't you?"

"Yes. The whole supervisory system is messed up because of the administrators' manipulations."

"You've got your hands full with taking care of Eric's troubles right now. I'm a big girl, and to tell you the truth, I'm happy with the new location for the diploma program."

"There's something else that I want to talk to you about before I hang up, Jan. You know how Lindner always comes in and takes over my computer without asking or apologizing or anything. We wondered about it because it never seemed to make sense. Well, he's been using it all the time for some project or other, something to do with money for a Mrs. Morley and construction. I'll tell you all about it when I get back from Montpelier."

That sounded ominously like Jake's last transaction, Jan thought nervously. "Wait a minute before you hang up, Ginny," she said into a dead connection. It was to be hoped that Ginny wouldn't say anything to Lindner about the files she had stumbled on, or God forbid try to question him. Jan tried to call her back, but she had left for school to join Lindner and friends for the ride to Montpelier.

Just as she turned to pour herself another cup of coffee, the phone rang again. This time it was Greg, and Jan was glad to hear his voice for more than one reason. She told him about Ginny's phone call with emphasis on what she had said about the computer in her office and the files. The way Ginny had ended the conversation made her very nervous, she indicated, like certain conversations she had had with Jake before he was killed.

"I'd certainly like to take a look at that computer and now would be a good time," Greg told her. "Do you still have your keys to the voc wing and the adult ed office?"

"I was going to turn them in today before I went down to the employment office to arrange my things," answered Jan. "I can meet you somewhere and give them to you. I don't have any problem with that. What are we going to do about Ginny and her big mouth, though?"

"I'm in the coffee shop at the motel," replied Greg. "Can you meet me in a few minutes? Bill is here with me eating breakfast, and then he's driving back to Montpelier to attend Mr. Frost's funeral as an unobtrusive observer of the proceedings. He can speak to Ginny about keeping her mouth shut. Let's hope it's not too late to surprise Mr. John Lindner with her discovery. By the way, Bill said to tell you that I was whistling and actually smiling when I got back to the motel room last night. What do you think he meant by that?" he teased.

"I'm sure I don't know, but tell him from me that I'm glad to hear it," Jan teased back. They said their good-bys and Jan ran to the bedroom for her jeans and sweater.

It took only ten minutes for her to wash her face, brush her teeth, and comb her hair to head out the door for the Escort, which was parked outside. She automatically looked around for Dickens as she backed out and drove down the hill to the main street. There was no sign of the big black cat.

Greg was waiting for her at the cashier's counter when she arrived at the motel coffee shop. Bill winked at her as he grabbed the report envelope that Greg had failed to mail the night before and ran to the door. "It's just as well he forgot to put it in the mailbox because I'll be going to the Montpelier office before I go to the funeral parlor," he said. "The mail doesn't go out until five o'clock this afternoon anyway. What a system."

"Hey, I never forget anything, and don't you forget it," Greg replied. He turned to Jan and

201

said, "Well, almost never. I had trouble with my concentration last night for some reason or other."

"Poor you. I slept like a baby and didn't wake up until eight thirty. I've been feeling awfully happy all morning in spite of the distractions that have developed, though. Is it something in the air today?" Jan leaned close and gave him a discreet hug before they parted at her Escort door. She didn't really care who saw them together. There had been no man she trusted even this far for several years.

Greg took the keys to the voc wing in his hand as Jan explained which ones to use. "Do you want to go with me?" he asked. "After all, you've been in on most of the school stuff since the beginning of the investigation."

"I don't think I'd better go near the school again until I have to for graduation," she answered. "Are you going to be all right with the computer?"

"Didn't I tell you that I'm a computer whiz? I only need to see what the files look like, and if it's what I expect, I'll take the whole thing for evidence. Lindner screwed up somewhere."

"Ginny's machine was one of the computers not networked throughout the building. She used it for data input, names and addresses mainly and letters. I'm flabbergasted that she found anything of Lindner's that he wanted hidden."

Greg helped her into the car and gently shut the door. "Drive carefully. I think that we should have dinner together again tonight, don't you? We will have a lot of talking to do."

Back at the condo, Jan walked to the edges of the property on two sides and behind the garages looking for Dickens. She was really beginning to wonder where he could be. He's been gone for longer stretches than this, she told herself as she walked back to her front door. It's like worrying about a close relative, though; I want to know that he's all right.

The bedroom and kitchen were in a mess from her hasty departure to meet Greg at the motel dining room. After an hour's concentrated effort, she had both rooms straightened up, a pot of fresh coffee made, and a load of washing going. Her inner drive to keep busy would not let her rest, however. Maybe she should give in and go down to the employment building to straighten out her new office after the laundry had been dried and folded. A quick lunch with the fresh coffee would also keep her going until it was time for dinner with Greg. Making decisions and plans for the afternoon helped quiet the thoughts of Greg, the worry about Dickens, and the wonder about what was going on at school, she thought.

She was wrong. Thoughts of Greg kept right on coming while she folded laundry and put it away. They intruded as she mixed tuna and Miracle Whip for her sandwich and then sat down to eat. What's happening to me anyway, she wondered; I feel like a teenager with a new crush. I'm either about to make the biggest mistake of my life or find the greatest happiness I've ever known or both of the above. Do I dare, after all these years of pretending that I am independent, needing no one else to make me feel secure and happy?

All at once she knew what she had to do to get her thoughts and emotions in order. There was a noon Eucharist service at St. Luke's, and she had ten minutes to get there on time. When she was working, there wasn't time at noon to attend, but today she was free to do anything she wished to do. Rushing from the condo to her car, she drove down the hill and through town to the little white church with the red doors. The service usually was not well attended beyond the twelve parishioners who were sitting together, but separately enough for privacy, in the front pews on this Wednesday. Jan sat and then kneeled to pray in the fifth row on the left-hand side of the church, hoping no one would come and join her. Father Gareth and a lay minister came in quietly after she had been there about five minutes. The service was low key and reached out to comfort or strengthen each person there for whatever reason.

The thoughts of Greg stayed with her all through the service. She remembered what he had told her about his wife and her lingering death. The guilt and sorrow connected to her passing had made him look so stern and serious when she first met him. Now she thought of him as a happy person who liked to tease and make jokes. Was this his personality before his wife became ill? Jan thought so and was pleased to think that she had something to do with the change for the better. Then she wondered how she had appeared to him at first meeting. Did she look overly serious and concerned with her students? They had joked about her following a person who was a stranger into an office at the police station. That's how they met, making a joke together to break the ice. When Jan rose to take communion at the altar rail, a person came from behind her to kneel at her side. When she looked from the corners of her eyes to see who it was, she was astonished to see that it was Greg.

Back in the pew again, sitting close together, Greg whispered that he always tried to attend Wednesday's service when something was bothering him about the police work or when he had thoughts that needed clarification. Jan felt like a great weight had been taken from her shoulders. Her thoughts were indeed clarified.

After the closing prayers, they sat and talked for another half an hour. It was difficult at first for both of them. Jan confessed that thoughts of him had been with her all morning even though she tried to keep busy enough to quiet them. Greg told her that when he spoke of his lack of concentration while he was doing his paperwork, it was because he kept thinking of her.

"I feel like a twenty-year-old kid again when I think of you and at the same time like I've found the other half of myself that's been missing all these years. I couldn't wait until tonight to tell you."

"You make me feel happy and at home like you're someone I've known and loved for a long time," Jan replied to his confession. "But how can this be happening to us so fast? Here you are investigating murders and finding out all kinds of bad things about the school administrators and prominent people in town.

Who else can tell such a story about how they first met?"

"Not very many, I'm sure." It was Father Gareth who had been waiting for them to leave so that he could lock up the church. "I couldn't help overhearing your last few remarks to each other. I'm sorry to disturb you when you're at an important point in your lives. Do you want to come over to the parish house to continue?"

Greg and Jan looked at each other for minute and then both declined the invitation with thanks. They hugged and kissed at the red doors while Father Gareth locked up.

"We're meeting for dinner tonight; after that, we both might want to make an appointment to talk with you," Greg told him and Jan nodded in agreement.

"Where's your car parked?" asked Greg, as they started down the front walk of the church. "I'll walk you to it, and then I'm headed out for Montpelier with a big box in the back of my Volvo containing you-know-what."

"I'm parked right here nearly in front of the church," Jan replied. "This means that you were successful, doesn't it? What time will you be back, or should I just wait to hear from you?"

"I would say that six thirty seems about right. I'll see you then. We'll go to the same restaurant as last night, if it's all right with you."

"It's still not prime rib night, but it sounds good to me." They kissed again before parting with a little more intensity than they had at the church doorway.

"Things are heating up," said Father Gareth to himself as he looked down on them from his office window in the second story of the parish house. He had known Jan for many years going back to the days of Joe Madison and the famous flying sales trips. A smile came to his face as he guessed what was happening in her life.

Greg walked to his office, which was only a block away from the church. He then loaded the box containing the adult ed computer into the back seat of his car and drove off to Montpelier. He was whistling under his breath again without realizing what he was doing.

Jan drove home slowly. How was she to endure the hours until it was time to meet Greg for dinner? What was happening to the wall of dignity and reserve that she had so carefully built up around her body and soul in keeping with her position in the community as teacher and devoted St. Luke's parishioner? She was in a limbo of pleasure and fearfulness combined until the questions could be answered, but her heart was telling her to let the past go as she enjoyed the present. There was a smile on her face when she drove into the condo parking area, got out of the Escort, and walked to the post office boxes to check her mail.

Thankfully noting that there was no strange-looking envelope in amongst the bills and several personal letters, she returned to the condo to change clothes for the trip to the employment office.

After showering and dressing in slacks, turtleneck, and sweater, Jan heated a cup of the morning's leftover coffee in the microwave oven and sat at her dining room table writing checks for the bills that had accumulated over the past week.   Then she went on to answer letters, particularly the one that had been nagging at her thoughts for several days to her cousin Liz in Seattle.   She thanked her for the Easter card and apologized for not sending her one, giving the gist of the situation in New Venice as an excuse.   Meeting Greg and liking him came in the second last sentence on the final page of the letter.   Knowing Liz, she was sure that she would be getting a phone call from Seattle as soon as it was read.

With her thoughts once again on Greg, she looked at the clock to check how long it would be until she saw him.   There were three and a half hours to fill until six thirty.   Could she bear it?   Getting the letters ready to go in the mail and donning her light khaki jacket occupied her for five more minutes.   With a glance out the porch door for Dickens, and not seeing him again, she left for the employment office on River Street.

It was necessary to speak to Grace Evans before she did anything else, Jan decided as she walked into the lobby and front desk area of the large employment office.   She introduced herself to the receptionist, who used the phone to buzz Grace that Jan was there to see her.   Her office was the largest enclosed room beyond the huge partitioned space for the ten employment counselors, and Jan went down the aisle near the windows so that she could get another look at her own space on the way.   The room was so clean and light in contrast with the grubby conditions in the vocational wing it made her spirits soar in delight.

Knocking on the doorjamb because the door itself was open, Jan announced her appearance. Grace was seated at her computer dressed in a severe-looking gray pantsuit, white blouse with the collar on the outside of the jacket, and old-fashioned black, sturdy shoes. Her smile was sincerely welcoming, in spite of what she might have been told by John Lindner or Ms. Watkins about Jan's leaving the high school voc wing. I would guess that she's seen a lot of in-fighting and office political maneuvering in her day, thought Jan. My little battle probably doesn't mean beans to her. Besides that, she knows that Lindner is being audited and is in big trouble with the state ed office.

The two women greeted each other and chitchatted for a few minutes until Grace called her assistant on the phone to ask if she would give Jan a guided tour of the building. This was to include what Jan had access to in the way of office machines and supplies. The tour was short and to the point with introductions to the counselors who were not busy with clients as they proceeded around the office.

She felt at home when the formalities were finished and she was at last viewing her own office space. The student files were quickly lifted from the boxes where they had been stored and placed in the drawers of the new beige-colored cabinet at her disposal. She arranged her books and supplies on the shelves above the electric typewriter. The space was going to work out just fine. Jan eyed the windowsill and imagined several green plants sitting there before she went out to her car to retrieve the two cartons of small

items for her desk and shelves. With the
addition of colorful posters pinned on the
burlap-covered partition, the place would
actually look spiffy, she thought.

Just then, Grace came by to tell her that
everyone had to be out of the building by four
thirty because there had been a break-in the
night before. Grace herself could stay late, at
her own discretion, but everyone else had to be
out of the office by the deadline. Jan's heart
sank as she thought of the search of her old
office in the school building. Her eyes fell on the
metal file box on her desk where Jake had left
his evidence message, and she wondered if the
break-in at the employment office had anything
to do with the bad things happening at the high
school. Somebody knew a lot about what she
was doing and where her student files were
stored.

There was no way she could speak to Grace
about her suspicions, so she just asked if
anything had been stolen or trashed.
Fortunately, Grace told her, the break-in had
been related only to change jimmied out of the
soda machine in the employees' lounge and
money extracted from the big box of snacks food
sold by the honor system. Jan was relieved to
hear that, but a nagging doubt in the back of
her mind said that the juvenile style burglary
could have been a cover-up for a search through
her papers again. Whoever it was could have
been looking for Jake's presumed evidence.

It was four thirty when she glanced up at the
clock. All the counselors were dutifully putting
their jackets on and collecting lunch bags in

preparation of going home for the day. Jan was accustomed to staying into the early evening hours at her former office when she had a student who couldn't leave work until five o'clock or later, but this was not going to inconvenience her or her students greatly. There was always the public library to use for a meeting place until eight o'clock and all day Saturday when appointment times became difficult to arrange. She made her own schedule for the month and then turned her hours in to George when it was over. Of course, there was never money in the program's coffers to pay overtime, but she used the comp time to her own advantage to balance out a thirty-six hour work week.

Saying good-by to her new colleagues, Jan turned the Escort toward the business district. She had letters to mail, and there was just time to get to the post office before the mail went out at five o'clock. Joining the secretaries with boxes of bulk mail, Jan thought about Bill Rainey's comment about the system.

That made her think about Ginny and the phone call she had made to her before leaving for Montpelier to attend Dan Frost's funeral with John Lindner. She wondered if Bill had spoken to Ginny in time to prevent her mentioning the strange computer files she had found. Jan had no confidence in Ginny's ability to keep news to herself, but maybe it would be all right.

The traffic outside the post office was in a tangle, as everyone tried to back out to leave the parking lot at once, and the in-coming vehicles had no place to go after turning from the street.

Jan waited patiently until the five o'clock rush sorted itself out and then slowly drove homeward. Killing time was getting to be a pain in the neck, she decided.

What she should do is stop at the mini-mart at the bottom of her hilly street to get the newspapers to read while she waited for Greg.

It was getting dark by the time she reached the small store. She purchased the two papers and a Kit Kat bar to eat as she read and left the oasis of outside lighting for the condo. When she reached her parking place, she looked back at the mini-mart glowing in the darkness and noted that it looked like a UFO with problems stranded on the planet earth for repairs. That's pretty fanciful thinking for an older type adult education teacher, she thought.

Letting herself into the small hallway of the condo, Jan automatically expected to see Dickens sitting near the door waiting for her return. He's been gone too long this time, and I'm beginning to get really worried about him, she told herself. There were so many possibilities for pet disasters: poisons, cars, kidnapping, and abuse by people who did not like cats.

She peered out the sliding glass door to the porch after turning on the outside light, but there was no sight of the big black cat there either. I miss him being parked inside the front door when I get home from work. Where in the devil can he be?

Letting the newspapers down on the blue chair, she took off her jacket and walked to the kitchen to put on a fresh pot of decaf. I'll sit by the door and read, and maybe he'll see me, she thought when the coffee was ready.

At six o'clock her doorbell rang and when she went to open it, there stood Marianne, who had stopped in to see how she was faring after the move to the employment office.

"I was at an afternoon meeting in Derby Line for Sunday school directors that dragged on and on," she explained. "And there was no coffee. I'm exhausted and need some to get me the rest of the way home. I could see your lights from the street, and all of a sudden the car was turning up the hill. I can't stay very long though or Sam will get worried about me."

"I'm glad to see you." Jan explained about the cat being missing, and how she was afraid something had happened to him. "It's the old intuition again, I guess."

"The move to the employment building was easy, and I had lots of help," she continued. "George Wright came up from Montpelier and my friend, Greg Whitehouse, helped us carry the heavy boxes into my office space late yesterday afternoon. Today I went over to put things away and arrange my stuff. It's going to be great with all those windows and brand new rest rooms and all. And it's so clean I hardly know how to react. You've seen how dirty the vocational wing is."

Jan poured Marianne a cup of coffee and they split the Kit Kat bar. "Do you really think Dickens isn't coming home?" she asked. Marianne knew that Dickens was like a member of her family and had been since Joe was killed.

"I wish I didn't have this feeling of dread when I think of him, but that's how I feel. Of course, he could show up at any time, all battered and filthy dirty like he has in the past." Jan felt tears forming in her eyes and closed them for a moment.

Marianne quickly changed the subject of their conversation. "Is the person who helped you move the same man you told me about last Sunday?" she asked.

"Yes. Greg Whitehouse. Before you hear any gossip about us, we're getting to be more than just friends. It's making me a little nervous, but I shouldn't be, because he's a wonderful person who's had a lot of sorrow in his life. I told you about his wife dying and the way it affected him. We also did a little detective work on the Jake Patenaude mystery together and came up with something concrete to explain why I've been harassed and threatened. I hope that ends now that there's evidence in the hands of the state police."

"Oh, I'm so glad it's over," exclaimed Marianne. "I was going to insist that you come and stay with us, but I guess there won't be any more trouble now. Are there going to be arrests soon?"

Jan frowned in concentration. "I don't know all the details, and I hate to sound like I'm prying when I talk to Greg about what's going on. He's pretty stern when it comes to the police business. They're still putting the pieces of the puzzle together, I think."

Marianne finished her coffee and stood up to put her jacket on. "I hope that things work out for you and this Greg. He sounds awfully nice, and I'd like to see you happy with someone like that." She gave Jan a quick hug and turned to leave.

Jan walked with her to the door. Just then the doorbell rang, and Jan told her that she was probably going to meet Greg, if that's who it was. "We're going out for dinner," she said.

They opened the door to find Greg standing in the hall. Jan introduced them, telling Greg that Marianne was her best friend since the days before Joe was killed. Marianne and Greg gave each other a good surveying glance before smiling, and then Marianne turned to hug Jan again. "I can see what you mean," she whispered in Jan's ear as she left.

Greg was in the living room when she returned from seeing Marianne off. "I should have said 'my best woman friend,'" she said to him. She looked him straight in the eye.

"It's nice of you to say that, if I've got your meaning straight," he replied, as he leaned forward to enfold her in his arms. "I've wanted to do that all afternoon. I missed you." This time their kiss was long and deep, lasting until Jan felt her knees wobble a bit.

"If we're going out for dinner, I think we'd better leave right now." Jan grabbed her jacket from the couch where she had thrown it and ran out the door.

Greg laughed and followed after he made sure she had her keys. He turned her to face him as he helped her into his car. "Are you afraid of what's happening to us?"

Jan thought about what he had asked as he walked around to the driver's side and slid in under the steering wheel. "I'll tell you the truth. It feels better than the first time around when I was too young to appreciate anyone as good as you are. I think we are two lucky people who have found each other in the middle of crazy circumstances, and I think that we can handle it without making a major scandal in town."

"Maybe you can Ms. Madison; I'm not having a bad time worrying about making a scandal in this town,"

"I love it when you tease me, Inspector Whitehouse."

"Thank you very much, Ms. Madison. Just for the record, I know what you mean. There's already been enough scandal in this town to satisfy the viewers of an on-going TV melodrama of the worst kind."

"I missed you, too," said Jan, as she pushed herself across the seat to be closer to him.

They drove to the restaurant in companionable silence; there were no words necessary to express what they were both feeling. After parking Greg's Volvo, they entered the warm lobby and waited to be seated. Jan's former student, Susan, was on duty as hostess, and she kept turning to smile at her as she led them to the same booth they had occupied the night before. Everyone in town knew that Jan was a widow who did not wish to date the few available men in the area.

Jan sat down and shrugged her jacket off her shoulders. The atmosphere of the restaurant was cozy and filled with the aroma of good food cooking on a huge open grill. Greg excused himself to go to the men's room, and then returned with their waitress in tow.

"I thought this would speed things up," he said. "I'm starving for the big steak dinner with all the trimmings. How about you?"

"I'm starving to hear all the news, the news you can tell me according to proper police rules, of course." Jan studied the menu in front of her. "I think I'll have the grilled chicken salad with ginger dressing while I listen."

"You're a card, Ms. Madison," returned Greg, with a grin. "I think I can trust you not to spread the word all over town." He then told her about the bogus plans for an agricultural school presented to a Mrs. Morely of Barton by the three high school administrators. The deal was supposed to be a secret using cash they had taken from construction kickbacks. More land purchases followed that first one, but things started to get out of hand along the way as another elaborate scheme was presented to them. They needed ever more cash as the scheme became wildly grandiose, involving other people in the state legislature and out-of-state gambling interests.

Jan thought about what Greg was telling her. "The computer files that Lindner was working on must have gotten on the hard drive to be saved for posterity," she surmised. "I've heard of strange things happening along those lines. Old Lindner thought he was safe when he carried away his disks and hid them from his secretary. Does anything match up to the figures on that piece of paper we found in Andre's folder?"

"It sure does. The evidence is so blatant that it's pitiable that anyone in a responsible position of trust could have such contempt for a rural community's business affairs. Toward the end of the last file, it sounded like someone we know was losing his mental health, you know, delusions of grandeur." Greg paused. "It's happened here before. Remember the real estate scandal involving several well-known brokers?"

"How is all this tying in to the two murder cases?" Jan asked.

"I've tried to reason it out. One seems compulsive involving passion, and the other is cold-bloodedly premeditated murder to keep someone quiet. We haven't found the murder weapon or weapons yet." Jan had finished her grilled chicken salad while Greg was speaking, but he was lagging behind on his steak dinner.

"Did Bill speak to Ginny when he got to Dan's funeral?" asked Jan. "Did anything weird happen?"

"I guess he got to her in time, if she's telling the truth," replied Greg. "There were men present that Bill couldn't place. He's doing some research right now on the strangers who sat in the back of the room away from everyone else."

"I'll bet he's got his suspicions though. Would they have anything to do with the grandiose plans that got out of hand?"

"Probably. Bill said that they looked and acted very confident and free from worry. It seems they don't know how far we've come in our investigating. Sometimes I don't even know because the evidence is being coordinated out of Montpelier. I'm supposed to concentrate exclusively on the murders from now on. Sources for keeping up-to-date are available to me under the table, so to speak, but it's time consuming to do business that way."

"You're too good for the politicians in Montpelier. They should let you head the whole investigation because I know you don't play games like they do. You're intelligent, as well as good at listening and paying attention to your hunches. And you treat people fairly when you question them, like the people down in Barton. More than one person has told me so."

"Thank you very much for the kind words, ma'am," replied Greg. "Now for your reward. How about another big piece of that delicious lemon meringue pie?"

"I think that I shall accept graciously, sir, although I want you to know that I had no ulterior motive when I spoke those kind words." They both laughed as Greg signaled the waitress to order the pie and two more coffees. "However, I did think ahead and have salad for my entree. Am I smart, or what?"

"Or what, most likely. The steak here is excellent. But you're right; we have to watch the old figure, don't we?"

They laughed again. There seemed to be a lot of things to laugh about this evening, Jan thought to herself as she ate her pie and drank the last of her coffee. I love it when Greg loses that darn serious look he carries around with him so much of the time. She felt bubbly and happy herself, and hoped it showed.

"Did you know that your face just glows and your eyes sparkle when you're happy and laughing?" said Greg, leaning over the table to hold her hands.

Jan looked at him with amazement. "Did you know that you're a mind reader? I was hoping that you could tell how happy I am right now."

"Let's get out of here and go somewhere private where we can do some more research on happiness." Greg helped her with her jacket and placed enough money on the table to cover their dinners and a generous tip for the waitress.

The April air outside the restaurant was crisp and clear. There were a million stars visible in the midnight blue sky. They wrapped their arms around each other as they ran to the car, pausing briefly to breathe in the crispness and gaze at the stars.

There are advantages to living in a rural area, thought Jan as she slid into the passenger seat of the Volvo. The stars were beautiful, but it was just a tad too crisp out there. Greg turned the heater on as soon as he had the engine going, and they melded into another one of their deep kisses.

"That warms things up, doesn't it, and I don't mean the heater," he said, as they reluctantly pulled apart. "I feel like a kid on a date, but I'm a lot more appreciative than I was then."

"I was thinking about that, too," Jan replied. "As long as we're doing happiness research, think how compatible and contented we'd be as old married folks, but here we have the magic again like a gift. I want it to last as long as possible. We're not kids, and we already know what love and marriage are all about, what with all the day-to-day stuff that wears away the wonder of it all. I intend to be darned appreciative, if you don't mind."

"Sounds good to me," laughed Greg, as they drove off to her condo to do some more happiness research.

"Should we park the Volvo in the garage so as not to offend the neighbors," Jan asked casually, "or are we honest and forthright about our seeing one another and to hell with it?"

"Ms. Madison, I'm shocked by your wanton attitude," Greg laughed again. "Have you no pride? Let's go for the honest and forthright though. It saves a lot of time explaining and slinking around, and we are two adults of an age and marital status that qualify us as people who know what we're doing."

They hugged again before entering the front door, clearly wanting to be a lot closer than their bulky clothing permitted. Jan was surreptitiously looking for Dickens on her way indoors, however. Even at a romantic time like this, she couldn't abandon her hopes to see him come to the door to be let in. She told Greg what she was doing while they were taking their jackets off and getting close to another embrace. They both went to the front porch to look for the big black cat as Jan explained the circumstances and timings of his periodic disappearances.

"You're really worried about him this time, Jan. Let's go out on the porch with the overhead light on to give it a good search. He may be sick and lying out there waiting for you to find him." Jan got her flashlight out of the

kitchen drawer and passed it over to Greg, who
went through the slider first.

He shined the light into all the dark corners
of the porch behind the lawn chairs and a plant
stand that were stored against the wall. Greg
then went to the railing and peered down into
the bushes that crowded against it at the
farthest end. "Don't come over here," he
whispered softly. "Get a towel and I'll wrap him
up. We need a box to put him in, too. He's
dead, Jan."

Jan did what he asked, feeling numb all over.
How could Dickens be dead, she thought. When
I let him outside, he was well and sassy as ever.
She took one of her best blue towels from the
closet shelf and rummaged around for a box that
would be the right size to hold a large cat.

Greg took the towel from her when she
arrived back at the porch. He had his pocket
knife in his hand, and was throwing some twine
and a piece of paper onto the porch floor. What
is he doing, she thought to herself, not willing to
believe that Dickens was indeed dead. Forever,
just like that. Here today and gone tomorrow,
just like Joe. Dead.

After wrapping the body of the cat in the blue
towel, Greg placed him in the box. It was a little
short, but it would do for a cat that was going
nowhere. Jan saw him shining the light around
the bushes where damp, partially frozen dirt was
bare.

"Your cat didn't just die, Jan, he was
deliberately hanged along the side of the porch
from the bottom of the railing where the bushes
covered him up. He tried to get loose, but his

struggles apparently made the noose around his neck pull tighter and tighter. The sicko that did it left a note for you."

They left the box out on the porch where it was cold, and brought the twine and piece of paper indoors. Greg read it to her. I TOLD YOU TO MIND YOUR OWN BUSINESS, was printed in large penciled capital letters on a piece of heavy gray paper. Jan shuddered. She wanted her cat back. She wanted to put her hands around the neck of the person who had killed her cat and squeeze as hard as she could. It wouldn't help Dickens, though. He was dead.

Greg took the flashlight and went outdoors to look at the damp earth near the bushes that lined the porch. There was a partial heel print of a work boot visible, and although he couldn't identify it, it looked familiar. Copying it down in his ever-present small notebook might prove useful later, however.

Walking back to the condo front door, he thought of the ten years that Dickens and Jan had been together, since her husband's death, in fact. The significance of the cat's death was that it would bring back memories of Joe's accident and the hours of searching before his downed plane was found. He felt angry and disgusted with the person or persons who had killed Jan's pet in such a cruel way, and surprisingly so, angry with Joe for being such a damned fool, flying over the Allagash when there had been so many small plane accidents that year.

Greg had to ring the doorbell to get back into the condo. They sat together on the couch and talked about Dickens and Joe and why did bad things happen just when a person was not prepared to deal with them, like this evening when they were so happy and ready to take the next step in their relationship. Jan's face was swollen from all the weeping, and when they kissed he could taste the saltiness of tears still streaming from her eyes.

They talked about his wife and her terminal illness. He told Jan that even though he knew that she was going to die, he couldn't let her go and kept hoping some new cure for cancer would come along in time, just like in a happily-ever-after movie. That was a large part of his guilt, he said, pretending that she could get well even when she was at peace and ready to go. His pastor had tried to explain to him that he was being cruel, but he wouldn't listen at first to the gentle words of admonishment.

They kissed again, and it was Jan's turn to comfort him as they lay on the couch in a close embrace, tasting each other's tears. Their kisses intensified until there was no denying what they wanted for release from their acute feelings of grief.

Later that night, they lay together in Jan's bed and talked and made love again. It made them laugh softly, remembering how they had rolled off the couch onto the rug where they had frantically disrobed enough to press flesh on flesh in consummation of their first loving.

"We are well and truly bonded, Ms. Madison," Greg whispered in her ear, as he smoothed her long bangs away from her eyes.

"We fit together like we were made for each other, Mr. State Policeman," returned Jan. "I have been chaste in my lonely years, and I thought that was how it would be for the rest of my life what with AIDS and all the complications of beginning a new relationship. It just wasn't worth it until I met you."

"Tonight was the first time I let my guard down all the way since Gail died. It's hard to believe that I've been so angry all this time under the sorrow. When I thought about how I made Gail's last days difficult and about the person who killed Dickens and Joe's flying all over New England in that plane of his when you were afraid for him, it hit me right where it hurt the most. I guess I was waiting for you to come along to help me get it straightened out."

"We can make up for lost time once we get our lives sorted out after the next couple of months. I'm not going to be able to live without you, no matter how we have to figure things out to be together. I've got my students to get ready for graduation, and then I'm free to do whatever I want to do."

"And I've got a double murder investigation to complete. We know that we want to be together, so we can make it happen. It's hard on us to have the real world intrude right now when we're so happy, but that's how it is." Greg moved closer and they made love again.

CHAPTER TEN

He left her bed in the early hours of the morning. Jan got up and helped sort out his clothing from hers where they had left it in the living room. It was like another lifetime from where they were now, she thought. How had they ever endured the lonely years until they found each other at last? Those years were firmly in the past, thank God.

Before Greg left, they had coffee together and talked about possible consequences of their bold adventure into togetherness. His car had been parked outside her condo nearly all night, which fact may have prompted the other owners to wonder who was staying where into the wee hours of the morning. Another such person was Bill Rainey, who had the watch on her place last night. Jan was grateful that it wasn't the local police's turn, but who knew what went on with the patrol cars of New Venice at night. At the last minute, she remembered to tell him about the break-in at the employment office.

"It's not clear to us whether the people looking for Jake's evidence are still at it, or if they've moved on to the revenge stage. We need to keep tabs on each other's whereabouts during the day, if we can, and plan on having dinner together in the evening. If it's possible, we can meet for lunch; it depends on what's happening for each of us. Right now, I don't want to go, but I've got to relieve Bill so's he can get some sleep."

"I'm going to cancel my appointments for this morning and sleep in a little. Then I'll go out to Marianne's with Dickens. The ground's still too hard to bury him, but I know she'll keep him out in the barn shed until I can. She loved him too, and they've got a spot out there where their pets are buried. Take care. I'll be here or at the employment office in the afternoon until four thirty."

They hugged and kissed at the door. Jan watched Greg's headlights vanish down the hill and around the curve from the front windows. At that moment, she felt more alone than she ever had when she was truly living alone by choice. Life is so strange, she thought, but her glow of happiness was a reminder of what had transpired during the night.

Half asleep, she moved to Greg's side of the bed and slept with his pillow clutched to her chest until the alarm clock went off at seven o'clock. There was no way she would be getting out of bed until it was a decent time to call her two students to make new appointments. Then she could call Marianne to tell her what had happened last night. Some of it, anyway. She dozed off again until eight o'clock.

At eight o'clock she went out to the kitchen to use the phone. One student was at home, and Jan told her about moving to the employment office and the necessity for making a new appointment. The young woman sounded slightly apprehensive about the change, so Jan told her that it would be easier than it was when she went to the high school. "Just ask the receptionist for me, and I'll come out to meet you in the lobby for the first time. It's really nice," she assured her.

The second student she called had stepped out to the Grand Union for some milk, her husband said, so Jan left the message about the change in location with him and arranged a tentative appointment for the coming week.

Holiday weeks were always crazy, Jan thought, but this one was good enough for Guinness. What else could possibly happen? Changes to her schedule usually bothered her, but they were most often put upon her by the students, who were not all that impressed by appointment times. It would take awhile to get the work week regulated because of the location change, for one thing. The other reasons were connected to the situation at the high school, the killing of her cat, and last but not least, her constant thoughts of needing to be with Greg.

After breakfast, she called Marianne to make sure she was home. "Come ahead," Marianne said. "I've got to stick around all morning to take in UPS stuff for Sam."

Dressing in jeans and sweatshirt and straightening up the bathroom after her shower, Jan decided to go ahead and tidy up the rest of the condo for an hour before she left. It would be hard to find time later in the day. Retrieving the box holding her poor Dickens from the porch, she took one minute to gaze out at the lake and mountain view. It didn't seem fair, but the weather was still holding with plenty of blue sky and sunshine, no matter how sad she felt about her errand to Marianne's house. Her spirits soared again when she thought how fortunate it was that Greg had been with her when she needed him.

The state highway and the gravel road leading to Marianne's were still in bad shape with frost heaves and potholes evident in every mile along the way. Moreover, the gravel town road seemed to have lost its bottom in places where water had undermined the foundation. It took great care to arrive at the Mackenzie driveway and make it safely to the top over cascading rivulets and loose stones. How did they put up with it on a daily basis, she thought.

Leaving the box in the car, Jan went through the garage to the steps leading to the kitchen hallway door and knocked. Marianne called for her to come on in.

"That's okay," she added when Jan stopped to take off her shoes. "There's no way I'm going to keep the mud out of the house until the middle of May at the earliest. The road and driveway are a mess, aren't they?"

"I wouldn't lie to you, my friend. I made it here safely, though. One thing about a Vermont winter. We all forget how bad it was once it's over and summer's here." Jan had told Marianne about her cousin Elizabeth wanting her to move to Seattle this year before the snow fell again in Vermont.

"It's sort of like giving birth," replied Marianne, with a smile. "How're things going with that nice friend of yours? I certainly liked the looks of him. He reminded me of Sam with that quiet face of his. From what you told me about him, he's earned the right to look dignified and a little sad. Are you really getting serious about him after knowing him such a short time?"

"Well, Marianne, how long did it take you to know that Sam was the one for you? I've heard your story about meeting him on the street in downtown New Venice when he was wearing his navy uniform, and it sounded like love at first sight to me."

"Okay, okay, you win. Thank God that he's turned out to be such a wonderful guy. I was definitely smitten."

"I think he was, too," Jan replied. "And he is a wonderful guy. My intuition works well when it comes to picking out the great men, you know. I hadn't met any that impressed me and were available until I met Greg. It's strange, but it's like we were looking for each other as if we knew our other half was out there somewhere waiting to be found."

"Aren't you a little afraid that one of you is taking unfair advantage?" Marianne frowned. "You know what I mean. Two lonely and sad people who have had unhappy experiences in the past and can't get past the memories enough to have relationships with the opposite sex long enough to get even remotely serious."

Jan pondered how to tell Marianne what had happened to get them past the awkward part of showing serious mutual affection, even though the walls of reserve had been slowly crumbling for both Greg and her by their laughing and joking together. They worked well together, too, in finding Jake's last messages and trusted each other's integrity. Jan thought that Marianne deserved to know; she and Sam had been so kind to her.

"It's too late to worry about seriousness. We've slept together and thoroughly enjoyed ourselves. Greg is a trustworthy, dignified, and competent serious person who also likes to tease and have fun, may I add. It was like a dam burst for both of us when something awful happened to Dickens. Greg was consoling me because he realized how much that cat meant to me, and the next thing we knew we were comforting each other by making love. It happens that way sometimes, I guess."

Jan's eyes grew misty as she told Marianne more about Greg's wife's death. "He'd never broken down enough to really cry until last night because of the anger and guilt. You know, being strong and manly. They must have had a wonderful marriage until she got sick. He couldn't bear to have her leave him, but he couldn't make her well either."

"You said something happened to Dickens. What was so awful?"

"He's dead, Marianne. Some horrible person tied a cord around his neck and hung him from the railing of my porch. Greg found him and cut him down to wrap him up before I saw him, thank God."

"Do you think that it had anything to do with the phone call and warning note you got?" Marianne was as furious as Jan had ever seen her.

She nodded. "There was a note attached to the cord. We don't know whether the people behind this warning business are getting revenge for our finding Jake's notes or if they are still trying to scare me into being quiet about what I know. How could they know I'd found anything unless someone clued them in?"

"They don't sound smart," replied Marianne. "Just vicious, empty-headed jerks doing what someone suggested to them in order to frighten you is what they seem to me."

"The people behind whatever plan has been in progress all these weeks are in for a rude shock and soon. Greg hasn't told me everything because he can't, but I have a feeling that he's on the right track. When all the information out of Montpelier gets coordinated with what's been happening in New Venice and Barton, they'll be up shit creek without a paddle."

"But what a way for Dickens to die. I'm so sorry for you. You got him right after Joe died, didn't you? He was like a part of your family. I'm glad that Greg was there to be with you. Don't mind what I said about your getting serious this fast." Marianne's eyes were wet with tears for Jan and for Dickens.

Jan hugged her and told her that she understood that the words were spoken with her best interest at heart. "Let's have some coffee while I tell you what I want to do with Dickens' remains. Maybe you won't go for it, but it seemed like a good idea to bring him out here to bury in your pet cemetery when the ground thaws out."

"We can put him out in the barn shed where it's cold," said Marianne, as she set out the cups of coffee and fixings. "Did you have a box the right size to put him in?"

"Yes I did, and thanks to both you and Sam. Life won't be the same without that big black cat waiting for me when I get home from work every day. It's hard to understand why cruel people pick on innocent victims when they want to make a point. My guess is that they're cowards who are afraid to confront other people directly when they want to hurt them. Anyway, Dickens is dead and I can't bring him back. Last night I felt like I wanted to murder the person who did it and I still want him punished, but good."

The two women drank their coffee in silence for a moment. Jan was hoping that Marianne really did understand her affair with Greg, and Marianne was thinking that she shouldn't have said anything about their seriousness because Jan was obviously happy about finding someone she could love and trust. If Greg hadn't been there to help, Jan would be in much worse shape today.

Finally Jan broke the silence. "It's strange how things happen, isn't it? Greg is here in the area to solve two murders, and I keep forgetting about that when we're together. We have so much fun talking and making jokes, I think we both forget. It must be hard for him to stay balanced with all the bad stuff going on around him. If I can erase that sad look off his face, even for a little while, I'm happy."

Jan looked up at the clock suddenly. "I'm going in to work this afternoon until four thirty, so I'd better get going. Thanks for the coffee and everything else. I'll keep you posted about what's going on, I promise. Maybe then we can talk about Ginny and what she's been up to. I really shouldn't talk about her right now although she's on my mind along with all the other stuff."

They hugged again and went out to Jan's car to get the box holding the body of the big black cat. Jan put the box in the farthest corner of the barn shed where Marianne told her it was coldest and said thanks one more time before leaving the yard. She wasn't looking forward to the drive back to town, but her mind was much relieved after her conversation with Marianne. It paid to have a friend like her. It was much cheaper than going to a psychologist, and what's more, it was a reciprocal arrangement.

It was early enough for a possible call from Greg about lunch, so Jan drove to the condo to wait. She had to change clothes before going to the employment office anyway. She also needed to call Sis Vachon at the vocational wing about passing the information of the program's new location along to her students. When Jan got through to the vocational office, one of the shop teachers answered the phone to say that Sis was away from her desk.

"Is anything wrong?" Jan asked, because there was a strange note apparent in the teacher's voice.

The teacher, a Mr. Dixon, wasn't sure. There was a meeting going on in the auditorium and he had been pressed into service to answer the office phone. "I came in this morning to pick up some manuals for planning, and here I am until Sis gets back."

"I'll leave a message for her, then," said Jan, as she passed along her request slowly so that he could write it down. "She knows that I'm over at the employment office if she wants to talk to me about this."

After she had replaced the receiver, she found herself looking out at the porch door to see if Dickens wanted to come in. I wonder how long it will take to get over that habit, she thought sadly.

Greg had picked up the cat's dishes and scrubbed them out for her some time during the early morning hours, knowing that the sight of them on the floor near the refrigerator would make her feel bad. The leftover cat food in the fridge and the new cans in the cupboard were gone too. Jan wished that she had him right there in her arms so that she could show him how appreciated his thoughtfulness was. With that wish she felt a throb of desire for him course through her body. The pleasant, but urgent, feeling made her wonder how she could wait to be with him that evening. And to heck with dinner, she thought and laughed at herself. It reminded her of situations when couples had to work instead of going on honeymoon vacations to be by themselves after the marriage ceremony. At our ages, this might even get embarrassing as well as scandalous.

The phone rang, and when she picked up, it was Greg calling through the dispatcher on duty at the police station.

"I won't be in town this noon," he said. "There's been an accident out on I-91 that is connected to the high school business. It's the principal, Dorothy Watkins, this time, a one-car affair into the ledges. You know what that means."

"It usually means suicide, doesn't it? I just tried to get Sis Vachon at the high school, and everybody was attending a meeting in the auditorium. I knew something was wrong. If you get a break at dinner time, I'll be here. I can get some groceries for a quick meal at the condo instead of our going out to eat. You'll probably be worn out."

"That sounds great. I'll tell you all about everything when I see you. Take care."

"I will be careful and you do the same." She wanted to say I love you, but decided that wasn't for the dispatcher's ears.

When Jan arrived at work, she knew that something was up by the way the receptionist was looking at her with a smile hovering around her mouth. Wondering what the big deal was as she walked back to her desk, she found out as soon as she turned the corner around the file cabinet. There was a vase of red roses on her desk and two plants were placed on the windowsill where she would see them right away. Knowing who was the gift-giver of the roses, she slid the accompanying card out of its tiny envelope and read the words, "I love you, from Greg." One of the plants was also from Greg and the other was from Marianne. Jan's heart sang with happiness all afternoon at work and all the way to the Grand Union at four thirty.

Not knowing exactly what kind of food Greg liked beyond the steak he'd ordered the night before and the meat loaf of several days ago, Jan played it safe by picking up ground beef, chicken breasts, and a pot roast as well as salad fixings, raw and frozen vegetables, and sandwich meat. She had fresh fruit at home and some desserts in the freezer. It had been awhile since she had shopped for anyone other than herself and an occasional guest. Carrying the brown paper bags out to the car, she could still feel the smile on her face and in her heart.

The hassle at the doorway to the condo didn't faze her today, trying as it was with her purse, bookbag, and grocery bags to get inside to the little hallway. After removing her outdoor clothes and putting away the groceries, she decided to call Marianne to thank her for the beautiful plant she'd gotten her for the office windowsill.

Marianne was fixing dinner for Sam and kept right on as she conversed with Jan. He had come home with news of a horrible crash out on I-91, she told her. It looked like a one-car against the ledges. Jan filled her in with what Greg had said earlier that afternoon.

"By the way," Jan said. "That was some nice surprise I had when I got to work and saw the plant you bought for my windowsill. Thank you so much."

"You've waited all these years to have a window for plants," laughed Marianne. "I just couldn't pass up a chance to put a smile on your face for your first day at the employment office."

"You did a good job. I'm still smiling. I can't help thinking that Lindner did me a great big favor pushing me out of the high school building."

"Too bad it wasn't possible long before this. Mr. Lindner is the one who is in hot water, however. Maybe it made him feel better to pick on someone else. You know, misery loves company."

Jan grimaced. "I'm making a face here where you can't see it. There's enough misery going around right now to cover everyone in town. You took it away for me with your thoughtfulness this afternoon. Thank you again."

After hanging up, Jan put the pot roast on for dinner or late supper, whichever it turned out to be. It would make good sandwiches if it didn't get eaten tonight, she thought. Potatoes could go in the microwave at the last minute and with vegetables cooking on the stove top plus a green salad, she was all set for whenever Greg got off work. She had a feeling that it might be very late when all his reports got written.

At seven thirty Greg finally called from his office at the police station to say that he would be able to come to the condo for something to eat. What he had said was "come home" and Jan's heart felt like it was bursting. Can there be such a thing as an overdose of joy, she said to herself. In spite of all the horrible things that have happened at school and to me personally, there is this wonderful feeling of happiness.

At fifteen minutes to eight, Greg was ringing her doorbell and Jan ran to open the door for him. She took one look at his haggard face and pulled him to her in a close embrace. They sat on the couch and continued the embrace, kissing deeply and thoroughly as if they had been parted for days instead of hours.

"It's been that bad, has it my dear?" Jan whispered around another kiss.

"Yes, I'm afraid so," he murmured back, as he held her closer to his heart. "Dorothy Watkins is very dead. She committed suicide."

"Did she leave any kind of letter to explain why she was doing this accident thing?"

"Yes, we found it in her purse after the coroner and his assistant got through with the body and evidence at the scene. There were no skid marks on the pavement, and she must have been doing close to a hundred in that Cadillac of hers."

"Has the letter she left helped with the details of the murder cases?"

"Oh yes, it certainly does clear up some of what happened the night Dan Frost was killed, and Dorothy was sure she was responsible for his death. We're not going to be positive about that until we find who the out-of-control person is."

"Don't tell me any more. I'm not supposed to know anything beyond what the general public is privy to. Besides, it's hard to tell you thank you for my beautiful roses and plant with Dorothy Watkin's death intruding." She initiated the next kiss and let it linger until they both wanted more contact than a clothed embrace.

Greg groaned. "I have to go back to the office in a little while. I left half of my reports unfinished, but I can get them finished if I stick to it later on. There was too much happening this afternoon to have time for that." He stroked her bangs out of her eyes and kissed her forehead and both cheeks before he gently pushed her away. "I've been out on the highway supervising the troops nearly all day, or at least it feels that way. I'm grubby and sweaty and hungry. Let's wait. I'll be back after I stop in at the motel if you want me to, I promise."

"All right. A promise is a promise, and I do want you to. Dinner will take a minute if you want to wash some of road grime off first. There are plenty of towels and things in the cabinet over the washer and dryer in the hall. This isn't the first time I've seen grubby and sweaty, I want you to know."

Greg headed for the bathroom with a grin on his face. It made Jan's heart sing to see him set aside the horror of the day's business, and she wanted to see more of it.

"Your flowers made my day," she called to him. "I had a smile going all afternoon at work, in the supermarket, while I fixed dinner, and right up to the present moment."

They sat close together while they ate, not wanting to be apart even for a short time. "I wish I could have been there to see your eyes light up when you saw the roses on your desk. Only the call of duty would get me to miss the glow on your face when you're happy, and I've missed one chance already. The picture of you in my mind kept me going all afternoon while I was climbing rock ledges and sliding down embankments at the scene. It wasn't a good place to be."

"When you get back, I'll show you my happiness," Jan replied. She wished he didn't have to go and was surprised at her mixed feelings of pleasure and sudden fear of the unknown person out there in the darkness thinking up ways to hurt her again. "I have to confess something to you. I'm afraid to stay here by myself tonight even for a little while. The person who killed Dickens the way he did must be a monster, and he obviously likes to slink around in the dark when nobody can see what he's up to."

"Come with me then. I'll find you a comfortable chair and you can read a book or a magazine while I finish the paperwork. Have you been nervous all day about that person?"

"Not really," she answered. "I went out to Marianne's like I told you I would. We took care of the arrangements for Dickens and had a good talk. She's been worried about me, the two of us, I mean. I did my best to explain the circumstances and feelings of how we met and seemed to know each other right from the start. She and Sam like to look after me because I don't have much of a family left. And then there was work."

"You're lucky to have such good friends. We don't exactly understand what happened when we met, either. It must have been hard to explain it to someone else."

241

They picked up their plates and went to the kitchen together to rinse them and the pots and pans for the dishwasher.

"We work well as a team here in the kitchen, too," Jan laughed up at Greg's serious face. His eyes met hers with a smile that melted her heart.

"Methinks I hear a double meaning there, Ms. Madison. Am I right?"

"I wouldn't lie to you, Sir Inspector," she answered. She turned him all the way around to face her before she reached up to put her arms around his neck. "Thank you for being so thoughtful. I noticed right away this morning that Dickens' things were gone."

They kissed. "And one more for my roses and plant." They kissed again and held on tightly to each other.

"We'd better get going out the door or we won't get to the office at all tonight," Greg said with pretended gravity. "Suddenly I don't seem to care about paperwork at all."

"We knew the rude world would keep us on the straight and narrow, didn't we? Forward to the office and reports. Just write fast, okay?"

They collected Jan's red jacket and her hot virus book and left for the police station. The conversation about the rude world intruding on their happiness continued. Greg thought that it would be a good idea for him to speak to his commander about his feelings for Jan before the two of them became an item of gossip that would hurt their relationship. Jan agreed.

"We go back a long way, the commander and I. And he's been a good friend right through all the bad times when Gail was sick and then dying. If I needed to go and be with her at the hospice, he found a way to get me extra free time." Greg paused with sadness returning to his eyes. "He's tried to help me get on with life although he never said it directly. You must know how men are about having that type of conversation; we're not as good as you and Marianne, for instance."

"I do know what you mean. Men think intimate conversations are for women only," Jan sighed. "It would cost me a fortune to go to a shrink if I didn't have Marianne to help me straighten things out. She's needed my help from time to time, too."

"That's a good deal you've got going there, my dear."

The police station was very quiet when they walked down the hallway to Greg's temporary office. He turned on lights and went to scrounge up a comfortable chair for Jan to use while she read. Background sounds from the dispatcher's office came from beyond the inner door in a muted, far-away fashion. It was almost as eerie as the high school building when Jan had stayed late for appointments.

Greg returned with an orange plastic lounge chair. Jan took off her jacket and got comfortable as possible. But before she started reading and he started in on his reports, she looked up. "Say it again and I promise to be quiet as a mouse until you're finished."

"What's that you want to hear?" he asked, smiling at her as if he knew.

"Say 'my dear' the way you said it ten minutes ago."

"I'll do better than that," he said and walked over to her, kissed her, and murmured "my dear" into her ear.

"What a romantic fellow you are," she teased him gently.

Settling down to write reports wasn't easy for Greg after that exchange, but Jan was as good as her word about being quiet as a mouse while she read. The sooner the work was done, the sooner they could go "home."

It was eleven o'clock when he finished the last of his paperwork. There was more to it than the accident scene, although it was the catalyst for several other related reports. Jan had slipped sideways in the chair with her head pillowed on one arm, sleeping, when he looked up. Her glasses were on the floor next to the book on hot viruses. Oh boy, he thought. It's been a long day for both of us.

Waking her quietly with a kiss, he helped her into her red jacket and picked up the glasses and book. Jan was not fully awake when Greg handed her into the Volvo and drove to the motel to give the reports to Bill.

"I picked up some clothes and told Bill that I would be with you all night. It was my turn to watch over you at the condo, by the way. I think he is quite satisfied with the arrangement."

"He's a good friend, too, isn't he?" said Jan sleepily. She had liked him from the time he had winked at her with a big smile on his face.

Greg pulled out of the motel parking lot and headed down the hill toward the business district. "He's much younger than I am, but he's smart and practical at the same time. He'll be a good inspector for the department when the time comes."

Traffic was almost non-existent as they traveled up the hill on the other side of town to the condo. New Venice rolled up the sidewalks on weekdays after the shops closed at five-thirty. There are many law-abiding people living here, Greg thought, but it was amazing how much turmoil and trouble the place generated in spite of that. The state police knew that the aura of isolation from more-generously populated areas made it seem like a small kingdom to those in power, a small kingdom to manipulate for their own benefit.

They left Greg's car in the parking space next to Jan's condo in another bold statement of togetherness. Hand in hand, the two lovers walked swiftly to the front door, ignoring light switches, and made a direct route to Jan's bedroom, shedding clothes as they went along the hallway.

"My dearest," Greg whispered.

"My dear love," Jan gently breathed as she pulled him ever closer to her warm, naked body.

The energy that had all but disappeared by the end of their busy day returned magically as they made love. It didn't seem possible to them that any two people had ever been so completely happy in spite of the odds against it.

Afterward they cuddled and talked about all the things they hadn't gotten around to telling each other about family and childhoods that were remarkably alike. His mother had been a teacher and his father a fireman. They died together in a car accident when Greg was eighteen. A much older brother and sister had been surrogate parents through his college years. There had been time in the Air Force and then a marriage and a position in the state police. The only disappointment to a very satisfying life was that Gail did not get pregnant no matter how they tried for babies to make that life complete.

Jan's beloved father had been a teacher and her mother the high school librarian. "That's how I got to be such a serious reader," she told him. "I was always too afraid to disappoint my parents by being naughty, so I went home to read the books I picked out when I visited my mother. The recklessness of my friends got heavy at times, and some of them were slow learners about it. My mother died of leukemia when she was in her early forties. It was tough on Dad, but he managed to get me to college and see me graduate before he died during a massive heart attack. They were both far too young to die."

She told him about meeting Joe right after graduation. "We weren't really right for each other, but we stuck it out anyway when our friends were getting divorced. I was pregnant twice, but miscarried in the third and fourth months. The last time I was sure I was going to have a beautiful baby after I passed that third month, but it didn't happen. I decided to stay at home and help Joe with telephone orders and paperwork to see if that would make the baby machine more efficient. There didn't seem to be any particular reason for my not getting pregnant; it just didn't happen," she repeated.

"We've both had enough of sadness. When we're together, I feel so happy that I could shout it from the top of my cruiser to everyone in this crazy town." Greg laughed softly into Jan's shoulder. "I'm afraid it's going to be hard not to show it. Maybe we should make an appointment with Father Gareth."

"I'm willing to go anywhere to talk about you and us and the situation we find ourselves in. Going to work tomorrow is the last thing I want to do. Couldn't we just stay right here in bed all day and forget the rest of the world and its problems?" Jan sighed, and then laughed too. "I'm being silly, of course. If it hadn't been for our work, we might never have met. Think about that."

"I can't. It scares me when I think how much of life seems to be dumb luck."

"A good subject for conversation with Father Gareth, I'm sure." They both chuckled at that thought and drifted off to sleep. It had been a busy day, indeed.

Jan slept soundly until four thirty when she suddenly found herself wide awake. "There it is again," she said to herself, being careful not to awaken Greg. It was a tinny sound, like a metal pail hitting wood. Carefully and quietly she slipped out of bed and peeked out through the mini blinds.

Someone or two someones were standing near the front corner of the condo garage building. She couldn't see what they were doing at first. The metal container one person was holding was being drawn back and forth along the wall in an arcing motion. Jan could not see

247

their faces. Their attention was completely concentrated on pouring something all over the side of the garage. Her garage unit. Where her car was parked. A tiny spark appeared, and then the wooden wall burst into flame.

"Greg, wake up," Jan screamed, and then plunged back onto the bed to shake Greg's shoulder. "Wake up, wake up. Someone's burning down the garages."

He woke almost immediately and grabbed his sweats from the athletic bag on a nearby chair. Slipping on his shoes as he pulled the slats of the blinds apart, he quickly and accurately assessed the situation and dashed for the front door.

Jan called 911 to report the fire, standing naked at the telephone. Her sweats were in the bathroom, and she swiftly donned them and thrust her feet into a pair of sneakers without tying them. Her first thought was that Greg would need some help if there were indeed two or more someones out there by the garages. Running out her front door, she paused long enough to punch the doorbell of her first floor neighbor.

A garden hose could be used to put out the fire, but it was too late to open up her garage for the one she used to wash the Escort. She hoped her neighbor was good in a crisis situation and could figure out what was happening quickly enough to help.

Where was Greg, she thought as she ran in the direction of the blaze. Then she saw him chasing one of the persons who had set the fire as he attempted to make a getaway by reaching an old pickup truck parked on the end of the gravel driveway. She screamed for the benefit of the neighbors who had come out to see what all the ruckus was about.

"Get a hose from one of the garages before it's too late."

"Gotcha," yelled someone.

The sound of a siren could be heard in the distance, drawing nearer by the minute. It would be a local cruiser coming to see what the problem was before notifying the alerted fire department that there was indeed a fire, Jan thought.

Just then a dark shape emerged from the evergreen planting behind her where Dickens had used the thick shrubs for cover when he was out hunting. The thought of Dickens and what had been done to him galvanized her into action, and she ran toward the shape to fling herself, arms outstretched, in a strong tackle around his blue-jeaned ankles.

The dark shape fell and then dragged Jan along the gravel in another attempt to get away before the authorities reached the condo. She held on although her arms were being scraped and one booted foot got free from her grasp to plant a kick on her jaw and collarbone.

Greg returned to the condo entrance with the other culprit in tow just in time to see Jan go flying at the shape emerging from the shrubbery. Turning the miscreant over to one of the young male neighbors, he ran to her assistance.

"Let go, Jan," he yelled as he pulled the second fire-starter up to his feet in one powerful swift motion. He shook him to make sure that he understood who was boss. The officer from the cruiser arrived with handcuffs as Greg read him his rights. They repeated the operation with the first arsonist and led them off to the cruiser for the trip downtown.

The one fire engine that had been dispatched to the scene quickly had the garage fire under control. It had gotten a good start that was only slowed by the garden hose hooked up to the outdoor spigot by one of the neighbors. Everyone stood back as Jan's garage door was opened to check the inside for smoldering wood. The Escort's right side was a mess of blistered paint and broken windows.

Jan did not care about the car. She had insurance to cover the loss, whatever it turned out to be. As Greg helped her to feet and held her close, she was crying for Dickens and glad they had caught the two men who were probably responsible for killing him. Her left shoulder and upper arm felt strange, bringing more tears to her eyes.

"Let's get a jacket to put around your shoulders and head for the emergency room," Greg said after they both gave short statements to the local police patrolmen. "If they need any more information, we can give it to them down at the station after we try to get some sleep."

"It's almost morning now." Jan watched the neighbors slowly disperse to their own homes. They looked like they wanted to know more about what had happened, but it would have to wait. Most of them smiled and waved as Greg helped Jan into the Volvo for the drive to the hospital. It was obvious to them that they were a couple deeply committed to each other, Jan thought, but they don't know when or why.

She knew Greg was angry with her for some reason. He didn't say a word as they drove to the emergency room parking lot. "Why did you tangle with that big galoot?" he finally asked her when they got inside the double door system. He looked very stern, like he had when she first met him at his temporary office at the police station.

"Well, it seemed like he was going to get away. All of sudden I had a flash of anger when I thought of one or both of those guys killing Dickens, and I tackled him. And I caught him. You got one and I got the other one. We're a team in catching bad guys, too." Jan smiled at him, hoping to see his grin appear.

It didn't appear. "When I saw that boot coming toward your head, I nearly went crazy. I was angry and scared that he had really hurt you." Greg's eyes teared as he led her to a chair, and then he turned to speak to the nurse on duty.

When he returned, he kissed her gently and then helped her fill out the paperwork necessary for identification and insurance. "I can't help it if I'm the athletic and courageous type. Maybe I got too strong a dose of adrenalin or something."

Then Greg grinned. "Save the athleticism. I do have to admit that we make a pretty good team though."

Jan's doctor arrived. "Well, what happened to you, Jan? Let's go back to a treatment room and take a closer look at your face and shoulder."

He looked suspiciously at Greg as if he had something to do with her condition. Jan introduced him as they walked along and laughed to herself when he realized that Greg was the state police investigator.

While Dr. Morris examined her, they explained together what had happened and the circumstances that led up to the catching of the two arsonists. "We consider ourselves to be a magnificent duo of teamwork." said Greg with a wink in Jan's direction.

A private joke, thought the doctor as he worked on Jan's face. "We will need an x-ray of your shoulder area. While we wait for the technician on call, let's clean up those arms where they're abraded. Did you get dragged through a gravel pit? Just kidding."

The nurse brought an ice pack for Jan's face and started working on the arms. In a short time, the technician arrived to take her x-ray. Greg pushed her to the neighboring radiology department in a wheel chair, not paying attention to her comments about there being nothing wrong with her legs. As a matter of fact, she was feeling a little woozy by the time they returned to the emergency room to have her broken collar bone aligned and a sling applied to her left arm. "One more thing before you leave," Dr. Morris said. "The nurse will give you a tetanus shot, and then you're all set."

They thanked the doctor and the nurse and left for "home." Jan would not be going to work this Friday morning after all. More cancellations, she thought, but thank goodness it's Friday.

CHAPTER ELEVEN

Greg had helped her into bed when they returned to the condo and brought her a glass of water and two painkillers. "Might as well get a head start on the soreness you're going to feel when you wake up," he said with authority.

After they kissed, Jan reminded him that she had to get up to cancel her eleven o'clock appointment. Greg took the comforter from the end of her bed and arranged it with one of the bed pillows on the couch for a short nap until he had to report to his office. He also took charge of the alarm clock intending to wake first and let Jan sleep as long as possible.

As she closed her eyes, Jan thought that she would never be able to relax enough to go to sleep, but she had promised Greg that she would try. He had helped her undress and found a baggy pair of pajamas for her to put on over bandages and immobile arm. It wasn't hard for her to tell that he had cared for his wife in the same tender way when she was too sick to help herself. She found herself feeling loved and cared for in a way that she had not experienced before, and she drifted away into a deep sleep.

Greg found the couch tolerably comfortable no matter how much he wanted to be closer to Jan, to hold her in his arms until she slept. A smile flickered on his lips as he thought again of her courageous, but also foolhardy, actions in stopping the arsonist. We are indeed a magnificent duo, he thought as he closed his eyes and slept.

When the alarm rang at nine thirty, it seemed to be only five minutes later. Greg quickly turned it off and went to the kitchen to make the coffee. Peeking in at Jan on his way to the bathroom, he saw that she was still fast asleep. He hoped the shower wouldn't wake her as he went through his morning routine and dressed in another pair of sweats he had brought from the motel last night. There were a couple of phone calls for him to make this morning, too.

Last night seemed like a week ago, he thought as he got off the phone and poured a cup of coffee. Sitting in a blue chair conveniently placed near the sliding glass door to the porch and swiveling to the left a bit he could see the lake shining in the sunlight. The mountains in the distance were pink with leaf buds, and his heart began a prayer that rose to his lips. It was almost spring. He had found Jan. Thank God.

Hearing a slight noise, he turned and saw her standing behind him with a smile on her face. She had been up a few minutes he noticed, with her cheeks fresh and pink and her hair combed.

"You wouldn't have wanted to see me when I first got up," she said. "I didn't want to see me in the mirror. With a cup of coffee and a couple of aspirins I'll be good as new. Well, almost." Her chin and jawline were black and blue, but not noticeably swollen.

They fixed breakfast together with Greg staying on the opposite side of her broken collarbone. First pulling up another chair for himself near the slider to the porch, he seated her in the blue chair with their breakfast on a wooden tray table between them.

"I'll bet you eat breakfast here by the window every morning," he said.

"You'd win the bet," returned Jan. "If I get up early, it's still dark and I can see the lights of the cars and trucks going by or pulling into the mini-mart. And then it gets lighter and I can see what kind of a day it's going to be by watching the lake and the sky."

Greg smiled at her. "That's what I was doing, and it's going to be a great spring day with lots of blue sky and sunshine. It's too bad to waste it on police business, but we might as well get it over with."

They finished eating in companionable silence while they gazed out at the view, which was becoming more spectacular by the minute. "I'm canceling everything today," Jan said. "I can't sit at a desk feeling like this, all battered and bruised. Nobody will expect me to, I'm sure. That's the first thing for me to do, make the phone calls, and then I'll need a little assistance getting dressed. You don't mind, do you, Sir Inspector."

"Jeesum Crow, lady, give me a break, will you?" grinned Greg with a twinkle in his eyes.

Jan made her phone calls to the students who needed new appointments for the later part of the following week. I'm going to give myself at least five days before I go back to the office, she told herself before she called George Wright and spent ten minutes explaining everything that had happened and then went through the same explanation for Grace Evans at the employment office. Her last calls were to her insurance companies.

The sound of the dishwasher running told her that Greg had picked up the breakfast things and found them to be a sufficient load with the dinner dishes from the night before. The magnificent duo strikes again, she thought.

They picked up the bed clothes from the living room and made the bed together, Jan's one-handed aid proving to be more of a hindrance than help. "This is not going to be fun," Jan told Greg with a hint of frustration in her voice.

Together they wound plastic wrap around her bandaged arms and carefully took off the sling so that she could shower. It proved to be impossible for her to shampoo the gravel out of her hair in the shower, however, so Greg helped her do that in the kitchen sink after wrapping her in a beach towel sarong. With a little more assistance, her hair was dried and arranged in some sort of an acceptable "do." There goes the last shred of my independent attitude, Jan told herself.

Getting dressed proved to be an occasion for fooling around when Jan couldn't figure out how to get her bra on and decided to give up on that idea. They also had to look through her closet for a blouse that was loose and buttoned down the front, and she got a kiss with each button, in reverse of the usual tradition.

"If I'd known it was going to be this much fun coping with a broken collarbone, I'd have done it long ago," she teased Greg. Her face, except for the black and blue chin, was shining with happiness. The frustration was in the past, as if it had never been.

Greg smiled at her happy face. I didn't miss this one, he thought. "You had to wait for me to come along to make it fun. But I don't want you going around breaking your collarbone every time you get a chance to tackle some jerk out in the parking lot just to enjoy all this again."

"Ahem, sir, don't you have to report in for work this morning?"

"I called in to the local police about finishing our statements early this afternoon. I don't think they were expecting us right off anyway after what you went through last night. I also called my commander and told him everything about our meeting like we did and working together to find Jake's evidence. Of course, I told him that the reports that Bill brought him didn't tell the whole story because we caught the two guys who had been harassing you later on in the morning. When I told him that you tackled one of them and got hurt, he said to take as much time off as necessary to make sure you were all right. He understood that your welfare was my number one priority, but he had trouble with the tackle business until I explained about the cat."

"There's a lot more to this business than catching those two dummies and the cat getting killed," Jan stated. "I'm not presuming to think that it is my right to know more, but it would sure help me to understand what you've been doing and what Montpelier's up to."

257

"The note that Ms. Watkins left behind after her death will be public knowledge soon. All the financial stuff on land purchases and plans for that land is being put together in Montpelier, using evidence from John Lindner's questioning and what Watkins left for us. Your harassment was carried out by those two idiots we captured. The one I caught is singing his head off. They work for Smithfield Construction Company, by the way. I'll get out of these sweats and then let's go somewhere for lunch so that you can show off your black and blue marks and the sling. We can start some more rumors in town, and I'll tell you about all the dirty deals while we eat."

"Guess whose car we're going in," said Jan.

"It's the Volvo or nothing at this point in time, and besides you need to give that collarbone a chance to knit." Greg changed into civilian clothes and found a light denim jacket in the hall closet to drape over her shoulders. "I think spring is really here this time, but you never know about Vermont weather. Do you think you'll be warm enough?"

They both looked out the front windows at the same time. "Doesn't seem like there's a blizzard brewing out there today. I'll take my chances with the light jacket." They walked out the front door and stood gazing at the mess in Jan's garage a moment before leaving for the restaurant.

It was a glorious spring day. Jan even thought she spied crocuses peeking out of several flowerbeds as they drove through town. When they arrived at the restaurant and were seated in a booth near the window, she mentioned to Greg that it didn't seem appropriate to be talking about murder and greed on such a beautiful day when the hope and promise of Eastertime were so evident.

He told her then how he had felt that morning, seated in her blue chair and looking out at the lake and mountain view. Then reaching for her hands and holding them tight, he told her how grateful he was that there was a Jan Madison for him to love and care for. "Just don't ever scare me again like you did when you tackled that guy this morning."

"I've got some good reminders on my poor body to help me make that promise right now." She held up her bandaged arms a fraction off the table. "But if I ever saw you in trouble, I'd rush right in to give you assistance, I'm sure. The old adrenalin was flowing this morning when I thought of Dickens, and I'm probably always going to feel the same way when I need it. Can't you see me some time in the future, at seventy-five years old or more chasing down a burglar or a mugger? You read about those tough old ladies every day in big time newspapers." Jan laughed at his expression of mock horror.

"You're kidding, of course, aren't you Jan?"

Their waitress arrived at the table with glasses of water and oversized menus. Jan turned to the salad selections at once, as was her habit of long standing. When she told Greg that she would like a small chef salad and some coffee, he tried to talk her into a burger and fries, so she told him she'd have a few of his fries to bolster up her health. "After all the doings of this morning, I could use some, I guess," she agreed.

They ordered and received their lunches as Greg explained some of the background of the financial dealings of the New Venice people involved.

"The state legislature works in strange ways depending what combination of men and women show up after elections, you know. Sometimes they're a large group of lawyer types, and sometimes there are cliques of businessmen and women predominating. The friends and supporters of the elected legislators expect some pay-off down the line when bills are researched and written, even to the point of presenting entire plans clandestinely to their pet legislators. Then they expect to profit from them because they are all set to move the minute a particular bill is passed and signed.

Jan sighed and told Greg that she knew of one case herself that involved a tourist appropriation bill and a brochure printing company that had a whole winter ski campaign in place with all the literature ready to go the same week the bill passed.

"That's exactly the kind of thing I mean," Greg replied. "This past winter there was a push to expand gambling in this state. You know, first we got the lottery, and then there was this idea going around the legislature, in confidence of course, that it would great for state revenues if a piece of land could be designated as gambling territory with casinos and all the trappings confined to one area only so that it could be controlled. It's happened in other states."

Jan looked up from her salad and helped herself to several of Greg's French fries. "Do I hear you saying that you've been investigating this for some time?"

"I didn't say that, but you've picked up on what I've been doing. When I got onto the New Venice part, it seemed like a modest plan that Frost, Lindner, and Watkins first had in mind when they had the kickback money for their land purchases, starting with the deal with Mrs. Morley. It's possible that they even entertained the idea of founding an agricultural school."

"The terrible three was really the terrible four because they needed the business manager of the junior and senior high schools to manipulate the books and set up a dummy company for them. In order to hide the money, they devised more land purchases. The plans got complicated when Smithfield wanted in too, or he blackmailed his way in. Their ideas got more grandiose every time they held their secret meetings at the high school until it became apparent that someone was over the edge mentally."

"It was too much for Ms. Watkins, who was beginning to regret that she had ever thought of cheating the supervisory region. I know that she went along with Frost's ideas in the beginning because she was in love with him. That's what she wrote in her suicide note." Greg paused for breath. "She said that she was the one who hit Frost on the back of the head when they had a confrontation on the stair landing, but she thought Dan must have gone over the railing by himself because he was momentarily out of it. We know someone else must have helped him over the railing a little later. She hit him with the big battery lantern they used for the meetings, you know, and dropped it there when she heard someone coming along the upper hallway. The lantern has disappeared. Fear of that person and remorse led her to commit suicide because there seemed no way out of her dilemma."

"She couldn't take the pressure after she realized that Dan was using her, and then there was another murder, possible evidence against all of them floating around, topped off by fear of someone in their group who was out of control," Jan thought out loud. "How did the five get in touch with the pro-gambling faction in Montpelier? Do you know what the connection is?"

"We don't know for sure, but there are several possibilities involving corruption of the last election. There is also the murder of Jake Patenaude to figure out yet. His funeral is tomorrow at eleven o'clock."

Jan was eating some more French fries off Greg's plate, but her hand stopped in mid air as she thought of poor Jake. "You know," she said quietly, "I think that Jake was trying to play with the big boys and got caught when he tried to blackmail his way into the scheme right after Mr. Smithfield pulled the same stunt. Whoever it was who killed him wasn't going to stand for that. Things must have really gotten crazy when the cover-up became the main agenda. Was there out-of-state gambling influence?"

Greg looked at her with admiration. "You've got a pretty good head on those dilapidated shoulders of yours."

"Thank you kind sir," she replied. "Please eat the rest of those French fries before I fall any farther off my diet."

"What you really want is for me to put on some weight, around the middle for love handles, right?" They both laughed as a signal to change the subject away from murder and cheating. Enough had been said for the time being, with the meeting with the local police to complete their statements about the fire in the early morning still to come.

On the way to the police station after lunch, they discussed the complications of telling too much about the background of Jan's harassment. She wanted to know whether it would mess up the state police investigation if they said why the two construction workers had sent her the threatening letter, made the phone call, and killed her cat before they made the arson attempt.

"Mr. Smithfield has been questioned in a preliminary way this morning. One of the construction workers implicated him in your harassment. The guy stated to the police that they were just supposed to warn you, but when you didn't do what they wanted, Smithfield got mad and threatened to fire them. They decided on their own to get revenge." Greg thought a minute. "Just play it straight, starting with Jake wanting to tell you something that Smithfield wanted suppressed, but you had no idea what it was that you were supposed to know. Does that make sense?"

"I think so," Jan replied. "It was like that in the beginning before I figured out that Jake must have left me a note somewhere in his son's paperwork. How much do the local police know about the proposed gambling concession and a possible connection between the legislature and out-of-state interest?"

"I would say what they know about the big picture is non-existent right now. They are very concerned about Jake's death and Smithfield's involvement in your harassment. Mr. Smithfield has a large amount of clout in this town, and that's making them nervous as hell."

"When the whole thing gets aired out to the public, there's going to be a terrible scandal. The state's attorney general's investigation in Montpelier about the election and the pro-gambling group and the out-of-state casino owners will have to be put together with the events here in New Venice and the murders." Jan shuddered. "Some of those people aren't going to be happy about your investigation."

"We're going to close them all down pretty soon. That's part of the consequences for them, and if they lost a bundle of money, too bad. The governor and the old-line, conservative legislators definitely do not want out-of-state gambling interests in this state, no matter how lucrative the pro-gambling group makes it sound." Greg shook his head sadly. "I don't think they're even happy with the way the lottery has turned out."

FROST HEAVES

The chief of police and the patrolman involved with the capture of the arsonists were waiting for them when they arrived at the station. The preliminary conversation was directed at Jan and how she was feeling after the tackling exhibition. They exclaimed over her black and blue chin and broken collarbone until she felt as if she was up for a civilian purple heart medal. But there was also the same air of disapproval about her behavior that Greg had expressed to her earlier.

"It just happened when I thought about my cat being killed by one of those guys," she told them. "I couldn't stand to see him get away, and all of a sudden, there I was hanging on to his ankles for dear life. I don't plan on a repeat performance, but what can I say about the effect of adrenalin while under that type of stress?"

Greg made a groaning sound and said he hoped with all his heart that other situations of the same kind never arose to test out her theory. The chief and his patrolman were looking at each other out of the corners of their eyes obviously wondering about their relationship, and why it called for so much protectiveness on Greg's part that he had stayed overnight in Jan's condo. They did not comment on their thoughts, however.

Between the two of them, Jan and Greg explained about Jake Patenaude and his unkept appointment with Jan and how she was sure that he wanted to talk to her about strange things happening in the high school building in the early morning hours when he was on duty as nightwatchman.

"Had you seen either of the two men before, around town, I mean?" asked the chief.

"I think that I saw them one day in Wendy's," Jan replied. "I kind of ran into them when I was in a hurry to get out to my car. They were looking at me afterwards with funny expressions on their faces. It wasn't important enough for me to remember until right now."

"The inspector told us about the letter you received, and we have a fingerprint that can be used when the time comes. The threatening phone call got us involved in keeping an eye on you, as you know. What do you think was behind their behavior?" the chief questioned.

"Well, there was something going on at the high school that didn't seem right to Jake, and he was seen talking to me at school. It follows that Mr. Smithfield has a connection to that person, and they used two of his employees to threaten me out of telling anything Jake had perhaps passed along regarding his suspicions. They searched my office when it was in the vocational wing, too. The only thing is, I didn't have any idea what it was that I was supposed to have or know. My boss helped me to move my office to the employment building on River Street right after that and I had police protection, so I thought the harassment would be over. Then they decided to get even with me by killing my cat and burning my garage and car."

Jan didn't dare look at Greg when she professed to know nothing about Jake and his suspicions. She hoped that her face wouldn't betray her skimming over the truth.

The chief looked as if he knew that there was more to Jan's explanation, but he had to stay with the business at hand. "One of the guys you captured has confessed that Mr. Smithfield hired the two of them to harass you, and predictably, Smithfield has denied it. Of course, we've got them for the arson job. They've been arraigned and are in jail for the time being until trial. The school connection to Smithfield and the reasons for all the things that have happened here in New Venice over the past week are a part of the inspector's investigation, so we'll stick to our business and he'll tend to his for now."

Greg looked relieved at the outcome of the interview. "We'll be available for any further help we can contribute when the time comes to put those two losers away."

They said their good-bys and left to go to Greg's office down the hall.

"Whew," exclaimed Jan in expression of the relief she had seen on Greg's face a moment ago. "I was afraid that the questions were going to get a little more to the point there for a minute." She sat in the orange lounge chair that was still in the corner of the office.

"It's going to be hard to hold back from now on until everything comes out in the open," Greg replied. "You did a good job skirting the 'why' of your harassment, but I don't think they bought it. Jakes' murder is under my investigation, but the local police are deeply concerned about it."

"I was afraid to look at you when I answered the big 'why' question. Unfortunately or fortunately, however I look at it, my thoughts are registered on my face making it difficult for me in situations like that one. I just kept telling myself that the overall investigation is the one that is important now, and the rest will follow." Jan's face was flushed from remembering the interview with the police chief.

"I wouldn't have it any other way," professed Greg, putting his arms around her carefully and kissing her lips soundly and then tenderly and then deeply. For a very satisfying interval, the present melted away from them, taking with it the grubby office and all thoughts of greed and murder.

A soft knock on the office door and a polite cough interrupted their reverie. It was Bill Rainey, pink-faced and grinning from ear to ear when he saw the two of them pull apart with their dreamy faces showing exactly what had been happening.

"Sorry to intrude, folks. I'm bearing news and instruction from Montpelier. The investigation is heating up from their end."

"I'll take you home, Jan, and then come right back here to get the word," said Greg, gently helping Jan up from the lounge chair. "Get everything lined up so we can go over the instructions with as little time lost as possible, Bill."

On the way through town to Jan's condo, their loving mood persisted in spite of the intrusion of the rude world, as they called it. The sun was shining in the blue sky and the temperature was definitely spring-like. "I will be so happy to see this investigation ended," murmured Jan. "The people responsible for all this misery in New Venice should be put in prison for the rest of their lives."

"Someone is going to be put away for a long time, and that's for sure. I have a feeling that Montpelier wants me to come down strong on Mr. Lindner, using the information left to us by Dorothy Watkins. We're getting to the nitty gritty part of the investigation, Jan." She leaned over and kissed him one more time as he helped her from the car and closed the door.

"I can manage the rest of the way. Be careful, Greg. Somebody is getting desperate."

"Do something for me this afternoon, will you Jan?" asked Greg before he pulled away to return to his office. "Call Father Gareth and make that appointment we've been talking about and then get some rest. I would like our relationship formalized; I guess that's the word to use for us older folks, if you agree that's what you want."

"I told you that I would go anywhere and talk to anyone about the way I feel when I'm with you. It's going to be wonderful to be formalized." Jan laughed. "What a proposal, but I'll take it and cherish it." She gave him a last kiss loaded with promise, and he drove away with a smile lighting his face.

She walked over to her garage and looked into the burned out interior. Her car was more of a mess than she had thought when she first saw it, all blistered paint and charcoaled upholstery and shattered yellowed glass. A crime tape was still affixed across the open door and extended to include the outside end where the arsonists had begun their work.

Jan was not the type of person to personify an automobile just because it was hers. But she still felt anger and sadness about her loss. First had come the killing of Dickens and now the Escort was demolished to a burned-out shell. With a shiver of intuition, she wondered if the revenge were truly over as she let herself into the condo. The arsonists and probable killers of her cat were in jail awaiting trial, but she felt the chill of apprehension return.

While she was putting a pot of decaf on, the telephone rang. It was her insurance representative on the line asking if it was a good time to come over to assess the damage to her car and garage. She said yes and warned him that the crime tape was still in place. Checking with the police would be a good idea before driving to her condo from the office in St. Johnsbury.

That's one thing out of the way, she thought as she lifted the receiver to dial Father Gareth's office. When he answered the phone, Father Gareth professed to be delighted to hear from her at long last. He was a great teaser, as Jan knew, and she laughed before telling him what she and Greg were requesting.

"I'd love to hear the story about how you two got together," he told her. "I was watching you from my office window last Wednesday, and I swear I could feel the heat all the way across the lawn and up to the second floor where I was standing."

Jan was embarrassed at that statement and said so. "It's a good thing I know you as well as I do, or I'd be mortified," she told him.

"Don't be embarrassed, Jan," he said. "I kept my little secret to myself, and now it looks like I don't have to anymore. That's right, isn't it? You sound so happy."

"We'll tell you how everything happened. It was just one more connection for us when he came to the Wednesday Eucharist. I felt the need to be there on my own, and so did he without either of us saying anything. He can tell you himself how he got in the habit of attending an extra service during the week. I'd guess it's hard to keep a good balance of emotions when a person deals with the ugly side of humanity on a daily basis like he does. In a lesser way, it's hard for me, too, when I get involved with students more than I should."

"And for me, even though my parishioners expect me to be a rock to cling to in time of trouble. I sometimes feel overwhelmed with sadness or anger." Father Gareth gave a sigh, but his voice soon assumed its normal sunniness.

"You do a good job of keeping us all together and on the right path."

"I've got a spare hour after the ten o'clock service on Sunday, if that's a good time for you both," said Father Gareth. "And thank you for the kind words. See you on Sunday."

Jan hung up the receiver and began to feel her emotion of apprehension abate somewhat after speaking with Father Gareth, but it was still there niggling at the back of her brain later when she poured a cup of coffee and went to look out the glass door to the porch. It was impossible for her to rest.

She thought of Dorothy Watkins with a sympathy that she couldn't have dredged up before Greg told her what the suicide note contained. Dorothy hadn't been what men call a good-looking woman, but she had been stylish and intelligent. In fact, she and superintendent Frost would have made an interesting couple with similar backgrounds of education if they had played it straight and kept their greed under control. It was apparent that wasn't enough for good old Dan, however. Dorothy was going to have her revenge on the whole unsavory group when Greg got through with his questioning of the ones who were left, Jan thought to herself.

She stepped out through the slider with her cup of coffee in hand to savor the last of the day's springtime warmth. The beach and soccer field in front of the high school were still visible through the leafless trees to the east of the condo. Bays of the lake and openings of the in-rushing rivers were outlined between spits of land extending into the water. She could identify the school complex and other prominent buildings from her porch and would be able to until the foliage of summer intervened. That is one good point about living here, she thought; the views are ever changing with the seasons, and there is always beauty to be seen in a widespread arc from the porch. It was hard not to think that Dickens should be springing up through the bushes and through the railings to rub against her ankles in mock adoration, so she stepped back through the slider and closed it.

The thought of Dickens brought back the feeling of apprehension that had been temporarily stilled at the back of her mind. Darn this intuition thing, she thought. It was almost impossible for her to stay at home and do nothing while Greg was out there somewhere interviewing a person who might be an out-of-control killer. It could be Lindner. It could be Smithfield, who was probably feeling quite smug about dodging allegations of wrong-doing, or it might be the out-of-state person. Jan felt a headache coming on, and her collarbone started to throb with beginning pain.

It's time for more aspirin, she thought. I promised that I'd stay ahead of the pain, and here I am coming from behind already. There hadn't been much with the schedule she had put herself on, and that was the problem now. Jan didn't like to take pills unless she felt the dire need of something for headache or sinusitis already in progress.

She poured another cup of decaf after swallowing two aspirin tablets with a glass of water, and settled into her blue chair to read. Within half an hour, she had slammed the book down and was on her feet pacing back and forth in front of the door to the porch.

When the telephone rang, she was almost grateful for the distraction. It was an Officer Viens calling from the police station. She recognized his gravel voice from the day she had gone to the station to get in touch with Greg after finding Jake Patenaude's note.

"Inspector Whitehouse wants you to meet him at the high school in the vocational wing," he said. "He told me to tell you that he'd be in the director's office."

Jan thought it was a strange request, but she was eager to do something, anything active to quiet her feelings of restlessness. Maybe Greg needed a bit more of confrontation about Jake's evidence to push Lindner over the edge. The rational side of her brain was telling her to be careful because Lindner might already be over the edge, but she ignored it. She called the one cab company in town and flung the denim jacket over her shoulders as she ran to the front sidewalk to wait for her ride.

Her intuition fought with the logical side of her brain all the way to the vocational wing of the high school. When the cab driver had let her out at the janitors' door, she remembered that Greg had her set of keys to the building. This worried her for a minute until she realized that she knew several ways to enter one of the other wings and could then walk back to the vocational section.

The janitors' door opened easily to her tentative pull, however. Making her way down the murky gloom of the hallway, she was wishing that Greg had met her at the door. It was unusual for him to forget that she did not want to be in this building for anything less than an emergency. Turning the first corner to the left and pulling the glass-windowed fire door open, she could see light coming from the doorway of the voc office spilling out into the next corner of the hallway.

Her intuition was clanging away in her head and her knees started to feel weak. This whole scenario was not right. I've done a foolish thing by coming here, and I'm leaving right now, she admonished herself. Greg would never ask me to do this. She turned and was beginning to run back to the janitors' door when a hand bearing a white cloth came down over her nose and mouth. She had one second to identify chloroform before passing into complete darkness.

Jan did not know how long she had been out. When full consciousness returned it was not that different from being out of it; for about five minutes she strained to make use of the little light that permeated the room. Underneath her body was a narrow cot with several small pillows propped against the wall to her left. An afghan was pulled up over her knees and Jan recognized the scent arising from it. She was in the severely handicapped classroom on the second floor of the voc wing. Upon attempting to sit up, she found that her hands were bound behind her, tightly; too tightly, and her wrists hurt at the same time her fingers felt numb. A wave of despair washed over her when she saw the furniture piled around her cot, completely concealing her from the classroom doorway. The janitors must have stacked the tables, chairs, and big standing chalkboard at the back of the room in preparation for redoing the floor, she thought. How would anyone find her here? Her mouth was dry and a wave of dizziness brought her body back down to rest on the smelly cot. The pain from her shoulder was excruciating, and she slid into unconsciousness once more.

CHAPTER TWELVE

After Greg had left Jan off at her condo doorway and driven down the curving hill to the main road, his undertone whistling began. "It's a Wonderful World" could just barely be recognized by someone close to him because that was what he always whistled when he was happy. "Imagine that," he said to himself as he made the last turn into the parking lot at the police station, "I'm on my way to an interview with a real crook and I'm about as happy as I've ever been."

Bill Rainey met him just inside the doorway. They were driving the cruiser immediately to the vocational building to pick up John Lindner for a questioning session that would probably bring some closure to the crime spree at the high school. The word had been passed on to them that he was in his office waiting. As distasteful as it was, a deal was going to be offered for full cooperation. Lindner was a crook and a coward, but he was being practical about his situation, not over-the-edge as Greg had first thought him to be. It's either Smithfield or the out-of-stater we've got to stop before more mayhem happens. "It could be all of them are nuts, though," Greg told himself.

Lindner was indeed waiting in his office for him when he and Bill arrived at the vocational wing. He got up slowly from behind his desk and pulled on his suit coat as they left the building. With his computer files on land deals and plans for the casino complex already confiscated by the state police combined with the information left behind by Jake Patenaude and Dorothy Watkins, he had little choice left to him but to implicate Smithfield and the shadowy stranger from out-of-state. Greg fairly ached to get the name and the connection down on paper. "Be patient." he said to himself. "It will all come out with some good questioning."

Back at the police station, the three men gathered around a battered old library table in the interrogation room, and Greg began his questioning after the preliminary introduction into the cassette recorder of names, date, time, place, and circumstances of the procedure about to begin.

John Lindner started by confirming the computer files were his and that he was indeed implicated in land sales that were bought with a fraudulent intent to set up a gambling area in the state with connections to a faction of legislators who were in turn obligated to an exclusive group of out-of-state investors with questionable integrity. Yes, the land had been partially purchased with money bilked out of the New Venice school district by kickbacks from the Smithfield Construction Company and the missing federal funds. Yes, Dan Frost and he had originated the plan with the help of Dorothy Watkins and Reg Lessette, at first. Yes, they had had secret meetings in the high school rooms during the early hours of the morning when Jake Patenaude had spied on them for blackmail

information. No, he did not know who killed
Dan Frost after one of the heated arguments
that had ensued.   Yes, he did know how
Smithfield got on to their plans through some
shrewd guessing and snooping around the land
sales deals and putting two and two together.

Lindner stopped his confessing for a moment.
There was extreme uneasiness showing on his
usually stonewalled facial features. He would
not go on without being assured that he would
have protection from Smithfield and his,
Lindner's, friend from New Jersey, Lanny Ross.

Aha! Greg wanted to know why Lindner was
afraid of the two remaining members of the
group and who was this Lanny Ross, but he
acted as if he had known all about them for
weeks.

Sweat broke out on Lindner's face as he
talked about knowing Lanny from prep school in
New Jersey.   Lanny's real last name was
Rosselli, a good old boy name from organized
crime for three generations. Ross was of the
generation that craved legitimacy by way of
college careers and professions, but Lanny
preferred his grandfather's way of intimidation
and fraud.   Of course, the professions and
legitimacy came in handy at times. He and
Lanny had pulled some good ones at school until
they both were asked to leave or be prosecuted
as felons in their senior year.

They hadn't met for years until Lindner saw
Lanny in the bar after skiing at Jay Peak one
Sunday. In fact, it turned out to be strange that
he and Ross hadn't met sooner as Lanny had
been skiing at the area often throughout his

college years and for the last fifteen as well. The family owned a terrific lodge near the ski area. He loved Vermont. Of course, the family didn't approve of hanging around bars when they had that nice lodge out in the woods. Lanny, however, preferred getting away from his family for some real fun whenever he could manage it.

They drank too much that evening, and Lindner had spilled the beans about how smart he was at pulling a shrewd deal on the school district. Lanny replied that he could top that, and filled him in on the gambling area idea that he and his father were working on as a project to get Lanny in good with the family. It seems that the family was not all that pleased about how Lanny was maturing. They still called him Sonny, and here he was thirty-seven years old. He needed a successful deal to make them sit up and take notice of his capabilities. Maybe they could work out a deal for the land that the New Venice people had picked up. It would make Lindner and friends very rich and get Lanny in solid with the family. "That's how it started," said Lindner.

Greg had kept his face quiet as Lindner spoke into the recorder. They paused as Bill changed cassette sides. Both of them now knew why the vocational director was frightened. The "family" he had spoken of had been involved in murders of all types in the big city when expected favorable outcomes for them got messed up. Sonny Ross had screwed up again, and his friend John Lindner was part of the screw-up as soon as Dan Frost had been killed. The state police investigator and state's attorney general

were tuned into what was happening in the
legislature and became more focused when
another New Venice murder occurred. The
family knew by long experience that it was only
a matter of time until the whole project
unraveled when they learned that Lindner's
computer files had been accidentally found by a
secretary. Leave it to Sonny to hook up with
such a loser, they told each other with knowing
shrugs. They'd have to cut their losses. It was
over for now they told his father. Give Sonny the
word.

"Lanny Ross has disappeared, probably to
Montreal," said Lindner. "And I'm holding the
bag. The family is not going to like it when they
find out that I'm talking, but I'm not taking the
rap for everything and letting Smithfield go scot-
free. He's the one who caused all the trouble
when he insisted that his company be the one to
build the casino buildings. The family has its
own contractors and contacts and wouldn't go
with his plans as a matter of business policy.
No way."

Greg asked him point-blank if he had
anything to do with the two murders. Lindner
answered in the negative vehemently, saying
that it was Smithfield who was responsible.
Greg was inclined to agree, knowing Smithfield
as he had come to know him. Now, all they had
to do was catch up with that busy contractor
and nail him to the wall too.

Lindner was remanded to jail to await
arraignment. He had been advised of his rights
in an orderly procedure, but his lawyer would be
at work for him in a short time. Greg was

confident that the evidence he and Bill had gathered plus that of the state's attorney general's office was going to be sufficient to put Mr. Lindner away for quite a stretch, maybe even in spite of his deal for spilling his guts.

Finding Bob Smithfield proved to be another matter. The local police tried his home, office, and known hang-outs to no avail. They put his license plate number and truck description over the radio to all law enforcement vehicles on the road, but no word was received back on his whereabouts. Greg stayed in his office while Bill scouted around town for information on places to check out as possible hiding sites. They uncovered a current girl friend, but she hadn't seen him lately either.

Greg tried to call Jan at home at seven o'clock, knowing she would be upset with him for not calling sooner. When she didn't answer the phone, he became worried enough to leave the office and drive to her condo. There was no answer to the doorbell either. Deeply concerned, he climbed over the porch railing and looked inside the living room for a sign of her. It was dark inside making it obvious that she was not there, but he rapped sharply on the glass door to make sure she hadn't fallen asleep. There was no Jan there; he knew that by the emptiness in his heart, but he tried once more anyway.

When he got back to the office, there was a yellow envelope on the center of his desk top waiting for him. Absently tearing it open while he tried to think where Jan could be, he finally looked down to see a crude penciled message on a folded piece of cheap lined notebook paper.

"For the inspector" it read on the outside. He unfolded the note and saw words that took his breath away as if he had been punched directly in the solar plexus. "I HAVE JAN. WILL TRADE FOR GETAWAY." It must be from Smithfield, Greg thought. Lindner said that Ross disappeared days ago. His blood ran cold. Bob Smithfield was the one out of control, killing Dan Frost and Jake, and hurting Jan like he had. He was using her because he knew what effect it would have on Greg's manhunt for him.

Bill came in fifteen minutes later from his survey of the area's best-known hiding places.

"No dice, boss," he told Greg. Then he looked at Greg's face and winced visibly. "What's wrong?"

Greg tossed him the note. "It's got to be from Smithfield. He's the biggest fish not accounted for if we believe that Lanny Ross has been gone from the area for days. How he got Jan to stand still long enough to become a hostage, I have no idea. My brain is refusing to work property."

"The note doesn't say how he's going to contact you, but it could be the phone," said Bill in his no-nonsense voice. "We should set up some kind of recording device for the phone right now. It's all we have time for."

Greg stared into space for a moment, trying to gather his wits. "Bob Smithfield is a tricky S. O. B. and a dangerous one," he returned. "He's a native of New Venice and knows his way around in places we haven't even heard of. He might have some other method up his sleeve for contacting me."

"Poor Jan. Where can he have her stashed?" Bill was trying his best to be professional and practical, but it wasn't working well. "Do we just sit and wait for Smithfield, or what?"

Greg shook his head in frustration. "I'll arrange for a recording device to be put on the phone, just in case. I don't dare get too far away from the office right now. If you inform the local police what's happened and then call the commander in Montpelier we'll get things rolling. Oh, and see if the locals can do a trace on the call if it comes in to my phone."

Bill returned with his tasks completed in twenty minutes. The commander had affirmed their usual kidnap/hostage procedure of giving the perpetrator anything he wanted in order to preserve the life of the victim held in lieu of money or escape method. They would get him later. The local police would help under Greg's directions, but tracing a phone call from Smithfield would be impossible because of the time constraints. Ten minutes later the awaited message from the construction company owner came in to the instrument on the inspector's borrowed desk.

Greg gave a sigh of relief. The recorder was in place, and just maybe they could get a clue to work on. He concentrated on his voice as he answered, making it as cool and professional as he could with his insides churning with fear for Jan's safety.

"Listen carefully," a deep muffled voice directed, "because I'm only saying this once. Your girlfriend is safe for now, but she won't be if you f... this up. I want a small plane with full tanks available for my use out at the airport. Make the route through town to the airport open. No police. You have my license plate number. The locals and the sheriff's department men know my truck. I'll leave you word where to find Ms. Noseybody. I'll be on the road in one hour."

"How do I know Jan Madison is okay? Put her on the phone so's I can speak to her."

"This is no big deal like on TV. I want out of here and you're going to get it ready. Agreed?"

Greg's voice cracked with emotion. "Agreed." Smithfield hung up immediately. Greg slowly returned the receiver to its base.

Smithfield's desperate plans for escape were a tacit expression of his guilt. Greg understood who had shoved Dan Frost over the railing and hit Jake Patenaude on the back of the head before pushing him into the icy water of the river. Bob Smithfield had a history of going overboard with his actions if things weren't happening the way he wanted them to. He, Greg, should have gotten that message several days ago. In his case, the fraud and manipulation of people and money was going to be secondary in court.

He and Bill played the tape over and over after they had finished making plans with the local law enforcement agencies and at the airport. At one point in the taping there was a background noise that they couldn't identify.

Bill had grown up in a mill town in New Hampshire. "It sounds like the horn at the paper mill," he guessed, frowning. It wasn't exactly like that sound, but it set the two men on the right track with further conjecture. All at once they both looked up at the same time and said, "it's the CN train diesel engine horn."

Greg wanted to kick himself for not thinking of the train that passed by the high school sooner. It blew warning blasts as soon as it began to draw close to the small mall where Wendy's restaurant was located as there were no barriers or flashing lights there. Cars could turn off the causeway street and drive over the tracks in front of the slowly moving train. The main railroad crossing with barriers and lights was two blocks beyond. The sound of the diesel horn would reach the school buildings. Greg and Bill hadn't been in town long enough to appreciate the significance of the railroad tracks as the long train only passed through town twice a week. Smithfield had called from the school, and it was likely that Jan was there too.

"Cripes," exclaimed Bill. "We were at the vocational wing just a few hours ago. That guy's got a lot of guts, but he's not very smart if he didn't notice the sound of the train going by."

"I'll bet he's so used to it that it didn't even register," said Greg.

They glanced at each other with consternation when it dawned on them that there were myriads of hiding places in the high school complex where Jan could be kept out of sight for a long time even if they knew she was somewhere within the buildings. It was the only clue they had, however, and they had only a few minutes left to check it out.

CHAPTER THIRTEEN

Jan turned on her side and tested the rope around her wrists again and wiggled her fingers to bring back some of their circulation. Her head had cleared from the chloroform fumes, making rational planning possible. She knew where she was. She knew how she got there and guessed who was responsible for her particular problem. Bob Smithfield was the out-of-control desperate member of the fraud group who was unpredictable in his actions and as dangerous for her as he had been for Jake. It was a process of elimination that made sense. She sat up with her feet flat on the floor and thought some more.

Smithfield didn't realize that she knew this room almost as well as she knew the room two doors away which had been her office. If she could wend her way through all the piles of furniture around her, she might be able to find something to cut through the rope binding her wrists.

Thank God her ankles weren't tied together, she thought, as she dodged around desks, a kitchen table with chairs stored on its top, and the large, standing blackboard that had blocked her view when she first woke up from the chloroform. Losing her balance trying to climb around a rocking chair, she sat down heavily on the tiled floor, jarring her shoulder against another set of desks stacked haphazardly together near the blackboard. It hurt, but she thought that she had better not let out the scream hovering on her lips. Smithfield might be close by. She preferred that he thought of her as an unconscious lump lying on the cot where he dumped her.

The side of the room nearest the front entrance was set up as a kitchen with fridge, stove, sink, and cabinets arranged in a normal pattern. The cabinet drawers held flatware of all kinds, including kitchen utensils and knives. One drawer contained miscellaneous items and among those items was a pair of scissors, if she remembered correctly. Should she try the scissors first or a knife? How could she manage it? It seemed impossible, and indeed it was after she managed to open a drawer from behind her back to give it a try.

Maybe I can escape from the room, was her next thought. There were three doors; the front door was the obvious place to start. It was locked or wedged somehow from the outside. The door to her right in the back of the room as she turned around was blocked by the piled furniture, making the other rear door to the adult ed office the next choice. All the classrooms were interconnected in this way. Miraculously it opened, but she wasn't home free yet. A large filing cabinet was partially blocking her way; by sheer determination she squeezed into the space available to her and pushed the cabinet over enough with her backside to make it through the opening. Jan knew that the door to the hall would open from the inside even if it was locked, and she was right.

The hallway was dark with only the glow from the emergency exit sign showing to her eyes at first. There was an elevator down the hall from where she stood for the use of the severely handicapped students, but no matter how tempted she was to use it, she knew that it made too much noise for an escape. In fact, she was afraid to use the closest of the stairways because Smithfield would surely use that one if he came to check on her. The corridors on the second floor formed a box around the space reserved for the elevator and two stairwells. She could follow the back corridor and come around the end where the other stairwell was located to make her escape, but the bottom of the steps was closer to the voc office where Smithfield might be. It's six of one and half dozen of the other, she thought. From the bottom of the steps and the fire door of the first stairway it was only a short distance around the corner to freedom. It was definitely do-able. "Go, Jan, go," she yelled to herself as she prodded her legs into action.

Greg and Bill went through the final drill for Smithfield's exit with the local police and several men from the sheriff's department before they alone quietly drove to the high school complex without stating their intentions to the others. The nearest road up the hill led directly to the vocational wing and wouldn't do, so they drove beyond the school on side streets, arriving at the parking lot near the lawn adjacent to the auditorium/gymnasium building. They parked Greg's Volvo on the grass and tried the door on that end of the building, knowing that it must have been locked by a janitor hours ago.

It was locked. They crept along the back walls of that building and the academic building trying doors as they went along. The next brick wall held the door to the vocational classrooms' hallways, and it could have been left open for adults using the rooms. It wasn't likely, but the last resort would be the janitors' door, too obvious and open to scrutiny. Greg had the key to that door in his pants pocket.

Bill looked at the luminous dial of his watch. "There's only a few minutes left until Smithfield makes a run for the airport. Do you think he'll come this way if he's here or use some other door?"

"I've got this hunch that he is here in the vocational wing somewhere," replied Greg. "I can almost feel his presence. Don't ask me why. What we do have to remember is that we don't want to jeopardize Jan's chances whatever door he decides to use. His truck isn't parked anywhere in plain view, so he's got it hidden somewhere close by. If we had more time, we could probably find it."

Bending over double, they quickly ran along the wall to the janitors' door and then knelt down on one knee while Greg inserted the key and slowly tested the door. With their weapons ready, the two men opened the door enough to crawl through. When they had made their way into the dark hall far enough to keep from being silhouetted by the faint light coming through the glass panels of the door, they stood against the cement brick wall to listen for movement within the building.

All of a sudden a scuttling dark shape came hurtling around the corner, heading toward the outside door. The two state policemen were nearly startled enough to fire at the shape, but at the last second pulled up their weapons in readiness for the next move of the person running toward them in the darkness. Whoever it was did not have the look of a desperate criminal making a planned getaway.

Greg said clearly, "This is the police. Stop where you are."

A voice quavered out of the darkness. "Is that you Greg? It's Jan."

Both men cried out at the same time as all hell broke loose. "Get down, Jan, someone is coming." Another dark shape was crossing in front of them toward the automotive shop door on the right side of the corridor. A shot rang out and reverberated in the hallway and Greg grunted in pain. He kept to his feet, however, and managed to stay with Bill as they carefully entered the shop to see the fleeing figure opening a door at the other side to the outside. They were nearly to the outside door when they heard the motor of a pickup truck catch and saw the vehicle lurch from behind a maintenance shed headed for the hill to the main street.

Greg ran to get Jan, and Bill radioed to the local police that action had occurred at the vocational wing with the suspect heading toward town in a dark-colored pickup with white lettering and logo on its doors. The hostage was safe. There was no doubt that the truck was Smithfield's and that he was making a last desperate attempt to get away.

Jan was still on the hallway floor as ordered. When Greg came through the janitors' door to hug her to him, she carefully rose to her feet murmuring that she was okay, she was okay. They turned on the hall light and saw that neither of them was really in good shape. Smithfield's bullet had grazed Greg's upper arm on the left side where he was bleeding profusely, and Jan still had her arms tied behind her.

Greg managed to get his pocket knife out and cut the rope binding her wrists together. Jan ran to the first aid box in the janitors' office and then tore his uniform sleeve away in order to bind up his wound with the sterile pads and gauze she found. It was obvious, however, that they were both on their way to the emergency room this time.

As they were wondering how Bill was doing as he pursued the Smithfield pickup truck down the hill from the vocational wing, the screech of brakes followed by the scrunch of metal hitting an immovable object could be heard clearly to them as they sat in the janitors' office. Those sounds echoed at the bottom of the hill for several seconds when they were suddenly muffled by the cracking boom of an explosion.

They sat together, transfixed with horror and wondering until Bill came to find them with an ambulance medic in tow. The two of them took one look and ran to get blankets and stretchers for their wounded bodies that were in the beginning state of shock. Greg refused to let up until Bill filled him in on what had happened when he followed Smithfield down the hill from the school.

"First of all, it definitely was Smithfield in his pickup truck trying to make a getaway," Bill confirmed. "He forgot one thing on his way down the hill. There's a big frost heave and pot hole near the bottom, and he hit it just right to send him into the side of the train trestle down there. The next thing I knew, the truck was in flames, but I got him out in time."

Jan and Greg then noticed that all three of them were going to the hospital emergency room. Bill's hands were bandaged loosely in wet cloths, and his face was red under a very singed blond crewcut.

CHAPTER FOURTEEN

The next morning they met in Greg's room on
the second floor of the hospital. He had an i.v.
going and appeared very pale from his loss of
blood. Jan was on her way home to the condo
later that morning she told the other two. She
had her arm done up properly in a spanking new
sling, and her lower arms and wrists were re-
bandaged. The overnight rest had restored her
vitality and good spirits. Bill was being released
in the afternoon to go home to Montpelier where
his own doctor would examine his burns. All
three were glad to have the ugly scene at the
high school behind them. "Except for the
written reports," Greg groaned. "They never go
away."

Just as Bill left for his own room, Father
Gareth appeared from the hallway. "We had an
appointment for tomorrow, but I thought it
would be easier for both of you if I sneaked in
one this morning. How are the two of you
feeling?"

"I'm feeling much better now that I'm cleaned
up, re-bandaged, and rested," said Jan, looking
and listening for Greg's reply.

He answered slowly after a mental check of
his wound's condition. "I'm on painkillers right

now for the arm, so that's all right, but I'm tired right out from loss of blood, I guess, and the shock. I'll be back to normal soon's I heal up and rest a couple of days."

"Being locked up in a dark room with furniture piled all around me was a piece of cake by comparison to the way I felt when I saw Greg's wound," Jan stated gently. "Our friend and colleague, Bill Rainey, was a scary sight too when I got a good look at his burns. He saved the life of the chief perpetrator by pulling him out of his truck just in time to keep him from burning to death. you know. I don't know how I feel about that right now."

Father Gareth smiled at her. "You'll get it sorted out in due time. Don't worry about it right now. You both have quite a story to tell, or do I have to wait until I hear it on the eleven o'clock news?"

"We can fill you in on most of it now if you have the time to listen to a complicated mess of criminal activity," Greg said, with a lopsided grin. He and Jan took turns telling about the "Terrible Three" that turned out to be the "Terrible Four" with the addition of the business manager, Reg Lessette, who helped the group collect construction kickbacks from Bob Smithfield and set up a dummy company to buy prime land in the Barton area.

"We're not sure whether they actually intended to start an agricultural college on the land they bought, but we are sure that a very nice piece of it was bought fraudulently from a Mrs. Morely, an elderly lady who lives in the nursing home over there," said Greg.

"In the meantime," he continued, "a plot was thickening in Montpelier with certain legislators to set up an exclusive gambling area somewhere in Vermont to bring in more revenues like, say, Atlantic City in New Jersey. There were rumors that a crime family there was using influence and money to get it going. I had been working on that when I was called away to investigate the murder of Dan Frost, a leading member of the Terrible Four."

Jan took up the narrative. "One of my friends told me about the land purchases and who was doing the deals. Some concerned farmers in the Barton area noticed what was going on and told him while he was on his farm supply sales visits. What started the conversation was my tale of woe about how despicably I was being treated by Dan Frost and John Lindner, members of the Terrible Four. I didn't have nice things to say about Dorothy Watkins, either, who was the last member of the group. The adult secretary, some teachers, and I thought we were being spied on through the intercom system used as a listening device when we discussed our dislike of the group and the atmosphere in the school. I had had several run-ins with Dan; once at a meeting he clamped down his big hand on my thigh under the table where no one could see. We found out later that was a pattern for him, forgetting himself with women employees and then getting them dismissed before they could dare to think of suing him and the school."

Father Gareth protested, "You should have told me what was happening, Jan."

"I realize that now, but then I was intimidated and embarrassed. One of my friends, I thought she was a friend anyhow, someone you know very well, got together with the vocational director Lindner to discredit me. I retaliated by having my office moved to the employment building, a logical move in any case."

"Jan and I met after she had become concerned about the body found in the river," Greg went on. "She was sure that it was the body of Jake Patenaude, the night watchman at the high school, because he was supposed to see her on Saturday morning to talk about some strange meetings in the middle of the night in the academic wing. He had given her the names he said he recognized, and an idea of what the meetings were about, but actually he was doing some active spying on them and had found a piece of paper left behind by the group. You can guess who the members of the group were. New people joined the others as time went by. Poor Jake was sure he had been seen in the hallway one night, and he became very frightened." Greg paused and smiled at Jan. "We became friends almost at once while we worked together to find a message hidden in his son's paperwork. The Terrible Four had forgotten that Jake's son graduated from Jan's program."

Father Gareth laughed when he saw them smile into each other's eyes. "And that's where I came into the story when you both showed up for the Wednesday noon service. I knew something wonderful was happening to you."

"Well," said Jan as her complexion slowly changed to rosy pink, "we got to be more than good friends rather rapidly, but it came about because of Mr. Bob Smithfield's harassment of me. Lindner must have told him that Jake was talking to me, and they both thought that Jake told me what the Terrible Four were up to. They searched my office, sent me a warning letter, made a threatening phone call to me, and then strangled my cat to pay me back for continuing to talk to Greg. We had been out to dinner, and when we returned, I was really concerned about Dickens not showing up for several days. Greg found him tied around the neck and dangling from the porch railing. We took care of cutting him down and wrapping him in a towel together. I was devastated and couldn't stop crying. That's when we talked about the deaths of our spouses and the consoling went on to become more than friendship. We've become firmly committed to each other, but it has happened so suddenly and forcefully that we wanted to speak to you about what our situation could mean to other people. I mean we don't intend to stir up a scandal in the community, for heaven's sake, but we don't want to live apart while we get to know each other better either. There's just not time like when we were in our twenties."

"I found myself not able to concentrate on solving the murders, and Jan was feeling that it was definitely time for her to be on vacation. We called our jobs rude intrusion of the real world. On early Friday morning this week, the rude world in the persons of the two thugs hired by Smithfield really intruded. They set Jan's garage and car on fire as one more act of revenge. Lindner and Smithfield weren't positive that we had found incriminating evidence, but then someone at the police station informed Smithfield that Jan had probably found Jake's written testimony hidden away in her files where only she would know where to find it. Greg turned to smile at Jan again. "We call ourselves the magnificent duo because we work so well together, on ferreting out clues and in other more personal ways too." His eyes twinkled as Jan blushed furiously.

Father Gareth saw how happy they both were in spite of the battering their bodies had undergone in the past few days. "Sometimes a gift is given, like the gift of finding each other that you've experienced. You have both been married before and know the magic of romance as well as the pitfalls that occur with intimate daily co-existence. I know that you can handle what will come with the rude world intrusion with love and grace. But, that's not all there is to the tale you've given me, is it?" He gave a meaningful gaze at Jan's sling and Greg's bandaged upper arm.

Greg resumed telling the tale of the two arsonists. "I ran outside and chased one of the guys, and Jan followed me after she had called the fire department. When the other man came out of the bushes and started to get away, she tackled him and got her collarbone broken in the process. We got that fixed up and rested a bit, but the rest of the day went downhill very rapidly. I had a scheduled appointment with Lindner and used some held-back information to get him to confess his part of the fraud deal. It came from Dorothy Watkins. and some of his own computer files. actually."

"The whole story of Ms. Watkins' death was kept out of the papers because she had left a full confession of what the group had been doing and the startling message that it was she who had killed Dan Frost. At least she thought that she had killed him, but Smithfield finished him off. She loved Dan, but he was using her for his greedy schemes, so she confronted him that night in the hallway as they walked toward the stairs. Ms. Watkins thought Frost was dead when she hit him with the battery lantern they used for the meetings. Smithfield came along, picked up the lantern after Dorothy ran away, and carried it to his car after pushing Frost over the stair railing. We weren't sure who it was until yesterday. The choices had to be Lindner, a friend of his from New Jersey who had joined the meetings, or Smithfield. I believed Lindner when he said that he had nothing to do with the murders. The friend, who was in on the gambling area idea through contacts with his family, has disappeared. That left Smithfield, a rough guy capable of all kinds of mayhem, and sure enough, he conned Jan into meeting him at the vocational wing office where he kidnapped her and hid her away in one of the upstairs rooms when he needed a getaway scheme. He's responsible for both murders. Dan Frost was getting in his way, and Jake tried to blackmail him with the information he'd picked up. Smithfield used the lantern again to kill him with some idea of making Ms. Watkins the prime suspect. Nobody has said that Smithfield is particularly intelligent."

"You must have been petrified, Jan," Father Gareth exclaimed.

Jan did not want to think about the chloroform and the tied-up wrists, but she gave the minister all the details of her ordeal in the darkened special ed room. "I managed to wake up sooner than Smithfield expected and got myself downstairs, nearly to the door when Greg almost shot me." She frowned in mock horror.

"That's not funny, Jan," Greg told her. His serious and stern face returned as he remembered how close it had been indeed. "Bill Rainey and I figured out where Smithfield must be telephoning from when he called and gave instructions for his getaway in exchange for Jan's life. We went to the high school to investigate without telling anybody because it was obvious that we had an informant working out of the police station office. While everybody else waited to let Smithfield drive to the airport, we flushed him out right after Jan made her escape. I guess you know the rest about the Smithfield's accident and the fire."

Father Gareth let out a long breath of air. "You're right, it's a complicated story. Jan will have to write it up herself for the local newspaper. One thing though, how come Greg almost shot you?"

"I was just teasing Greg because it was a weird coincidence that I escaped and came around the corner of a very dark hall at the same time Greg and Bill entered through the janitors' door. Smithfield was apparently right behind me, heading for the stairway to the second floor to see if I was still out of it when he heard Greg yell 'stop.' I didn't look the part of an escaping criminal at second glance, but Smithfield sure did when he whirled around to shoot at Greg."

"I'm very thankful that you and Greg are all right, and I especially give thanks that Jan did not get shot, for both your sakes. It's been a harrowing week, so I'll understand if I don't see you tomorrow," Father Gareth replied as he got up to leave.

"We'll try to make it if I am released from the hospital in time." Greg's sober face was still in place, and Jan didn't like it. She'd have to learn to cool it with the teasing.

She stood up and leaned over the i.v. lines to kiss Greg full on the mouth. She wanted to see his happy face reappear. "I don't sing in the choir tomorrow as per tradition for the Sunday after Easter Day. It would be nice to sit next to you through a whole Sunday service for the first time if we can manage it."

"Sounds great to me," Greg and Father Gareth both exclaimed. Greg's face lit up with happiness once more as they laughed about their unison reply. "Just like show biz," Jan said. "But it's time to get this show on the road because my doctor's due in at any minute."

"I'm going to take a nap and be in really great shape when mine comes in." Greg had a little more color in his face, but he looked white around the eyes and nose. "I want to make tomorrow's service at ten o'clock."

A. M. BYRON

Father Gareth left the room after waving good-by, and then Jan leaned over to Greg and gave him a long satisfying kiss, which he returned with enthusiasm. "I'll tell your doctor that you're more than ready to go home if he asks, Sir Inspector. That was some kiss."

"It's the effect you have on me, Ms. Madison. Let me know right away if you're leaving this morning so that I can con my doctor into letting me go home, too, maybe later this afternoon. I'll tell him that I've got a really terrific nurse lined up to help me recover."

Jan laughed and gave him one more kiss of good-by as she left for her room.

She lay on the bed and thought about the events of the past weeks. It seemed incredible to her that two murders and a suicide plus major financial and governmental scandals had occurred in such a small town as New Venice undeniably was. The kingdom aspect of living in an isolated rural area had certainly contributed to the absolute power felt by the superintendent and his henchmen in crime, but that made their blatant disregard of their responsibilities even more despicable. She was glad that Greg's part in the investigation was nearly over as the court system took on the arrests and arraignments before trial dates were set. Dan Frost, Jake Patenaude, and Dorothy Watkins had already paid the highest price for their outrageous scheming, but John Lindner, Bob Smithfield and his two hirelings, Lanny Ross, and a group of shady legislators still had their punishment coming as the wheels of justice turned slowly to the conclusion of the affair.

302

I'm still tired, she thought, as she felt herself drifting off to sleep. A smile hovered around her mouth as she thought of finding Greg, her heart's desire, in the midst of all the chaos. Was it all just dumb luck, or was such a miracle pre-ordained. She'd have to remember to discuss that with Father Gareth was her last conscious thought.

A. M. BYRON

EPILOGUE

While their wounds healed, Jan and Greg lived together in her condo for most of the time that elapsed until Jan's diploma students graduated in June. Greg was on leave because of the gunshot trauma to his upper arm, but not officially until his dreaded paperwork for the unfortunate happenings in New Venice's school district was completed by tape and/or dictation in Montpelier.

On one of Vermont's perfect early summer Saturdays in the latter part of June, they were married in St. Luke's Church by Father Gareth. The small church overflowed with their special friends from the area, the Vermont State Police, the diploma program around the state, and a few out-of-state relatives. Kate's cousin Liz attended and had also extended an invitation to use her apartment in Seattle as a base for their honeymoon trip. She would be touring Europe for the remaining summer months.

It was a joyous occasion that Saturday. A reception (which included several decadent chocolate amaretto cheesecake pies contributed by Marianne), held mainly in the parish hall flowed outdoors where tables and chairs were set under the canopy of a large white tent. No one could remember a more perfect day for a wedding.

304

A. M.'s Chocolate Amaretto Cheesecake Pie

1 ready-to-use chocolate flavor crumb crust
2 packages (8 oz. each) Neufchatel cheese
1/2 cup sugar
2   tablespoons amaretto*
2   eggs
1   square (1 oz.) unsweetened chocolate, melted

Mix Neufchatel cheese, sugar, and amaretto on medium speed until well blended.
Add eggs, mix until blended.   Stir melted chocolate into I cup of the batter.**
Pour chocolate batter into crust.   Top with plain batter.
Bake at 350' for 40 minutes or until center is almost set.   Cool.

Makes 8 servings.

* I buy small airline-type bottles of amaretto.
**Can add a sprinkle of sugar to chocolate batter.